MY ONE
EXTRAORDINARY
LIFE *A Feline Memoir*

T.D. ARKENBERG

outskirts
press

For Barbara, our Brussels neighbor at Number 6
and
All others who love, protect, nurture, and rescue animals

Also by T.D. Arkenberg

Fiction
Final Descent
Jell-O and Jackie O
None Shall Sleep
A Belgian Assortment

Memoir
Two Towers
Trials & Truffles, Expats in Brussels

Contents

Introduction

It's often said that cats have nine lives. Considering myself something of an expert in the area, I don't buy into that nonsense. Humans, I believe, advance the nine-lives gibberish because they mistake quantity for quality. One can understand their misconception. They plod through bland existences whereas we felines lead marvelously complicated lives. The difference between grape juice and champagne, saltine crackers and avocado toast, bare, splotchy skin and fabulous fur.

The misguided human perspective is ironic, an example of not seeing the forest for the trees. They have more lives than they realize. Is the number three, seven, nine, or more? I wouldn't hazard to guess. It varies by person and personality. What are these multiple lives? Obviously, I'm speaking metaphorically. Yes, cats do that too—smarter ones, anyway. Many people linger in the past. You've heard the litany delivered with a nostalgic sigh: "Oh, when I was single; when I was thin; when I was happy."

Some folks reside in the future. You've heard their lament: "When I'm older; when I'm married; when I'm rich; when I'm retired…" The number of prospective personae is endless. Even those grounded in the present wander into one fantasy world or another, deluded by what might be instead of what actually is.

My contention that few humans lead a single, extraordinary life comes from years of scrutinizing the tribe of upright walkers. My credentials? I remined you, I'm a cat. We are keen observers, patience our virtue.

Unlike human beings, cats live in the present. The past is pointless and our future uncertain. Whether lounging on a sunny windowsill, snoozing in a comfy lap, or stalking a mouse, we live in the moment. Some of this philosophy, what might be called "catitude," is born of necessity. In our dog-eat-dog world, predators pose existential threats. Pity the day-dreaming feline snatched by a hungry hawk, chased by a cunning coyote, or cut down by a speeding sedan. Living in the moment means survival. There are no second chances, let alone second, third, and fourth lives. After cudgeling and conniving their way to the top of the food chain, humans could learn from cats.

I acknowledge the contradiction. I urge readers to live in the present yet offer up my memoir. Indulge me. My trip is a purposeful journey, not a destination with intent to languish. Perhaps my history will allow humans with whom I share this planet to abandon many absurd myths about my species. Maybe I can inspire them to recognize and appreciate their one extraordinary life.

Chapter 1
I Am Born

Charles Dickens penned one of the most recognizable opening passages in literature. His novel's full title evokes memoir: *The Personal History, Adventures, Experience and Observation of David Copperfield the Younger of Blunderstone Rookery*. Logic may tell our brains that his rich history of great adventure, experience, and observation is fiction, but our hearts embrace young Copperfield and his colorful journey as fact. Losing ourselves in the book's pages, readers form attachments to its vibrant characters. We accept the premise that the story might be true; Micawber, Uriah Heep, Peggotty, *et alia*, could be real people.

Call me a copycat, but I borrow from Dickens to jumpstart my story. Had I not decided upon a shorter, snappier title, I might have instead called my memoir: *The Personal and Abridged History, Adventures, Experience and Observation of Fluff the Runt, Feline of Brussels and the World*. Why abridged? My life may be complex but, like all cats, it's brief by human standards. Besides, I not only lack Dickens' dramatic flair and flowery prose, in the last 150 years tastes have changed. Today, sound-bites are digested more readily than chunky, long-winded treatises. But don't fret dear reader, you won't be left hungry. That is, as long as you don't mistake quantity for quality.

—◦《◉》◦—

Whether, as young Copperfield opines, I shall turn out to be the hero of my own life, or whether that station will be held by anybody else, human or animal, these pages must show. To begin my life with the beginning of my life, I record that I was born (as I have been informed and believe) on a Monday, at five o'clock in the afternoon. It was remarked that the clock of the Church of Saint-Gilles and that of the commune's Town Hall began to strike at the very instant my littermates and I first whimpered.

I entered the world with two brothers and a sister in the final summer of this century's first decade. I remember nothing of my actual birth. How many of us do? According to my mother, called Vanille owing to her white fur, I was the last and smallest of my litter. "Your fur's no less soft or fluffy because there's less of it," she remarked after my siblings made fun of my size. "On the contrary, it's because there's less of it that your downy coat's the most precious." As a result, she called me Fluff. The name, she cautioned, might stick to me only until another one came along. Unlike humans who require a string of names in which to wrap themselves, animals have simple labels. More often than not, these describe our appearance or behavior. Tags come and go as we move through life. But beneath our fur where it matters most, we retain the indelible traits that make us unique.

Our estranged father must have been black, gray, and tan for those were the colors that attached themselves in various shades and patterns to me. "You look exactly like your papa," my mother said. "Same green eyes and handsome markings. Mark my words, little Fluff, you'll break many hearts." The oldest of my three siblings by mere minutes was Auguste. He shared my coloring. Next came Licorice, a black-coated brother, and then Lily, my fair-furred sister who resembled our mother. Papa must have been a mischievous rogue because the four of us were pawfuls of naughtiness for our saintly mother.

My first memories are of a cardboard box. What became of the large piece of luggage that originally occupied the slightly squashed container, we never knew. Perhaps it, like my father, was off on some grand, exotic adventure. Its absence, however, allowed my mother and her four kittens to claim the discarded cardboard as our own. Although our flappy-eared home tended to take flight, especially on windy days, the sturdy box remained within the perimeter of a neglected plot of earth. This green space, a term I use loosely, sat in the heart of densely populated Saint-Gilles, one of nineteen communes that comprise modern-day Brussels.

In addition to harvesting a hodgepodge of wind-scattered garbage, the acre of patchy grass collected a jumble of transients of both the two- and four-legged variety. This included my own small family. The few trees brave enough to sprout from the ugly acre—crooked trunks, gnarled branches, and leaves that turned spotted yellow then brown long before autumn—were as sorry-looking as the vagabonds that sought shelter beneath them.

At the edge of this shabby lot, nature surrendered to urban necessity. Recycling bins gathered glass and a prefabricated waist-high latrine collected urine from as many as three men at a time. The open-air contraption was put to use regularly and repeatedly by the men of our camp as well as by patrons of the area's bars. How a trio of men could relieve themselves while staring into each other's face was beyond me. When doing our business, cats preferred privacy. Despite the best intentions of city planners, neither glass nor urine streamed into their respective receptacles with any degree of precision. Poor aims left the pavement dotted with glass shards and sticky puddles, and the air stale with acrid odors of sour beer, wine, and pee.

Ironically, unsightliness allowed our encampment to survive. Respectable residents of the neighborhood didn't congregate for picnics or sport. Most marched past the forsaken plot with purpose, their blinkered eyes focused on the path before them. Local police, in keeping with the laissez-faire attitude that characterizes Belgian personality, didn't hassle squatters—human or animal—as long as peace was preserved. Seizing on this apathy, a variety of vagrants and misfits flourished on this piece of unloved earth where I first came into this world.

To be sure, I've painted an unpleasant portrait of this urban landscape. But most things in life, I've learned, shouldn't be defined in absolute terms. Our world contains as many shades of gray as the Belgian sky. As long as boundaries were honored and competition for food minimized, strays and humans communed in harmony. My siblings and I found the area idyllic. The absence of rowdy children and social crusaders bent on taming our wild plot into respectability, meant freedom and security. We were masters of our own domain. Well, sort of.

Among each group, hierarchies formed—masters among equals. Perhaps that's the natural order of things. Amongst dogs, the mutt that rose to the top of their unsavory heap was the biggest and fiercest, the so-called Alpha. Only the bravest or dumbest dared approach the menacing Belgian shepherd who called himself Rex. A notch below the chestnut and black dog were a band of eager lieutenants vying for pack prominence. As happens with most creatures, insecurity afflicted them with restlessness, fear, and savagery.

Humans stratified similarly. The meanest, nastiest, and most blustering among them rose to the top. Money, the pursuit of which turns civilized beings into wild beasts, was equally sparse. Communal poverty was a blessing akin to paradise without apple trees. Instead of monetary wealth, physical strength, cleverness, and ingenuity set social position. The fiercest human was Bog. The brawny Syrian enjoyed great deference and authority among the upright tribe. Despite standing atop the social ladder, humans weren't all to be feared. Friendship rewarded me with food, caresses, and scraps of insight into their mysterious world. Peter and Sarah, a young couple from the Balkans, came to our encampment after losing their jobs and small apartment near the train station.

After keeping a cautious distance from people, one afternoon I decided to investigate. As the couple sat on a blanket, Sarah reached for me. "Come on, little tiger. Let me hold you." Sidling closer, I paused just beyond her outstretched hands. Brushing against her jeans, I skirted behind her and pressed myself against her nylon jacket. "My goodness," she said. "He's adorable. Look at those emerald green eyes. And he's rubbing against me exactly like our little Scotty did. Gurgles and coos as well."

Peter glanced at me, kindness in his eyes. "You sound like a little pigeon."

Sarah sighed. "If only we could…"

His expression turned sullen. "Honey, you know we can't…"

"But…"

He caressed her arm. "We can barely take care of ourselves. We don't have a home. And even if we did, he's a street cat. He wouldn't want to belong to us any more than that cloud." He gestured skyward to a passing puff of gray.

A tear ran down her cheek. "You're probably right. But how I do miss our little Scotty. His handsome face, silky black fur, soft paws."

Peter wiped away her tear. "We had no choice. Even the priest said he'd be better off at the shelter. Father Pierre has probably found Scotty a good home by now."

Instinctively, I hopped into Sarah's lap. Startled at first, she began to cradle me in her arms. Her soft sobs surrendered to light laughter. "I heard someone call you Fluff. We may not be able to claim you, but we can pamper you." Purring my satisfaction, I writhed in her arms and lifted my chin to draw her caressing fingers to the soft white fur of my throat.

Peter scratched the top of my head. "We certainly can shower him with love."

I visited the couple on my daily rounds. As I snacked on bits of their leftover lunch, they regaled me with stories of their simple life. I learned about the human home—a safe place where people and animals known as pets lived together as a family. They called it "heaven." I hoped Peter and Sarah would be only temporary strays. Their absence would sadden me, but the kind couple deserved a good home, a heaven with a beloved pet.

Cats recognized the concept of community, but we didn't meld into the same tight packs as dogs and humans. Our hierarchy had fewer rules; our protocols and rituals less defined or predictable. A few of the scrappier cats among us staked out territories. Sometimes they allowed passage through their claim. Other times and without provocation, they defended their turf with ferocity. Meandering into and out of camp, feline wanderers shared tales of the outside world. I befriended one such loner.

A gimpy leg brought the cat we called Grumps to camp. In exchange for food, the elderly feline with thinning gray fur and smoky eyes entertained me with tales of a long and adventurous life. Painting my imagination with rich colorful images, Grumps sparked my wanderlust.

Chapter 2

On Little Cat Feet

Despite Grumps' mesmerizing tales of adventure, for the first several weeks of my life I didn't stray far from home. The cardboard box adorned with an image of its former occupant, a suitcase covered with decals of exotic locales, meant comfort and security. Inside, we found refuge from the chill and frequent drizzle of the Belgian climate while Mama provided all the nourishment my three siblings and I could want. A clump of kittens consumed my days with endless play. Romping, rolling, and squealing with joy, we embraced life's simple diversions before returning home at night to snuggle in a cluster of downy fur.

After we weaned ourselves off Mama's milk, I became bolder. Inspired by Grumps, my prowling range steadily grew. Separating from my less adventurous littermates, I ventured ever farther from home. That was when my real education began. My first solo foray took me to the nearby parvis. Others called the place a square, plaza, or piazza. But it was rightfully a parvis, advised Grumps, owing to the presence of a church. Regardless of the name they gave it, camp humans considered the parvis the social center of Saint-Gilles. The place from which they staggered back with full stomachs, breath reeking of beer, and bawdy stories punctuated by uproarious laughter. Their chatter stirred images of a magical, jovial place.

"Gee whiskers!" Upon seeing the parvis for the first time, I marveled at its rich buffet of sights, sounds, and smells. Restaurants, cafés, and *two* butcher shops supplied luscious, savory food for paying clientele and scavengers alike. The square pulsed with more energy than my curious eyes had ever seen. It seemed as big as the universe. Up to then, it was *my* universe. Most humans on the parvis, however, sneered and shooed me away. After a few harsh lessons, I learned the feline art of dodging swift kicks.

The church at the top of the parvis, according to Peter and Sarah, catered to afflictions of the human spirit. Seeking atonement for misdeeds, worshippers hoped to avoid being stuck in a hot, nasty place called hell. Instead, they prayed for salvation to gain entry to a posh resort known as heaven. To this outside observer, the church was ineffective. Kindhearted people emerged with the same gentle natures they possessed upon entering. Similarly, those wearing scowls, kicking strays, and elbowing fellow worshippers on their way into mass, resumed those bad manners on their way out, untouched by sanctity or sermon.

The dearth of worshippers didn't dampen the spirits of the chubby white-haired priest who presided over the parish. Father Pierre was the very priest referenced by Peter and Sarah with regards to their surrendered pet. He paraded about the parvis daily with the same smile on his round pink face that he exhibited Sunday mornings on the church steps welcoming his tiny congregation. He extended friendly hellos and gentle pats to the heads of strays. His charity included offerings of croissant and sweet rolls, crumbs of which regularly dusted his black jacket, shirt, and trousers.

To one side of the church, a plain door led into a social service agency. Many of those I saw in line included squatters from our camp. The agency's results seemed far more effective than those of the church. More tangible anyway. Dirty, stinky humans exited clean and fresh; hungry people emerged with full stomachs. Standing shoulder-to-shoulder with those seeking basic sustenance were others queuing for cash. A device labeled "ATM" spat out money to those lucky enough to know its secret code. What twist of fate, I wondered, relegated people to one line or the other? Was it the same higher power that decided which humans ended up in heaven or hell and which kittens were born before a warm hearth while others came into this world in a cardboard box?

Between the church and social agency stood an ancient three-story building housing a police station. I can't say for sure which of the three establishments—social services, church, police station—my human neighbors frequented most often. But I can state with certainty which they visited the least. Except when bitter cold and pelting rain drove vagabonds inside, the church's varnished pews lost little of their luster. Specializing in past sins and future redemption, the little church didn't offer much to my desperate neighbors. Ignorant of the secret code that dispensed cash, for them basic survival was an immediate need.

A daily market added to the parvis' allure. Although stray dogs, cats, and birds weren't guaranteed warm welcomes, an influx of shoppers enhanced begging opportunities. A few vendors had kind hearts, throwing scrawny shrimp, discolored cheese, or slightly off meat to persistent four-legged tramps. On weekends, offerings tripled. Hundreds of stalls attracted families, couples, and pets on leashes. Fruit and produce peddlers, butchers, cheese and fish mongers, fresh juice and milk stands, and purveyors of roast chicken and ribs, rice dishes and curries, fried potatoes, and sweets tempted the nose and palate. Delectable aromas swirled in the air above the cobblestones on which a hungry cat could usually find some savory scrap.

My elfin cuteness, distinctive markings, and soft, silky coat garnered morsels from even the stingiest of people. Those who pet me often cooed when offering a treat. "Such a handsome boy. So soft and fluffy." Our mother glowed with pride when I reported the reactions to my satiny coat. She'd add a sly wink, a reminder of our shared secret that she considered my coat the finest of all her kittens.

I shared my adventures with Grumps. My exploits, however, paled in comparison to his great tales. His long, repetitive narratives bored other cats, but I never tired of his grand adventures. He opened my imagination to a large, vibrant Brussels beyond the parvis. A city full of interesting places and fascinating people. My eyes practically bugged out when he boasted about his residency at the Royal Palace. He'd known two kings, three queens, and countless princes and princesses… each more colorful than the next. People, it seemed, weren't that different from cats. Some were born in a marble palace while others had the grave misfortune to live in a cardboard box.

When speaking of his favorite places, Grumps frequently purred his words. "The palace grounds are purrfect. Might even say, splendiferous. Like nothing you've ever seen or could even imagine. Orchids, daffodils, and birds of every size, color, and flavor," he added, licking his chops. "Plump, well-bred vermin to satisfy any appetite. And the garbage, oh the heavenly garbage. Fit for a king!"

Many nights, I fell asleep to the rhythm of soft drizzle on cardboard, fantasizing about living in a purrfect, splendiferous palace. Sometimes, however, images of a more humble, heavenly home with humans as kind as Peter and Sarah tempered my dreams.

⸻ ◆ ⸻

Over the next few months, my daily routine remained pretty much the same. I wandered the parvis, mingled among camp humans, and soaked up Grumps' tales. One night, my life took a dramatic and unexpected turn. Returning from my adventures, I found our box empty. No one could tell me what became of Mama Vanille and my three siblings. Lying awake quivering, my whimpers echoed inside the lonely box.

The following morning, relief swept over me. My eldest sibling, Auguste, returned. Having spent the prior evening carousing on the parvis, he was also shocked by our family's disappearance. Together, we canvassed camp residents.

"Quite natural, young ones," an old maiden cat said. "Happens to us all."

"About time you were on your own," added her friend. "Stand on your own four paws."

Finding little comfort in hollow sympathy, we wandered the area for several hours. We didn't turn up any sign of our missing loved ones. Inside our cardboard home, I turned to Auguste. "What can we do?"

He licked my head. "You stay. One of us should be here if…er…I mean when they come back."

"And you?"

"Off to search for them," he replied before disappearing into the misty twilight.

———— ◦◉◦ ————

Days turned into weeks. Weeks into months. I heard nothing about Mama, Auguste, Licorice or Lily. The first anniversary of my birth came and went. Whether a result of misadventure or abandonment, I found myself orphaned. The forgotten little acre and nearby parvis lost their enchantment. Every corner of the plot, each piece of scruffy turf held painful reminders of my loss. I made up my mind to seek adventure.

"I'll start with the afternoon markets, that's what I'll do," I said to Grumps. "Tonight, the Town Hall and Wednesday, Châtelain. There's no limit to where I can go or what I can see."

Grumps shook his head. "Dear boy, I might boast about adventure and pine for my past but there's no better place in all of Brussels for a cat to thrive than right here."

Not believing my ears, I stared at him. "I wanna see the whole, enormous city. And the palace where I'll curl up on the velvet throne. After that, maybe I'll wander the world."

With a scowl, Grumps silenced the snickering cats who encircled us. After caressing me, he plucked from the ground a *pissenlit*, known also as a dandelion. "Dear Fluff, in a field of weeds this vibrant flower knows no equal. But should the same bloom dare raise its golden crown in the palace gardens, it will be trampled, plucked, and thrown onto a compost heap."

My mouth quivered. "B...but we can't all be orchids and daffodils."

"Maybe not. Yet the humble dandelion must know its place if it hopes to survive."

Chapter 3
Catatonic

"Crybaby, crybaby, when are you leaving?"
"Thought you skedaddled days ago."
"You a chicken or a scaredy cat?"
"Fluff's a fraidy cat. Fluff's a fraidy cat."

Fellow squatters taunted me about my boasted departure. Their insults pelted me like hail. "I'm *not* afraid. I *don't* cry." But my protests were false bravado. Fear *did* grip me. My paws *did* brush away tears that welled in my eyes every night. The loss of my family broke my heart but I didn't dare show it. Sadness was a luxury on the street. Strays viewed sorrow as weakness, picking up its desperate scent as they did the aroma of raw meat. Animals and humans alike considered the broken-hearted easy prey.

As I dithered, my confidence and resolve ebbed. What-ifs pounded in my head like pealing church bells. *What if my family comes back? What if Grumps is right? What if it's not as exciting as I imagine it to be? What if I get lost?*

Bold declarations provided cover. "I am going on my adventure. You'll see. Wouldn't stay around here anyway. Not if we had central heat, roofs that didn't leak, and all the roast chicken we could eat."

Auguste's vow to return, however, provided a convenient excuse to delay my departure. The only ones not to snicker at my puffery were Penelope and Odysseus. Pert, perky, and preened, the fine fur of the Siamese siblings retained a sweet scent that Grumps called the telltale mark of domestication. "Soon enough," he said, "those posh parlor kitties will stink of musty earth and stale ale like the rest of us."

The brother and sister spoke of their recent owner, an ancient Flemish widow with whom they lived in a spacious apartment in Uccle. After the woman died without an heir, her landlord sold her belongings. Instead of finding a new home for her beloved pets or even sending them to a shelter, the thin mustachioed landlord whose tailored suits reeked of cinnamon and clove pipe tobacco booted the two cats to the street. Chance guided the downtrodden pair to our camp.

Penelope and Odysseus padded lightly into our community. The dandy housecats lacked the confident swaggers of veteran street creatures. I tried not to be too judgmental as I had yet to perfect my own poised swagger. Mama Vanille's words echoed in my ears, "Don't fret, my kitten. You'll soon be strutting like a tiger." But who ever heard of a tiger named Fluff?

As newcomers, the siblings drew narrow-eyed stares from tenured residents. Other cats kept their distance, considering the posh pair too aloof even for felines. Their formal meows sounded stilted, even uppity, to our common ears. Opportunists were the exception. Shrewd hustlers tested boundaries to gauge threats and opportunities.

"Pampered pets don't fare well on the outside," Grumps said during one of our storytelling sessions. Nodding to a willow tree under which the brother and sister huddled, his voice dropped to a whisper. "I wager they don't survive six months. More like six weeks if they're lucky."

I gasped. "Good heavens! Isn't there anything we can do?"

Puckering his mouth shut, Grumps shook his head.

Having lost my family, their plight pained me. Their inexperience could be fatal. In light of my imminent departure, however, I didn't want to waste anyone's time befriending them. But until I set out on my adventures, I might be able to teach them something of the street. Coaching them to forage for food and steer clear of dangers such as Rex the dog king and Bog the human brute were relatively easy tasks. Schooling them how to handle my feline nemesis proved trickier. Scratch, a burly black and white cat, had already begun to bully Odysseus with taunts of "sissy." He wasted no time pursuing Penelope, spreading vicious rumors about her virtue when she rebuffed his advances. "Stuck-up prima donna" was his mildest taunt. Something had to be done.

In addition, their first forays into alfresco dining didn't go well. In their former life, salmon pâté appeared twice a day in silver bowls engraved with their names. In camp, they discovered the intense competition for scraps. Experienced street animals and desperate people were better skilled. As for potential prey, fleet-winged birds, street-savvy mice, and other nimble vermin outwitted the parlor cats. Bigger, meaner felines including Scratch snatched any food they managed to snare. Initially rejecting my offers of help, Odysseus' and Penelope's grumbling tummies softened their resistance.

Coaching them brought an unexpected reward. Further insight into the human/pet relationship. Unlike Peter and Sarah, they spoke from a feline perspective. In addition to a warm hearth, fresh food, and filtered water, they described unconditional love. Penelope mewled. "Our owner was so kind, so gentle. I can still smell her lovely scent of lavender and roses." I soaked up her vivid descriptions of domesticity. Their plush pasts filled me with awe. Odysseus misinterpreted my silent wonderment as envy.

He caressed his sister's head. "Be sensitive, Penelope. I know you're sad. We were lucky to live like that. But you mustn't boast. It's unbecoming. Not all cats have been as fortunate." He offered a subtle nod in my direction. "This camp, rustic as it may be, is our new life."

That night, I expected grand adventures and exotic locales to fill my dreams. Instead, my head churned with images of a comfy apartment and human family. Prompted by a vivid scene of tummy tickles from a sweet-smelling human, my own giggles awakened me. Adventure or family; excitement or security? What was my heart's desire?

One evening, I led Odysseus and Penelope to a dimly lit residential street off the parvis. "Listen up," I said. "Nights before weekly garbage collection are a veritable buffet. Loads of scraps. Pickup day isn't so bad either. Refuse workers aren't known for tidiness, speed, or precision."

A gaping hole in a white refuse bag aided my demonstration. Contents of a discarded tuna tin spilled onto the pavement. The intoxicating aroma twitched my whiskers. I nibbled only a bit when I noticed my two pupils standing back. I slid the tin toward them. "Go on. About as fresh as you'll find on the street."

Tucking into the flakes of pink fish, Penelope and Odysseus ate with voracious abandon. After ingesting the last morsel, Odysseus licked the edges of his mouth. With a look of satisfaction on his gray face, he glanced over the empty tin and into my eyes. "Good friend, do you suppose my sister and I may accompany you?"

My head shot up. "Huh?"

"On your glorious expedition, of course."

"G…gee whiskers! I…I d…don't know."

A single traveling companion wasn't in my plan let alone *two*. I didn't want anyone or anything to slow me down. Then again, companions had certain advantages—additional eyes, noses, and ears to help scavenge for food; more claws, hisses, and teeth to ward off aggressors; extra fur and body heat for warmth. For every pro, a con rose in my head. Dogs travelled in packs, not cats. We preferred solitary lives, the stealth existence of an aloof and nimble loner. Two molly-coddled newbies would make miserable travel companions. They'd leave the dirty work to me. Worse, their inexperience and untested survival skills meant danger.

"We won't be a bother, I assure you," Penelope said. Reflecting the lamplights, her eyes reminded me of violets. "It's only that—"

"We're inexperienced in the ways of the street," Odysseus added, interrupting his sister. "Why only a fortnight ago we…"

"…resided in a warm, comfortable home with a kind, refined owner." It was Penelope's turn to interrupt her brother. "With silver bowls of fresh food and water, soft satin cushions and…"

"…all the unsolicited affection we could ever desire."

"We were lavished with love."

"Our safety, secure."

Motioning toward camp, Penelope dropped her voice to a whisper. "This life is all quite new to us. And a bit frightening."

"Camp's okay," I replied. "Just have to get used to it, that's all."

I wanted to ground them in reality, especially since I hadn't decided whether to let them tag along on my big adventure. However, Grumps' dire prediction about their fate echoed in my head. Pangs of guilt bubbled up inside me. Conflicted, I recalled my mother's stark warning about survival: *Logic, Fluff, not emotion, must be your guide.*

Penelope fixed her bewitching eyes on me. "If camp's all right, then why are *you* leaving?"

"Maybe he isn't." Sarcasm purred out of Odysseus' sneering mouth.

I bristled. "What's that supposed to mean?"

"All I know is what I see," he replied. "Since arriving in camp, we've heard endless boasts of your plan to see the world. And yet, day after monotonous day, here you remain. *Grand plan* indeed."

I arched my back in anger as Penelope turned a stern face toward Odysseus. "Dear Odie, don't be so impolite. That's no way to speak to our new friend. Fluff's been a saint, a lifesaver." She looked at me, kindness in her expression, "Really you have. We'd have starved if it wasn't for you. You're a dear."

"Gee whiskers!" I shifted my eyes to the pavement hoping my embarrassment didn't show.

Penelope nudged her brother. "Now apologize, Odie." Impatient with his hesitation, she added, "Go on."

"Oh, very well. My sincerest apologies."

Turning to me, Penelope batted her eyes. "I'm sure you'll allow us to accompany you if we ask politely."

"I...I...I," I stammered aloud as Mama's words repeated in my head: *Logic not emotion.*

She prodded me with her head. Her silky fur retained traces of lavender and rose. "We won't be any bother at all. You won't even notice we're there."

"Oh, okay." My thoughts, however, went in another direction. *Jeepers! Logic, my furry butt. This pretty little kitten means trouble.*

Odysseus puffed out his chest; a look of triumph swept across his face. "Pleased that the matter is all settled. You won't regret your decision, good friend."

As we walked toward camp, the pair suggested an immediate departure.

"Er, um,…how about next week?" I replied. Although prospects of my brother's return had faded, I hadn't abandoned all hope. My companions exchanged a look, the kind of subtle communication that occurs between siblings. I braced knowing what was coming.

Odysseus cleared his throat. "We hoped for a more imminent departure. Can't put the bullies and ruffians behind us soon enough."

"How about Sunday? Day after tomorrow." Penelope nuzzled me, her sweet fragrance intoxicating.

I heaved a sigh. "Okay, okay. We can leave sooner. But Monday, not Sunday!" I had to put my paw down. "You two wouldn't know of such things, what with getting your food handed to you on silver platters. Sundays are the best market day, juiciest roast chicken anyway. Gotta stay for that. Monday, we can head over to the Town Hall. Grumps raves about that afternoon market."

Satisfied with the compromise, brother and sister nodded in silence. With plans firmed and stomachs full, we neared home. A light rain began to fall. We reached the edge of camp where pockmarked asphalt surrendered to patchy grass.

"Hey! You there!" Meanness laced the guttural tone.

The three of us froze. I recognized Bog's gruff voice. *Please don't let him be speaking to us.* Seeing the menacing brute glare in our direction, I shuddered. Penelope and Odysseus whimpered.

"Yeah, you three flea factories." Bog, a bearded man with dark unruly hair, listed from side to side. His threadbare trousers and ill-fitting shirt flapped in the breeze. A red beer can in his hand explained his wobbly gait. "Get the hell over here, *now!*"

Penelope quaked with fear. I inched closer to her side. Options percolated in my head. If we ignored Bog's command, we risked even greater wrath. Those who angered the brute regretted doing so. We could attack but we'd only raise his fury. An excessive intake of alcohol probably numbed him; he'd pummel us without suffering any pain. We could turn and run. He'd never catch us…*all* of us anyway. And there was the rub. Bog might be able to grab one of us. Penelope was most likely to be scooped up. Images of the pretty young feline in the grimy clutches of the brute sent shivers down my spine.

Bog took another step. The pungent odor of onions and sausage gusted from his oversized mouth. "Come on scaredy-cats, I won't hurt you." Artificial sweetness laced his voice making him more menacing. "Here, kitties, kitties, kitties." He bent down, flashing a ghastly gap-toothed smile. Gesturing us forward with an extended arm knocked him off balance. He stumbled, tumbling to the ground and summersaulting forward. As he came to rest on his back, we stared at his feet. Dirty orange socks poked through holes in his well-worn shoes. He moaned. Expletives in a variety of languages peppered his groans.

Penelope fretted. "Oh my. Whatever shall we do?"

"Get the heck outta here, quick," I replied.

Odysseus stammered. "Where to? Where to?"

Let me think, let me think… "Got it. We'll tell Grumps what happened."

"Can he assist us?" Penelope was barely audible over Bog's grunts and curses.

I shook my head. "Don't see how. But he's sure to have advice. Besides, he should know what happened just in case…"

"In case what?" asked Penelope.

"In case…in case…just in case, that's all." I didn't dare describe the terrible things I'd seen Bog do to others who got in his way—animals and people.

Odysseus shook with terror. "Maybe we should alter our plans. Depart tonight."

"No!" I held out hope that Auguste or the rest of my family would return. "We're not ready. And remember, not a word to anyone that I'm letting you two join me. Don't want to find myself playing tour guide to more runaways."

"Damn cats!" We jumped at Bog's booming voice. "Wait till I get my hands on the three of you." His flailing arms accompanied his bellowing rants as he struggled to right himself. "Made me spill my beer." He turned the can upside-down before crushing it in his palm.

"Run!" I shouted.

The three of us bolted through the fog. Taking the lead, I glanced back to ensure my companions were keeping up. Scanning the horizon, I saw a shadowy figure. *Grumps.* He hobbled across the shrouded acre. Drizzle intensified into a steady downpour.

I yelled to my companions. "Over there!"

I sprinted to the spot where I saw him disappear into a hedge. "Grumps, Grumps," I repeated. "We need your advice." Sprinkles of kicked-up dirt suggested that he was finishing his business. I spoke rapidly into the black void, sharing our predicament. "What should we do?"

A reply came through the bushes. "Not good my young friends, not good."

My eyes widened; my fur stood. It wasn't the slow, meandering voice of Grumps at all. The sinister snarl belonged to Scratch. Penelope, Odysseus, and I retreated from the bush.

Scratch's white head emerged from the hedge. "Don't run. You're in a terrible fix. And when a cat's in a terrible fix, ole Scratch is the guy for the job."

"Yikes!" I exclaimed. "We thought you were Grumps."

Scratch raised his rump and stretched his head forward toward his front paws. His red eyes remained focused on me. "And what would old Grumps do but shake his head and fret. No, my wise young felines, fate led you to the right place. Scratch is the cat you need."

My fur stood on end. I didn't trust him. But we had no choice. A glance back showed Bog on his knees. He'd soon be on his feet again.

Odysseus cleared his throat. "Good Fluff, we find ourselves in a precarious predicament. We are in no position to refuse succor." He turned to Scratch. "My fine feline, what prudent course of action do you recommend?"

Scratch looked at him with a glazed stare. "Huh?"

"He means, what should we do?"

Scratch pulled a face. "Then why didn't he say so? Lay low for a while. With luck and a few more beers, Bog might forget what happened. Wouldn't be the first time."

Penelope whimpered. "But where can we go?" Scratch leered at her. I seethed but urgency demanded restraint.

"Camp's got big ears and bigger mouths," he said, explaining his lowered voice. "Behind the church is a rectory. Its basement is a good hiding place. You know where it is, Adventure Boy." I nodded through clenched teeth. "Bog's not the church type. Won't go near you."

"How do we gain access?" asked Odysseus.

Scratch turned to him, self-satisfaction in his expression and annoyance in his tone. "Look for the broken window, Sissy Boy."

Oh, how I yearned to swat the bully. Summoning my best self-control, I kept my paw planted on the ground. A skirmish would consume too much time.

"How long can we stay?" asked Penelope.

Scratch pressed his face close to hers. "Father Pierre's a softy for strays."

Odysseus tried to speak, "But..."

Scratch hissed. "But nothin'. Scat! I'll send word how things stand with Bog." He glared at Penelope. "And when you can show your pretty little face back here again."

"Tell, Grumps, won't you? What happened, where we are. Same goes for my brother if…er, I mean when he comes back."

Scratch flashed a sinister smile. "You can count on ole Scratch."

As Penelope, Odysseus, and I dashed toward the parvis, the raw icy wind carried the spine-tingling echoes of Bog's curses and Scratch's hissing laugh.

Chapter 4
Refuge

Scratch was right. A missing window promised entry to the rectory basement. Observing my companions quaking with fear, I agreed to descend first. Inching my nose over the dusty ledge, I squelched a sneeze before gazing into the dark void. My whiskers twitched at the odor of stale rodent droppings. The path down included a short plunge onto the uppermost box of a tall stack. A tricky leap onto an old wooden desk followed. From there, the floor was an easy reach.

Descending slowly, I assessed risks. Enhanced by darkness, my nose detected aromas of a meal in progress in the residence above—roasted meat, vegetables, and potatoes. Rotating my ears, I picked up the sound of music—a violin on a radio or turntable. Footsteps plodded overhead. Some, no doubt, belonged to Father Pierre. Muffled voices kept identities of the other diners a mystery.

Safely on the floor, I called up to the window. "All clear."

Penelope edged onto the sill. She leaped. My hair stood on edge until she reached my side. I celebrated her descent with a gentle nuzzle. Beneath her coat of fine fragrant fur, her heart raced. "You did good, *ma chère. Très bonne.*"

A distressed meow drew our attention. The floodlit church presented Odysseus' arched-back in silhouette. He emitted another piercing cry.

"Shush!" My voice was slightly louder than a whisper.

"Your turn, dear brother." Penelope's tone was soft, encouraging.

"Come on, Odysseus. You can do it."

Backing away from the ledge, he stammered, "I d...don't know." If he disappeared from view, I knew he'd never muster the courage to make the tricky descent.

I bellowed, "Bog's right behind you. Hurry!"

He gasped. "Oh my!" He leaped from the windowsill onto the top box. After steadying himself, he puffed out his chest and beamed down at us. "I did it. I did it."

"Bravo, dear brother!"

He glanced up to the window, his gray eyes wide, his tail stiff. "Hey! Bog's not there."

I hunched my shoulders. "Sorry. Musta been a shadow. Important thing is you're almost down. Just a couple more jumps."

"You're incorrigible," Penelope whispered. "Good thing you're adorable."

My legs buckled, but a distressed meow drew my attention. The boxes on which Odysseus perched began to sway. The stack resembled a giant pendulum. With a pained expression and cries of terror, he teetered back and forth. His paws clawed at the cardboard.

"Jump! Jump!" I shouted, extending my paw to a quaking Penelope.

Preceded by an awkward jolt, Odysseus leaped down to the desk. His rear legs exerted so much counter force that the top boxes tumbled to the ground. *Nice going, hotshot.* Fearing that the commotion had raised an alarm upstairs, we remained still for several moments. But nothing stirred. I gazed up to the ceiling. "Music must have muffled the noise."

Odysseus surveyed the clutter of boxes. "Heavens! Never had difficulty leaping from Madame's china cabinet onto her grand piano. Nimble as an acrobat, I was." Raising his chin and puffing up his chest, defeat vanished from his chubby face. "But I did it, yes I did it."

You certainly did it all right. There goes our escape route.

Finding an alternate exit would have to wait until morning. Except for the puddle of light in which we stood, the basement was as black as pitch. Damp, musty, and cold too. Despite our unfamiliar surroundings, relief swept over me. I could think of no safer refuge from a deranged brute than a rectory belonging to a cherubic priest.

Odysseus looked up. "Nice to have a solid roof over our heads again. Madame claimed that fine mist worked wonders for her complexion. But incessant drizzle has only wrought havoc on my fine fur."

As he shook his damp coat, a flickering blue flame drew my curiosity. I sauntered across the cold floor to an ancient device. My companions identified it as a water heater. The rusty tank radiated warmth, a welcome oasis in an otherwise dank space. Languid meows informed me that brother and sister were fading fast.

"We've had a busy night," I said. "Best get some sleep. Our heads and next steps will be clearer in the morning."

"Sensible plan, good friend," Odysseus mumbled through a yawn. "Perhaps Scratch will bring good news. Although a bit crass for my liking, he seems a rather decent chap."

Penelope offered a faint meow; her eyes flickered shut. My drowsy companions plopped down onto the floor and dozed off. Sleep would yield to hunger. We'd require food and water soon enough. Perhaps good fortune would bless us with a few of those church mice Grumps described. I imagined them as plump and agreeable as Father Pierre. Dropping onto my stomach, I folded my paws and tail under my torso to conserve heat. Fighting off sleep, I considered our predicament. We needed a way out that didn't take us through the residence. Father Pierre was friendly on the parvis but I doubted he'd take kindly to permanent squatters in his basement.

I envied Odysseus and Penelope. Melded together in a mass of fine gray and black fur, the posh refugees slept as if they didn't have a care in the world. Gurgles bubbling within the ancient water heater couldn't disturb their peaceful slumber. With a slow and steady rhythm, their soft breaths wheezed through the darkness. Their handsome faces, lit by the glow of flickering flame, wore masks of serenity.

I shook their blissful ignorance from my thoughts. Parlor sophistication might have given them flowery speech and refined tastes but it hadn't prepared them for the street. Cruel lessons promised to haunt their futures. Predators, disease, accidents, empty stomachs, and loss awaited them. From pampered domesticity to homeless refugees, their lives had taken a dramatic turn. So, as a matter of fact, had my own.

Playful days and warm nights snuggled with Mama and my siblings in our cardboard home seemed a lifetime ago. In the blink of an eye, I'd gone from carefree kitten to purposeful cat. The encounter with Bog and our unplanned exile forced me to accept bitter reality. Mama Vanille, Licorice, and Lily probably weren't coming back. I lost track of how long Auguste had been gone in search of the others. *No, Fluff, you're on your own.* Well, almost. By agreeing to guide Penelope and Odysseus, I'd assumed a major responsibility. My job was to bring the three of us to safety…to keep us all alive.

Movement and aromas from the floor above faded. Soft music and the crackle of a fire suggested a quiet end to the evening. Perhaps Father Pierre nodded off to sleep in a comfortable chair, a favorite book in his lap, his feet toasting before the warm hearth. Did the slumbering priest assume a carefree expression similar to those I envied on my sleeping companions? To ward off anxiety, I rekindled a recent fantasy—a lovely life as a family pet. Images drawn from stories shared by Peter and Sarah transported me to their former apartment near the Gare du Midi. In this world, their beloved Scotty doesn't exist. Instead, I snuggle on a soft cushion, my stomach full from an evening feast, my fur warmed by a generous fire.

Sarah calls from the sofa. "Here, Fluff. Let me hold you." I jump onto her lap and gaze into her dark, kind eyes. She turns to Peter, her voice soft. "He's adorable, honey. I love him to pieces." Smiling, Peter appears content seeing his wife happy. He scratches the soft fur under my chin. I purr with delight.

My pleasant fantasy faded away. I rolled onto my side and braced against the cold cement. With my head resting on my paw, I fell into a deep sleep. Sweet dreams of domestic bliss surrendered to a series of terrifying *cauchemars*, nightmares. Bog and Scratch, grotesque exaggerations of their actual selves, featured prominently. Some nightmares took place in the present. Others were set in an unrecognizable future where my fur was white, my eyesight poor, and my step as feeble as Grumps'. The endings were all the same. The search for my family ended in heartache.

One terrifying episode included Odysseus and Penelope. Bog chased the three of us through camp and onto the parvis. Sure-footed and sober, the brute sliced the air in front of him with a bloody knife. As the pursuit continued, the blade grew in size. His eyes fired with hate; his nostrils flared with fury. I bellowed to my companions to quicken their pace. But instead of running faster, Penelope and Odysseus moved in slow motion. The knife, lengthening as if by magic, cut within inches of their backsides. The next swing would whack off a chunk of their tails.

As often happened in dreams, the scene suddenly shifted. Scratch stood at Bog's feet, a menacing sneer on his face. Following his upward glance, I gasped. The long steel blade glistened in his hand. His other hand held Penelope by the scruff of her neck. Except for her twitching legs, she appeared as lifeless as a rabbit on a butcher's hook. Letting out a blood-curdling howl, Bog thrust the knife toward Penelope's throat. I attempted to meow alarm but no sound came from my open mouth. My paws remained glued to the pavement. The sound of Father Pierre's cheerful voice filled me with hope. Would he save her?

"Wake up little one, wake up."

I stirred at the sound of Father Pierre's voice. His tone was no longer harsh. Disturbing images of Bog and the butcher's caravan vanished like a magician's trick. A hand caressed my fur. I cracked open an eye. Swinging from the ceiling, a single light bulb illuminated the pink dimpled cheeks of the white-haired priest.

Resting on one knee, he bent over me. "There, there little one. It's okay. You're safe." His breath puffed with a hint of scrambled eggs and altar wine. "You and your friends must be hungry."

Friends! Were they still beside me? A glance over my shoulder reassured me. Odysseus and Penelope were fast asleep in a tight clump of fur. I couldn't tell where brother and sister, or for that matter, head and tail began and ended.

Father Pierre smiled. "I'll send Cook down with food. Canned fish is about the best I can offer, I'm afraid. And cream of course, that we can do. How does that sound?" My hearty meow signaled approval. The priest continued to pet me, his soft touch fluffing my fur. "I've seen you on the parvis, haven't I, little fellow? Sometimes with your mama and littermates. You had a handsome papa too. Same green eyes." After an exaggerated yawn, I rose to my feet and rubbed against his black trousers. "Such fine fur," he added. "Such a handsome boy."

My head spun with wild thoughts. Would Father Pierre want a handsome feline like me as a pet? Rolling at his feet, I lost myself in fantasy. But dreams of a cozy life in the rectory came to an abrupt stop. Loud barking from the landing above echoed off the concrete walls. Deep and raucous ferocity suggested that the bark belonged to a big, cantankerous hound. Definitely not a cat lover. *Fine, I don't want to live in a crummy rectory anyway. I've got a city to explore. A life of grand adventure awaits!*

Father Pierre's expression hardened. He shouted up the stairs, "Quiet, Max!"

The commotion awakened Odysseus and Penelope. Rising to his feet, the old priest looked down at the three of us. Kindness replaced the stern glower that had flashed across his face. He pulled a phone from his pocket and snapped several photos. "Splendid, splendid," he muttered. "I'd invite you three beauties upstairs for breakfast but I'm afraid Max wouldn't like it. No, he wouldn't like it one bit."

On the contrary, Max sounded to me as if he might enjoy three cats for breakfast—as his entrée.

Chapter 5
Leap to Freedom

As hide-outs went, the rectory was pretty nifty. Although we spent our first day and second night sequestered without any news from Scratch or his minions, we didn't fret. Consequences of rebuffing Bog could wait. We were enjoying the warm hospitality of Father Pierre and his staff. Other than Max's spine-arching howls, our stay felt more like a holiday than a forced retreat.

Cook, a tall, slender Polish woman whose steel-gray hair smelled of strawberries and her fingers of garlic, provisioned three meals a day. Canned fish offered up for our first breakfast gave way to shaved chicken at lunch and ground veal at dinner. Our second breakfast consisted of smoked salmon and creamed herring. Cook served our meals on china plates and gave us fresh water and cream in crystal bowls. I was unaccustomed to such fine dining but my companions devoured the delicacies like street cats feasting on smashed rat.

Cook's husband, Jean, was the rectory caretaker. As jovial as his wife was severe, he was as fat as she was lean. On his frequent visits to the basement, he muttered in broken Polish, French, and English, often peppering his comments with gut-jiggling laughter. The gusts that blew from his mouth suggested a fondness for beer. Jean kept a workshop in the basement that a deadbolt rendered off limits to snoops like us. Locks also restricted access to a separate storage room and wine cellar, the latter frequented regularly by Father Pierre. Closed doors aroused my curiosity; locks represented an invitation. My current interest was more than mere feline nosiness. One of those rooms might provide an exit to the street.

On our first morning, Jean delivered a large crate. "The boss told me to treat his furry guests *très bon*. First order of my business...a litter box for your business." His boisterous laugh echoed through the basement. With a flourish, he presented a shallow black box of wood as well as a bag containing sand. No sooner had he set up the strange device than my two companions scurried over. Jean laughed and my eyes widened in amazement as brother and sister demonstrated its use.

A grinning Odysseus motioned me toward the box. "Your turn, friend."

"Wowee! An indoor toilet. Whatever will they think of next?" After sampling all the rich new food, I was only too eager for a go.

Jean also produced three cushions. As soon as he placed the plush squares on the floor, Odysseus rushed over and plopped down onto the thickest one. Closing his eyes, the chubby Siamese purred as if he'd swallowed a juicy sparrow.

About to follow her brother's lead, Penelope hesitated. She turned to me, kindness in her eyes. "Which would you like?"

"Any will do. In fact, the floor is fine."

Giggling, she pushed me forward with a friendly swat to my backside. "Heroes take precedence." Her words sent my stomach fluttering and my knees wobbling but I managed to totter forward. As soon as my body hit the soft cushion, I curled into a ball and fell asleep.

⸺«◉»⸺

Days and nights passed in exile and still no word from Scratch. I began to feel anxious, unsettled. Pacing for hours over cool concrete, I explored every corner of our refuge. Sniffing the thresholds of forbidden rooms, my nose detected a mix of strange odors including a hint of the outdoors. As comfortable as our hosts had made us, the basement began to feel more prison than safe haven. I'd never been cooped up for so long. If our banishment lasted much longer, I'd go crazy. Finding a way out became my priority. With the residence protected by Max and locked doors preventing us from exploring other exits, the broken window through which we entered was our best option. The distance from desk to sill, however, was too great. Thanks to Odysseus' clumsy descent, the boxes we needed to ascend littered the floor.

As I fretted about escape, Odysseus heaved a sigh of satisfaction. "Exile is marvelous. Scottish salmon, Norwegian herring, Limoges china, Baccarat crystal, soft plush satin." He seasoned his litany with deep purrs. "My fur is regaining its luster. Best of all, we have at our disposal a mahogany litter box! If this is heaven, I surrender to death."

I glared at him. *Don't give me any ideas.*

An amused grin swept across Penelope's face. "Don't get too comfortable, Odie. This is only temporary. We'll be back on the street soon enough."

He groaned. "Dear sister, *pleeease*. How can you be so heartless? Allow me to savor this genteel respite without a reminder of the banal fate that awaits us. Misfortune has dealt us a cruel hand. Yes, the cards must be played in due course, but for now let me keep my losing hand face down on this miserable table of chance known as street life."

Oh brother! I stifled an urge to spit up a fur ball. A child's stuffed cat with oversized eyes and chartreuse-colored fur made a less annoying companion. Yes, this fancy lifestyle was great. You'd get no argument from me. But I was satisfied simply with an indoor toilet. As long as Jean kept it tidy, which he did.

"Odysseus can be a bit melodramatic," Penelope whispered from her cushion. "As you may have guessed from my brother's flowery rhetoric, our dear Madame enjoyed her afternoon card games. Nips of sherry too with her lady friends."

Our worlds were far apart. The parlor games of the siblings' mistress were nothing like the cutthroat matches of Bog and his wretched cohorts. Back at camp when cards came out, sensible cats, dogs, and humans scattered. Games devolved into a muddle of shouts, skirmishes, and after repeated guzzles of cheap wine and beer, knife fights. Bog was a nasty loser. He recouped losses with force. No savvy opponent wishing to avoid a jagged scar or broken limb beat Bog a second time.

I pushed from my head, card games and images of our vastly different worlds—theirs of velvet armchairs and mine of wooden crates and broken glass. Odysseus' philosophy, particularly the bits and pieces relating to fate and fortune, intrigued me. A street cat like me didn't have the luxuries of time and an idle mind to ponder such lofty topics. Given his severe distress with our predicament, perhaps I was the luckiest among us. A life confined to a narrow band between peaks and valleys had advantages. A common stray like me might never climb too high in the world but I didn't have far to fall either. Our current situation was dire but not fatal, at least for a seasoned street cat like me. Maybe a warm hearth and comfy lap were foolish, a brambled path leading to misfortune, disappointment, or worse.

"Your brother's okay. His gripes are understandable. Your lives have been turned upside-down."

"Kind of you to say. Our changed circumstances have been quite a shock. We not only lost the only home we ever knew, we also lost our identities, our purpose. You must admit, we don't make very good strays. Maybe we never will." A gentle smile replaced her wistful expression. "I know we've been a handful to you. Much more than we promised. I'm sorry."

"You've been no trouble at all."

"Now, now. We all know Odysseus and I were Bog's targets. You've been a dear not to blame us."

"I considered no such thing."

"The brute never bothered you before our arrival, or so you said. That's irrefutable. Places your forced exile squarely on our shoulders."

Although I vigorously shook my head in disagreement, the notion had crossed my mind. There were several reasons why Bog might want to get his clutches on two parlor cats. But they were too diabolical to share with my companions. "Well, we're here now, together, that's all that matters. Get some sleep. We'll see what morning brings."

She yawned. "Hopefully, Scratch gets word to us soon."

I hoped she was right. Max's patience was wearing thin. Hair-raising snarls and growls continued to accompany the mongrel's menacing scratches at the basement door.

For the third night in a row, a dinner party in the dining room above sent aromas of roasted meats and sounds of muffled voices and classical music down through the floorboards. With a plush cushion as my bed and a stomach satisfied by roast chicken, I fell asleep.

Next morning, I awoke to a paw caressing my face. The scent of lavender and roses filled me with contentment. I cracked open an eye and smiled at Penelope.

"We have a visitor," she whispered.

Shaking off sleep with a wide yawn, I rushed through my stretches and jumped to my feet. Standing beside his sister, Odysseus stared up to the broken window and meowed loudly.

I swatted his tail. "Hush! Can't have Cook coming down with breakfast. We need to hear what Ollie has to say." I nodded up to the fat orange and white cat, one of Scratch's cronies. More brawn than brains, Ollie had lost the tip of his tail on a dare to tickle the twitching nose of a snoring dog. A week later, he lost the tip of an ear accepting the identical dare.

He inched his head over the sill. "Nice digs."

Uninterested in small talk, I simply replied, "What's the word?"

"Scratch says for you three to lay low for another day or two. But from the looks of things," he added with a glance at the steep drop, "don't appear you're goin' nowhere."

Mention of delay caused me to groan. Odysseus, on the other hand, purred with delight. He replied to my icy glare with a shoulder shrug. "Why the face? I'm in no rush to leave. Can't understand why you are."

Penelope scowled at him. "We should trust Fluff's instincts. This is his world, not ours."

I huffed my frustration. "We simply gotta get outta here."

"I'll be back tomorrow. Don't go anywhere." Ollie snickered.

"Wait! Wait! Don't go!" My panicked tone surprised me. "What about Bog? He still angry?"

The orange and white face returned to the window. "Scratch says he'll take care of Bog...but it'll cost you." His lewd glare directed at Penelope raised the hair on my back. "Gotta scurry." He disappeared a second time.

Penelope pressed her paw to her face. "Whatever shall we do?"

Odysseus scoffed. "You heard the messenger. Stay put. That's what we should do. And that's *precisely* what I will do." He plopped down onto his cushion.

I took a deep breath. "Let me think, let me think."

⸺⸻◉⸻⸺

As brother and sister nibbled at a breakfast of gray North Sea shrimp, I hatched a plan. It required luck, opportunity, and a distracted caretaker.

After slurping a measure of cream, Odysseus glanced up at me. "Heaven's sake, what are you doing?" Ignoring him and his milky mustache, I continued to shuffle the scattered boxes. "Hey," he shouted. "Don't block the litter box. I'll need to relieve myself at any moment."

Perfect! For my plan to work, it needed a loaded litter box.

After surveying my work, Odysseus nodded. "I must admit. Privacy is a welcome and civilized improvement. Perhaps we're rubbing off on you."

I stifled a snicker before the three of us, in rapid succession, shimmied between the boxes to do our business.

Preceded by a burst of laughter, the heavy-footed caretaker

trudged down the stairs. For my plan to succeed, Jean had to stick to his morning ritual of cleaning the litter box before collecting our dirty breakfast plates. As he approached the mahogany box, he scrunched his face. "What's this? How am I supposed to clean your litter if I can't reach it?"

He stooped, lifting the first two cartons from the floor. I screeched; he flinched. Turning to me with a worried look, he stacked the boxes onto the desk. *Success!* I darted from one corner of the basement to the other.

Jean released a boisterous laugh. "Funny fellow. Thought I stepped on your tail."

Bending down, he lifted a third box. I jumped onto the desk and screeched. He laughed again. "What the heck's gotten into you?"

I hoped my cries from the desktop would prompt him to place the box on top of the others. Three stacked boxes weren't ideal but they would provide enough height to reach the broken window. Jean hesitated; his hands clutched the box. I screeched even louder. He simply laughed louder. Still, he held onto the box. *Failure!* As I abandoned hope of escape, Penelope charged into Jean's calf. *Good Girl!*

Jean placed the box on top of the others before rubbing his leg. "Playful little critters this morning."

I needed him out of the basement. Dashing to the top of the stairs, I meowed and scratched at the door. As expected, Max responded with fierce barks and paw scratches.

Jean groaned. "Why'd you have to rile up the hound. The wife will be furious." Leaving the boxes on the desk, he picked up the dirty plates and trudged upstairs. "You don't want that kind of trouble. *Her* bite's worse than *his* bark." With a strained laugh, he disappeared through the door.

Penelope purred into my ear. "Clever boy."

Odysseus shook his head and scoffed. "Clever? We're stuck with a filthy litter box."

Penelope and I tried to convince Odysseus that our moment of escape had come. Although a nighttime departure was preferred, we had no choice. Jean might return any second to clean the litter box. If he also carried away the stack of boxes, we'd be trapped for good. I stood nose-to-nose with Odysseus. Our whiskers touched. "This may be our only chance. Do you want to spend the rest of your life down here?"

He shrugged.

"Alone?" Penelope asked.

He rolled his eyes. "Harrumph! Okay, I'll go. But only to silence your incessant badgering. Don't whine to me when we're dining on garbage and relieving ourselves in a prickly bush."

Penelope, we agreed, should ascend first. Then her brother. I insisted on going last. If Odysseus' climb was as clumsy as his descent, a wily street cat like me was in the best position to find an alternate path. They jumped from floor to desk, then onto the stacked boxes. Finally, up to the window sill. Every step without a hitch.

My turn came. After jumping onto the desk, I hesitated. Had days of fine dining changed my aerodynamics? My fur seemed a bit stretched around my midsection. What Odysseus dismissed as bloat, I called fat.

Odysseus meowed. "What are you waiting for? It's quite easy."

Penelope's tone was reassuring. "You can do it."

Taking a deep breath, I leaped toward the stack. My legs hit an edge. The box lurched forward. I tumbled backward onto the desk.

Penelope shrieked. "Are you all right? Shall I come down?"

"Stay put. I'm fine."

After checking my bones and joints, I surveyed the situation. Although less stable than before, the stack remained in place. My next attempt required precision, a pinpoint landing or the boxes would topple. Laughter suggested Jean's imminent return.

Here goes.

I jumped, landing on the top. The boxes teetered. I held my breath until the stack settled. At the sound of a rattling doorknob, I leaped toward the window. Arcing through the air, I moved as if in slow motion. My eyes focused on Penelope's blue eyes. Jean's feet pounded down the stairs. If I missed the windowsill, I'd hit the wall and slide down to the floor. There'd be no second chance. Willing myself onto a higher trajectory, I slid across the sill. Penelope and Odysseus greeted me with licks as the boxes hit the floor below.

"Let's get outta here."

We hurried out from the alley and toward the parvis. The fresh air exhilarated me. Despite the threat of Bog and his minions, a sense of freedom swept over me. *This* was my world. A bounce returned to my step as we roamed the market. Asking where I'd been, several vendors threw us scraps.

Odysseus cleared his throat. "An odd man is staring at us. Over by the fishmonger. Suppose he wants to feed us too?" I turned to look but no one was there. "Strange, he was there a moment ago. Hello," Odysseus added. "There's the fellow. By the cheese stall."

I shuddered. He was no fishmonger or cheese man. Despite the man's cap and sunglasses, I recognized the scrawny fellow as one of Bog's shady cohorts.

"We're in danger. Follow me." I led Penelope and Odysseus on a zigzag course through the market before pausing under a table of a bustling outdoor café. "I think we lost him."

Odysseus sighed. "Thank heavens. I'm so knackered I'd gladly sacrifice one of my lives for a lie-down on one of the rectory's plush cushions."

Penelope and I glared at him when a voice interrupted us. "Look who we have here." Extending his hand to pet us, Father Pierre crouched down. Desperate for affection, a purring Odysseus brushed up against the priest's trousers. "Wasn't the rectory to your liking, little ones?"

I hoped that after showering us with affection, Father Pierre would leave. Surely, he was relieved to rid his home of three freeloaders. But he kept petting and praising us. "Such beautiful specimens. Such soft fur."

Whenever I backed away, he scooped me closer to him. His caresses felt more like a grip. The hair on my back stood on end. Her puffed tail suggested that Penelope shared my concern. Odysseus, however, meowed softly, preening for more backrubs and praise.

Father Pierre shook his head. "We were shocked to find the basement empty. Even poor Max was distraught. And after all we did to make you comfortable. I was about to have Jean post *Chat Perdu*, Lost Cat, flyers around the parvis with your photos."

I wailed, my cry releasing the priest's grip. I turned to flee. Someone blocked my path. I looked up. Cook! I pivoted. In front of me stood Jean. He held a short leash with a dog, some mix of shepherd. Max! The hound snarled. Channeling my inner tiger, I roared my displeasure. But instead of tremors of fear, my bravado prompted only laughter and snorts.

"There, there, no one's going to get hurt." Father Pierre took the crate that Cook carried in her hands. "Back to the rectory with you. For your comfort and safety." Placing the carton on the ground, he ordered us inside. Max's growls warned us to obey. Penelope jumped in. I followed. That Odysseus hadn't leaped in first surprised me. Since our escape, he'd babbled on about missing the rectory's many comforts.

Father Pierre stared down at Odysseus "Your turn, pretty boy."

Unable to see the pavement, Penelope and I braced for her brother's exuberant arrival. We waited and waited. Concerned looks and frantic shouts of the humans gave us our answer. Father Pierre bellowed, "Get that damn cat." The lid of the box closed leaving Penelope and me to fret in darkness.

⟫⟪◊⟫⟪

A slamming door precipitated the lid's reopening. The scent of candle wax, incense, and silver polish replaced the bountiful and unrefined aromas of the parvis. We were back inside the rectory.

39

Cook's red nose dropped into the box. "They're okay. Maybe a bit hungry but otherwise fine. Let me feed them." Carting us to the kitchen, she carried us through the ground floor. I didn't realize how helpful that tour was later to prove.

After returning us to the basement, Father Pierre instructed Jean to remove every box to the storage room. He also ordered the caretaker to fix the broken window. We were prisoners.

"I'm worried about Odie," Penelope said when we were alone. "Where do you suppose he went?"

"He'll be okay." However, I remained dubious. "Gotta hand it to fancy pants. Didn't think he had it in him. The looks on their faces were priceless."

"What do you suppose they want with us?"

"Don't know."

"I don't think I can sleep." But she soon closed her eyes and fell into a sound slumber.

Sleep was a luxury I couldn't afford. I needed time to think, to figure things out. Why would a priest lock us in his basement? I paced the floor, sniffing at the thresholds of closed doors. As I recalled from my first look about, street odors wafting from the shuttered storage room suggested a door or, at the very least, a window to the outside.

I pushed against the storage room door, which to my surprise, opened. Perhaps in the chaos of our escape, Jean forgot to secure the lock. I tiptoed inside. Flashing lights on electronic panels cast the room in eerie green and amber glows. Boxes, wooden crates, and papers filled tables. Scales, photography equipment, and a giant safe lined the floor. At least two locks secured every cabinet and cupboard. Windows had thick blinds, bars, and padlocks. Something other than church business was being conducted out of the rectory.

Chapter 6
I Plot

I continued to search the room. Although I found a door to the outside, locks made it an unlikely escape route. My mind churned. Why all the security? Had I happened upon a secret operation run by staff, or was Father Pierre also involved? What did all this mean for Penelope, Odysseus, and me?

Unlike our cobweb-riddled section of the basement, the room was pristine. Shiny surfaces and fresh scents suggested a recent cleansing. A mop and bucket stood beside a stainless-steel sink. Despite the heavy clean, faint odors lingered. My senses fired. Traces of other animals. A drain in the floor spurred my curiosity. I edged closer. Odors made my nose twitch. *Cats and dogs. Many of them.* Gurgling water echoing up the drainpipe caught my attention. I gazed into the dark abyss.

Penelope stirred in the next room. I lifted my nose from the drain; my eyes widened. *Why didn't I see it before?* At the edge of the grate was a wad of fur. The same gray color and fineness of Odysseus. I sniffed the feathery clump. Cleaning solvent and fruity shampoo masked any trace of its former host. Something even more disturbing caused me to arch my back. Crimson droplets of dried blood stained the floor.

For Penelope's sake, I had to act nonchalant. Her brother's disappearance had frazzled her nerves so much that I half expected her fine fur to twist into the tight curls of a poodle's coat. Before sharing my discovery, I needed to understand the rectory's business. Needed to find out what Father Pierre and his staff knew about Odysseus' continued disappearance.

Popping my head across the threshold, I feigned a grin. "Hello, sleepyhead."

She turned toward me, her eyes scanning the room behind me. "Any sign of Odie? Have they found him? Is he here?" Assuming a sympathetic expression, I shook my head. "It's only that...we've never been apart," she added. "Not once in our entire lives. What kind of a sister am I? Falling asleep when Odysseus is out there alone. It's unforgivable." The despair conveyed by her tone and expression melted my heart.

Her lament echoed my own. Was I a terrible son and brother for not searching for my mama and siblings? Helping Odysseus and Penelope had given me purpose. Made me feel valuable. In truth, it numbed the guilt as well. Still, I couldn't stop asking myself whether I should have been doing more to find my family.

Shaking the nagging questions from my head, I refocused on Penelope. "Don't be so hard on yourself. From what I've seen, you're a great sister. Odysseus is lucky to have you."

"Nice of you to say, but...I don't know."

"I'm lucky to have you."

Her head perked up. Despair gave way to gratitude. "You're a darling to say so."

"I mean it. Besides," I added with a nod over my shoulder. "Your nap gave me a chance to explore. Someone left the storage room open."

Her eyes darted back to the door. "Find anything? Clues why we're here? An escape route?" After stretching away her lingering drowsiness, she strolled toward the entrance.

I roared, "No!"

She stopped to study my face. Surprise gave way to concern. "W... what's wrong?"

"Nothing." Affecting a smile, I inserted myself between her and the open door. "Nothing's wrong."

Her brow furrowed. "It's Odysseus isn't it? Something terrible has happened to him."

"No, no, no."

"Then what? What don't you want me to see?"

I wracked my brain for a believable fib. "Well… er…um…there's a door to the outside."

Her eyes narrowed. "That's great news."

I moved my head from side to side. "Bolted shut I'm afraid."

She stepped forward. "Let me see."

"Go ahead. You'll find several locks. Bars on the windows too." Her wrinkled nose suggested lingering doubt. "We're not getting out that way," I added. "Didn't want to raise your hopes, that's all. You're already upset by Odysseus' disappearance." A fib motivated by good intentions, I reasoned, was okay.

Her eyes ping-ponged between the storage room and me. I sensed her inner struggle. Strong-will pressed her to explore. But what would ignoring my counsel reveal about her trust in me? After a few silent moments, she backed away.

We settled onto our respective cushions before I spoke. "I gotta get upstairs. Figure out what's goin' on."

"How? If you manage to get through the door, there's Max." She glanced up the stairs. Behind that door, menacing growls and vicious barks fired our imaginations. "He's wanted to tear us to shreds since we arrived."

"Civility is our friend." I found myself borrowing more and more from my companions' posh vocabularies. "As Odysseus says, dogs are less refined than cats." I nodded to the litter box. "Max goes outside to do his business. I need to figure out his routine."

Her mouth curled into a grin. "Clever boy. If you go upstairs, I'm going with you."

"Oh no, you're not."

"Yes I am."

Having her accompany me wasn't in my plan. But doing so had

benefits. She'd stay out of the storage room. In addition, she'd make an excellent lookout. Increase my odds of finding a new escape route. Our lives, I instinctively knew, depended upon it.

———————◦((◦))◦———————

Having fortified the basement against a second escape, Jean adopted a confident swagger. He treated us as captives. His false veneer vanished. His nature, however, was so hardwired that spontaneous laughter still caused his generous belly to jiggle over his belt. I hoped to tap into that good nature and deflate his newfound confidence.

Cook's behavior sent up real warning flags. She rarely popped down to the basement anymore. When she did, she treated us coldly, avoiding eye contact and shaking with what I assumed was rage. From the top of the stairs, she once sniped at Jean. "You go down. I don't want anything more to do with those…" In my opinion, she spelled trouble.

Penelope and I still didn't understand why we were prisoners. The strange room, I assumed, held the answer. Shedding light on the mystery, however, required action—getting upstairs. My evolutionary lineage primed me for the challenge. Mistaken for idle curiosity, felines excel in matters of sleuthing and investigation—one might say, *purposeful* curiosity. Gathering intelligence was best done during one of Father Pierre's dinner parties. Conversations overheard during our first nights in the basement were intense, sometimes heated. Topics were definitely business—more commercial, less spiritual. Unfortunately, voices were too muted to comprehend.

To understand the rectory's daily operating routine, I sat on the top step pressing my ears and nose to the threshold. A two-day and -night vigil gave me insight into upstairs activities. A clock with deep and sonorous chimes somewhere beyond the door helped me understand patterns, routines, and timelines.

Cook ran a tight and predictable ship. As with our feeding schedule, she served upstairs meals with a regularity. Prep and cleanup times were consistent. Except for the evening meal when they dined after the priest, Jean and Cook ate before. Max's walks also held to a routine. Jean walked him no less than five times per day. Extended walks occurred three times per day—mornings, evenings after Max's dinner, and before bedtime. The post-dinner walk offered our best snooping opportunity. Jean and Max would be outside the rectory while Cook was busy in the kitchen.

One obstacle remained—the basement door. A simple distraction such as the antics that facilitated our first escape wouldn't work. Jean was wise to my wiles. I fell asleep wracking my brain for a solution.

<hr />

"Got it," I muttered aloud during my morning stretches.

Penelope looked at me sideways over her breakfast dish. "Got what?"

I winked. "Tonight, we go upstairs."

"What about the door?"

"Leave that to me." I didn't share details of my plan. Penelope might stop me. "When Jean fetches the wine, we move."

Most nights after clearing our dinner plates and cleaning the litter box, Jean made one final appearance in the basement—a trip to the wine cellar to fetch bottles for the evening meal. He didn't appear again until the following morning's breakfast. The extended period between his wine run and breakfast gave us our best opportunity to investigate. Remaining undetected in the residence from human eyes and canine ears and snout was the trickiest part of the scheme.

Penelope and I spent the day huddled together reviewing our mission. As we spoke of risks, dangers, and deadly outcomes, I sensed our relationship change. Our respect and admiration for one another intensified. She, I knew, had my back. Her faith and trust in me, she said, were beyond question.

Although neither of us had an appetite, we licked every morsel of salmon pâté from our fine china plates to avoid scrutiny and suspicion. After dinner, we perched on the floor in silence to await Jean.

Chapter 7
Curiosity

Trudging upstairs with two baskets of wine, Jean called down to us, "Okay, kitties. Sleep tight. Don't let the church mice bite."

Where his laughter ended and his belches began, I didn't know. But his clamoring gave me cover to climb the stairs behind him. An abundance of wine, two baskets instead of the usual one, was reason for optimism. His hands were full. He'd probably shut the door with a foot tap rather than his customary push. The amount of wine suggested a long evening, a houseful of guests, and plenty of uninhibited conversation.

He plodded through the door; I scurried onto the landing. Taking a deep breath and closing my eyes, I slid my tail across the threshold and braced. Jean kicked the door, wedging my tail between door and frame. I winced. Satisfaction, sacrifice for the greater good, made the pain tolerable. The door held fast but didn't latch.

Penelope bounded up the stairs. "You poor thing."

"I'm fine," I replied through gritted teeth. "Listen under the door." Dinner would distract the hound. Then once Jean opened the wine, he'd fetch Max for a long walk. That ritual offered our best chance to sneak out. "Tell me when Jean and Max go outside."

Nodding her understanding, she continued to mewl. "Poor boy."

Despite my throbbing tail, I mustered a smile. "I'm okay. Remember our task."

Jean and Max left the rectory. Cook turned on the kitchen faucet. With a nudge of her head, Penelope opened the basement door. Freed from its vise, we examined my tail.

"You'll end up with a permanent notch. And such a handsome tail. Brave boy."

Her words were welcome salve but her licks and nuzzles caused my injured tail to flick uncontrollably. Trying to quell the shooting pain, I reminded her of our mission. "We only have 30 minutes."

The long corridor into which we emerged ran between the kitchen at the back of the residence and the entry hall. Shutting the door behind us, we shuddered in unison. Deep frenzied scratches marked the base of the oak door. Reminders of Max's lethal capabilities.

"Don't worry," I said. "Brains beat muscle every time. It's a proven fact. Cats are smarter than dogs." Her raised eyebrow suggested disbelief.

My eavesdropping and Cook's earlier unintended tour provided me a basic understanding of the ground floor plan. Father Pierre's study was off the front hall opposite the dining room. A butler's pantry connected dining room and kitchen. The corridor in which we found ourselves contained a bathroom and a curtained coat closet. Both spots afforded excellent hiding places to spy as did the lavishly furnished entry hall.

Voices belonging to Father Pierre and his guests could be heard in the dining room. Running water and clattering dishes confirmed Cook's presence in the kitchen. Padding lightly in true cat fashion, we observed every detail of the foyer and study.

Penelope scoffed. "This place is posher than Madame's flat. The artwork and antiques, alone, are worth a tidy sum. Where does the good father get his money?"

Yet another question with no answer. I nodded toward the corridor. "Go back. Watch Cook. Keep an eye out for Jean and Max. If anyone comes, dart into the closet."

Alone in the entry hall, I slithered under the low seat of a red velvet armchair. It sat beside the entrance to the dining room. Concealed by the chair's long, silk fringe, I rotated my ears toward the closed pocket doors. The conversation turned juicy.

"When can we expect the next shipment?" The speaker's accent was similar to that of a Russian back at camp. The husky voice and heavy breathing suggested a big fellow.

"Soon, very soon," Father Pierre replied.

"We're expecting another three," said a second man the others called Grabowski.

"And another three you'll have. Tell Ivanovich I'll meet his deadline." Father Pierre sounded annoyed. "Have I ever failed?"

"Always a first time, *always*," said the husky-voiced Russian.

The veiled warning must have triggered the priest's anxiety. His voice quivered. "We have two specimens in the basement. Fine ones, very fine. We'll soon have the third. I texted photos of them all when they first arrived. The Siamese are brother and sister. The male escaped but we've spotted him nearby. Staying close to his friends. We'll use the sister as bait. Won't hurt her too much."

Although the threat to Penelope stiffened the hair on my back, the news also offered hope. Odysseus was alive, and nearby.

Expressions of approval rose inside the dining room. "Littermates are prized." The raspy voice belonged to a third guest the others referred to as Claus. I couldn't tell whether Claus was a man or woman, but the accent was Flemish. "More lucrative for you."

"Ivanovich said so but didn't tell me why." Father Pierre assumed an upbeat, almost giddy tone. "Reminds me. The other cat in my photos, the tabby, is related to the white female and two kittens already in transit. One black, one white."

"The three I pointed out to you on the street?" asked Claus.

"The very same. Ivanovich, you said, ordered those specific cats. Sending yet another littermate should make up for the shipping delay. His fur is the softest and silkiest of the litter."

"I salute you," Claus said. "Littermates have been the reason for

Saint Clovis' success." At the mention of Saint Clovis, I figured that Claus was a priest or, at the very least, someone associated with another church.

"Score another bonus for you, Pierre," Grabowski said before glasses clinked.

"Better to pay off your debts," Claus added with a laugh. "Indiscretions are so costly."

I didn't understand much of their conversation. It didn't matter. My stomach fluttered and churned with excitement and dread. They were referring to Mama Vanille, Licorice, and Lily. They were alive. I had only to find them.

"If what you say is true," the husky-voiced Russian said, "about the relation of this other cat, you must hurry. Specimens don't linger. We prefer everything exits Poland in a single shipment."

Poland! My family was in a place called Poland. I didn't have time to think. Barking informed me that Max had returned from his walk. Jean too, of course. Sounds of plodding feet came from inside the dining room.

"Down, boy," Father Pierre scolded.

"The Siamese is near." I recognized Jean's voice.

Father Pierre bellowed, "Then what are you waiting for, fool? Take Max. Hunt down the troublemaker. I'll follow shortly." Apologizing for cutting the evening short, Father Pierre turned down his guests' offers of assistance. "Max hasn't failed us yet. Tell Ivanovich that we have everything under control."

The sudden sound of Max's snout pressing against the doors terrified me. He must have picked up my scent. Father Pierre shouted, "What's gotten into you boy?"

Chairs slid across the floor. In mere seconds, doors would open. I scampered into the corridor. Penelope was nowhere in sight. I stuck my nose into the coat closet. She wasn't there. Clammy breath blew across my back. Arcing my head, I saw the ferocious hound. He'd nudged open the pocket doors. He snarled at me through gritted teeth.

Outrunning him was impossible.

My eyes detected movement. The grandfather clock! Its base opened a crack. "In here!" The voice belonged to Amelia. "Hurry!"

I bolted towards her. Max lunged at me, his hot breath warming my neck. His jagged teeth nearly caught my tail. With no time to spare, I scooted inside the clock. Max slid into the clock, his snout butting the door shut. As the clock teetered, Penelope and I held onto each other. Max clawed the door.

"Get back here!" Jean shouted.

"Get him away from there," Father Pierre bellowed, "That's a priceless antique."

Max's high-pitched wail suggested that Jean had given the leash a sharp tug. We heard the dog being pulled across the floor and the front door open. A swoosh of air rattled the clock. The retreating sound of Jean's heavy feet and Max's pattering paws indicated their departure.

"The clock was my salvation." Penelope explained that Jean had surprised her, entering the corridor to use the toilet. "I had to think fast."

"If you hadn't, I'd be Max's dessert. I've got good news, *ma chérie*. Odysseus is alive." She wriggled with joy as I shared details of the overheard conversation. "We must escape tonight. We have to help Odysseus or the three of us will be packed off in the morning. First, to a place called Poland. Then Russia."

Inching open the clock, I observed Cook retrieve coats. A wide-girthed man in a big suit exited first. Next came an athletic younger man with blond unruly hair, Grabowski. The third guest, Claus, turned out to be a tall, shapely woman with flowing hair that wasn't always blonde. Her lips were artificially red and her powdered cheeks were nearly as white as Mama Vanille's coat. When she walked, she wafted a cloud of floral perfume. Cook handed her a fluffy vest with matching hat and mittens. I shuddered. The fur was an exact match of my family's coats: a white hat like my mama and Lily; black mittens the color of Licorice; and the vest, the very mix of gray, tan, and black of Auguste and me.

Penelope stared at me, her eyes the size of saucers. "You don't suppose?"

I was too startled to respond. But if I hadn't heard with my own ears that my family was in Poland, I might have been more suspicious of the ensemble's origin.

Having shown the last guest out, Cook left the door ajar to fetch her boss's coat. When his short, chubby arm twisted in a sleeve of the black trench coat, I saw our opening.

I flung open the case. "Run, Penelope!"

The priest's face turned scarlet red; a vein in his forehead throbbed. "Bloody hell!"

Penelope and I dashed for the threshold. Behind us, Father Pierre shouted, "Quick, you idiot, shut that damn door."

We sprinted. Cook stepped forward. Her hand reached for the knob. *No!* We had too much carpet to cover. We'd never make it. "*Faster!*"

How we did it, I didn't know. We ran outside. Cook's slow-motion response and unusual silence got me wondering. Had she intentionally aided our escape? It didn't matter. We were free. Before getting two yards, we froze. In the halo of a streetlight stood a figure. Cold, menacing, sober eyes glared in our direction. We muttered in unison, "Bog the Brute."

Chapter 8

Reunion

Penelope sighed softly. "Sorry, Fluff. Don't have it in me to run."
My confrontation with Max and our mad dash from the rectory
had spent my adrenaline too. I offered her a gentle caress to soften our
surrender. "Gave it a good shot though. We're a darn good team."

She whimpered. "Poor Odie. What's to become of him?"

"At the moment, he's doing better than we are."

"Hey kitties, kitties, kitties. Why the long faces?" Bog's menacing
tone filled me with dread.

For a fleeting moment, I had the notion to turn. To march back into
the rectory. At least Father Pierre was civilized and far less malodorous
than the crude brute into whose clutches we were walking.

Bog motioned us forward. "Come on, come on. Don't got much
time."

We plodded toward him, our heads and tails drooped in surrender.
I mustered the courage to look into his dark, brooding face. His stare
was intense, his eyes cold, spiritless. I meowed our defeat. "You've won.
We'll go quietly."

His head tilted slightly; his brow furrowed over pursed lips. Being
human, he didn't understand me so I dropped to my stomach and
prepared to rollover to signal surrender.

The sound of a familiar voice made my ears perk. "What are you
carrying on about? Nobody's won anything," the voice added. "If you

two don't put more pep into your step, we'll all be losers. Move it."

"Auguste!"

Out from Bog's shadow stepped my brother. Yelps and hearty meows expressed my exuberant delight. I hadn't seen him since he left camp in search of our family months earlier. In the lamplight, his eyes glowed like iridescent emeralds. Black stripes stretched over his gray fur frame. He was far more robust than I remembered. I started to introduce Penelope.

My brother raised his paw. "Niceties must wait. We gotta get away from here…fast."

I followed his gaze back over my shoulder. Father Pierre raced down the rectory steps. Having spotted us, he dashed off the curb… and right into the path of a speeding car. The four of us offered up a collective gasp. We braced for impact. *An answer to our prayers.* Dressed all in black, the priest melded with the dark sedan. Machine and cleric became one. Anticipating a fatal thud, my eyes creased.

Tires squealed. The sleek BMW veered away from Father Pierre. Its engine roared as it accelerated and disappeared from view. Priest staggered backward; his arms braced for a tumble. But he didn't fall. Recovering from the near miss, he shouted to Bog. "Grab those cats. I'll pay. Big money."

Looking up into Bog's face, I expected to see interest in the reward. Our shared history filled my head with wild speculation. I imagined him grabbing us by the scruff of our necks and thrusting us toward the priest. A bleak future flashed before my eyes. Widening his stance, however, Bog let loose a torrent of harsh words in his native tongue before lifting his middle finger at Pierre. Looking down at us, he bellowed, "Run, kitties, run!"

Auguste nudged by backside. "He's right. Explanations and headbutts later. Hightail it outta here."

With a raging priest in pursuit, we dashed along the Chaussée de Waterloo away from the parvis and rectory. As we sprinted, we scanned dark side streets and shadowy patches of sidewalk. Jean,

Max, as well as Pierre's co-conspirators might be anywhere. I didn't dare look back until we reached a large patch of green. Below the peaceful oasis in which we found ourselves, the busy inner ring road burrowed through a tunnel. Before us stood the Porte de Hal. My mouth fell open. Grumps spoke of the massive stone tower, the lone surviving gate of Brussels' medieval fortifications. My mind conjured up images of the moat and drawbridge that protected the ancient city. If the ravages of time hadn't claimed them, they might have provided better refuge than the thicket of shrubs in which we huddled.

Auguste retracted his head from the hedge. "I think we lost him."

Bog spoke between winded gasps. "That f...fat priest...couldn't run...a single block. B...but be c...careful. He may have stubby... fingers, but his network's got...long arms."

"And his dog has big, jagged teeth," added Penelope.

Casting a bewildered look to my brother, I nodded toward Bog. "I don't understand... you...*him*."

Auguste shrugged. "Long story."

"We got a long night ahead of us."

Taking a deep breath and settling onto the cool ground, Auguste suggested we do the same. His search for our family, he explained, took him across Brussels. Using Grumps' campfire tales as a guide, he set out for the produce markets—Flagey, Châtelain, Place Sainte-Catherine, Saint-Gilles Town Hall. Finding no answers, he traveled next to the sprawling flea markets—Marche du Midi and the Place du Jeu de Balle.

"Markets attract strays—cats, dogs, people," he said. "Meandering crowds and idle time are fertile for gossip. Figured I'd find our family or somebody who knew something about them."

My eyes grew to the size of tea saucers. Although my family's fate was top of mind, my brother's grand adventure mesmerized me. Penelope too. She couldn't keep her eyes off him. As he spoke, she sighed and mewled. A mix of anger, confusion, and sadness unsettled me. To ward off what humans called the green-eyed monster, I focused on Auguste's story.

He chuckled. "Information was scarce but market scraps were plentiful. I didn't go hungry."

"Yes," I replied. "You look rather well fed…might even say fat." I regretted the words the second they left my mouth. I changed topics. "What's Bog gotta do with all this?"

"Patience brother. I'm getting to that."

"B…but I—"

Penelope raised her paw. "Ssh. Let him finish, Fluff."

Flashing a nauseating grin, Auguste described his harrowing visit to the massive weekend market outside the train station. Rushing to a pile of overturned dates, frenzied shoppers almost trampled him to death. After Penelope praised his courage, he lifted his chin. "Don't you fret. Simply a hazard of adventure. But alas, my brush with death didn't reward me with news about our family."

Auguste next journeyed to Jeu du Balle market. He plopped down for a nap on a plush carpet in a stall belonging to a bearded émigré from Saint Petersburg. Nicknamed Rasputin, the man peddled candlesticks, gold-leaf icons, ornate crucifixes, and other paraphernalia associated with Russian Orthodoxy. Exhausted, Auguste dozed off among brassware. Somewhere between sleep and consciousness, voices swirled in his head. He thought he was dreaming.

"Turns out," he added. "The voices were very real."

He recounted the conversation between Rasputin and a carpet seller from Istanbul that took place over Turkish coffee and pungent cigarettes. The men discussed another peddler, a purveyor of cosmetics and perfume named Vaclav. Like Rasputin, the perfume peddler also emigrated from Saint Petersburg.

Penelope gasped. "More Russians! They're multiplying like those little wooden dolls."

"Rasputin," Auguste continued, "knew Vaclav in Russia. Said he was so poor he couldn't afford a tram ticket. But his fortunes changed in Brussels. 'Tell me,' Rasputin says to his Turkish friend, 'what flea market vendor can afford a new BMW and a fancy apartment in Ixelles?'"

Penelope's eyes widened. "What do you know about Vaclav?"

"Seen his stall at a few markets," Auguste replied. "Unsavory character. Looks and smells like trouble."

Auguste dismissed Rasputin's story as ramblings of a jealous competitor. But additional details roused his curiosity. Especially references to 'stray catcher' and 'animal trafficker.' Rasputin told the Turk that Vaclav, in a vodka-fueled rant, admitted to belonging to a gang of smugglers. They captured strays and sent them east to Poland. Corrupt customs agents let illegal shipments slip across the European Union frontier. Their destination? Russia.

At the mention of Poland, Penelope and I flinched. I started to speak about the rectory dinner conversation when Auguste lifted his paw. "I know what you're gonna say. Patience please. I promise it's all connected. The story's about to get interesting."

Penelope and I drew closer. Auguste continued, "As Rasputin babbled on, his Turkish friend picks up two pieces of merchandise. 'Hey,' the Turk says. 'What gives? These aren't Orthodox.' Hemming and hawing, Rasputin stammers about buying them as a favor. From a priest in *dire* need. The Turk scoffs in disbelief. But before he can call out Rasputin's lie, a man appears. In khakis and flannel," Auguste added. "But his clothes don't suit him. Seem out of place. So does his sport cap. Looks familiar but I can't place him. A visor shades his face. By sheer luck, along comes a bird that drops a berry-riddled load on his head." Auguste shook with laughter.

I inched closer. "And?"

"The guy removes his cap to shake off the poop. I do a double-take. It's none other than Father Pierre. Always sugary sweet to us strays. But he's not sweet. Sour like a lemon. Demands the Turk leave before dropping a gym bag at Rasputin's feet."

My eyes widened. "What was inside?"

Auguste flashed a grin. "Church trinkets. Gold and silver. But not Russian Orthodox. Same kinda stuff that raised the Turk's suspicions."

Auguste learned that Rasputin's business with Pierre was more complex than he let on to the Turk. "Rasputin's blackmailing Pierre. In the same drunken rant, Vaclav spilled dirt about the dear Father. Seems the priest's in hock up to his pulpit with someone named Claus. She financed hush money for something illicit. Pressured him to traffic strays as payback. The rectory, as you two learned, is a base of operations. Maybe not the only one either." Unfortunately, Auguste didn't learn their reasons for trafficking strays.

"Must be for our fur," I said, sharing my suspicions about the origins of Claus's wardrobe.

"Don't think I want to find out," replied Auguste.

"Whatever their reasons, it's imperative we find our loved ones," added Penelope.

I nodded toward Bog. He stood several yards away, a glowing cigarette dangling from his lips. "What about him?"

My brother laughed. "You got nothing to fear from him."

I flinched. "But back at camp? His violent behavior?"

"He certainly scared Odysseus and me," Penelope said.

Auguste nodded. "Believe me, I understand. Thought the same until I went looking for Fluff."

Enlightened by the conversations he overheard on Rasputin's plush carpet, Auguste returned to camp. Finding me gone, he sought out Grumps. "The old coot knew nothing. Said you wandered off in search of food with two Siamese parlor cats and never returned. Rattled on about dandelions and palace gardens. I questioned every stray I could find. Nobody knew where you went. Couple of jokesters suggested you might have finally gone off on one of the grandiose adventures you always boasted about."

I cringed, hoping my embarrassment didn't show.

"What about Scratch and Ollie?" Penelope asked.

I seethed. "Scoundrels!"

"Very shady characters," Auguste replied. "Sensed they were hiding something. Told them so. They pointed their fingers at Bog. Merely a ruse. See that now. But based on experience, I believed them." Falling for Ollie and Scratch's red herring, Auguste observed Bog closely. "Turns out he's not as bad as he lets on."

I knitted my brow. "Then why is he so mean?"

Auguste gestured toward the Porte de Hal. "Like this old gate, a defensive wall."

I scoffed. "He's the strongest, meanest man in camp. Why does he need protection?"

Auguste flashed a judgmental sneer. "He thinks he's a failure. Feels helpless. Wracked with guilt."

Lowering his voice, Auguste shared Bog's history. In Syria, he was a trained professional with a wife and young daughter. They lived comfortably until civil war brought their neighborhood to the verge of destruction. They fled on foot, trekking through Turkey then sailing to Greece. Many companions died but Bog and his family reached the Balkans. A melee with armed guards at a makeshift border fence separated them. Bog heard nothing for weeks. He considered returning home but the border was closed. With Brussels their ultimate goal, he forged ahead. But when he arrived, he found no trace of his wife or daughter. He feared the worst. Medicating his anguish with alcohol, he grew meaner and angrier by the day.

"And the card games?" I asked. "The beatings when he lost?"

"Fueled by self-pity and frustration," Auguste replied. "Bog needed money to pay for information about his family. Losing only made him feel more guilty and inadequate."

"The night we went missing," Penelope said, "He chased us. He's the reason we ended up in the rectory basement."

I shook my head. "He approached us, yes, but Scratch is the reason we ended up in the basement. Remember?"

"You're right. And Ollie's the one who told us to stay put."

"Exactly!"

"The night he chased you," Auguste said. "Recent arrivals, migrants from back home, told him that his family was in route to Brussels. He got drunk celebrating. Wanted to greet his little girl with a cat like the one she had to leave behind."

Penelope nodded. "Explains why he wanted Odie and me."

My brother shook his head. "He wanted Fluff."

"Me?"

"Uh huh. Wanted to adopt you. You're like the cat left behind. Looks and personality, or so he says."

Emotions flooded me. I'd dreamed of a human family. But I hadn't seen any of the world yet. I had Penelope, Odysseus, and my missing family to think of too.

My brother swatted the air with his paw. "Don't worry about that now. His family is in Poland. Fears they'll be sent back to Syria."

"But how did you find us?" Penelope asked.

"Finally got wise to Ollie and Scratch. Followed them to the rectory. Saw how chummy they were with Pierre and Jean. Back at camp, Bog understood my distressed meows. Agreed to help. Hates traffickers…of any kind. I led him to the rectory tonight."

Penelope pawed me. "Your brother's so smart and brave. Brains and courage run in the family. But you," she said, whispering in my ear, "you got the looks and sweetness." Her nuzzle caused my still-bruised tail to thump but I didn't mind the pain.

Auguste cleared his throat. "Time for that later. Here's what we gotta do."

According to his plan, we'd divide and conquer. Penelope and I would search for Odysseus in Brussels. Bog and Auguste would head east where they hoped to rescue both families—feline and human. Despite the risks, the plan was our best hope.

Traffic noise awakened us to a golden dawn. We said our goodbyes with hugs and wishes of success for our respective missions. With luck, Auguste and Bog would reach Poland in a week's time. Less, if they caught lifts on trains and transport trucks.

As they disappeared from view, Penelope turned to me. "Where shall we start?"

"The markets, of course."

"Which one?"

"Saint-Gilles Town Hall. And if we don't find Odysseus there, off to Châtelain." *And if not there, then Sainte-Catherine. Flagey too, at the weekend. If all that fails, then onto the Royal Palace gardens at Laeken.*

I could hardly contain my glee. I was finally getting a chance to see the world...at least as much of it as my four short legs would allow. For Penelope's sake, I stifled my head-swooning wanderlust. She was preoccupied with finding her brother. Although I shared her commitment, my mind churned with vibrant images of Brussels, especially the markets that Grumps called "pawsitively magnificat."

Chapter 9

Super *Marché*

"The day has come, at last, *ma chérie. Allons!*" The prospect of rich, savory market fare caused my stomach to leap with delight. We'd not been starved. Far from it. But Cook's delicacies left a bitter aftertaste knowing we dined under the roof of evil traffickers. By contrast, shrimp tails, mussel shells, meat scraps, and waffle crumbs nibbled off cobblestones under an open sky promised to taste heavenly.

After hearing Grumps describe the Monday afternoon market, I yearned to experience it. Although tragic circumstances prompted our visit, I finally got my chance. We chose a route to Saint-Gilles Town Hall that detoured around the rectory and parvis. Father Pierre's shadowy network probably had many watchful eyes, some aware of his evildoing and others naively willing to aid a man of the cloth. Mama's warning echoed in my ears, "Nothing's more sinister than a dark soul hiding behind a dimpled smile."

Towering above rooflines, the town hall's red brick belfry served as a beacon. Capped by a stone cupola, each of its four sides featured clocks and gilded statues. My heart raced with each step. Grumps spoke of afternoon markets with uncharacteristic cheerfulness. Sensitive to Penelope's anguish over her brother, I tempered my excitement. An easy feat, I readily admit, for any feline.

Nearing our destination, Penelope and I found ourselves at the edge of a traffic circle, the Barrière de Saint-Gilles, site of a 17th century fortification. Our eyes darted from street to street, car to car, and tram to tram. Belgian drivers considered lane markings, speed limits, and traffic signals optional. Sidewalks weren't safe. Erratic drivers regularly jumped curbs to park. Navigating a single street proved challenging for pedestrians—human and animal. Risks multiplied at the Barrière. Seven roads and multiple tramlines converged in a chaotic maelstrom. Looking like frightened rabbits, pedestrians scampered across the circle's many spokes.

One street, Chaussée de Waterloo, recalled Grumps' wayfaring tales. He'd spoken of taking the road, an ancient route linking Brussels with the town of Waterloo, and beyond that, southern Belgium and France. "Glorious days," Grumps had said, contentment sweeping away his customary frown. "Fresh air, an open road, and the sweet taste of freedom. An endless horizon fueled my spirit; my future had no bounds. But alas, dear kittens, my eyes were wider than my stride." Grumps reassumed his dour disposition. "After two days and nights with only scrawny country mice for food and run-ins with territorial bullies, I turned back." He heaved a sigh. "Too old for adventure."

Wouldn't stop a spry young tiger like me, I thought at the time. Now with Penelope beside me, I closed my eyes. I pictured myself skipping towards Waterloo and Paris. Grumps' cautionary tale of uppity dandelions, however, soured my daydream. Adventure had to wait. Crossing the Barrière without losing a limb was our immediate challenge. With Father Pierre's near fatal run-in forefront in our minds, Penelope and I studied the traffic circle. The safest course involved shadowing a human, especially one with gray hair. Trams didn't slow for any creature large or small, but most cars respected the elderly.

Jackpot! Two sour-faced women pulling empty shopping carts passed us on their way to the market. Preoccupied with litanies of aching joints, the human magpies didn't notice us tuck in behind them. True to their Belgian natures, they scowled at smiling passersby delighted with our sidewalk parade. The women's thick ankles and calf-length frocks obscured our view. Despite the scent of menthol balm wafted with each of their lumbered strides, a surge of savory aromas penetrated the medicinal veil. The market was near. My lips quivered and my stomach growled in anticipation.

Our guides veered toward an outdoor café for coffee and, I presumed, more droning tales of ill health. With our visual obstruction removed, the marvelous spectacle of the market revealed itself—tents, caravans, and canopies. "*Magnifique!*"

As backdrop to the stunning set, the Town Hall reigned in majestic splendor. A palace worthy of princes, not the hive of dour administrative drones that camp humans described. The clock tower that guided us to the marketplace was but a single gem in the building's glorious crown. At each end of the main structure, two wings reached forward gracefully—arms embracing the market. Scanning the structure from one wing to the other, I shared my wonderment. "A cat could live like a king. Months to explore every room. And we'd never go hungry."

Penelope shot me a sideways glance. "How can you be so sure?"

"Camp humans griped about the town hall's rats. Called them fat, lazy, and 'offissus,' whatever the heck that means."

She giggled. "I don't think they were talking about rodents. W… what's th…that?" A look of terror swept across her face.

I followed her gaze to the roof. Above the double staircase that ascended to the main entrance perched an eagle, its wings readied for flight. Had the creature also been lured by delectable aromas and promises of food? Perhaps vendors employed him to ward off freeloaders like us. Were we *his* market fare? I despaired. We stood no chance against his sharp talons and razor-sharp beak. After nearing the market of my dreams, must I retreat?

Backing away, I kept my eyes fixed on the predator. He didn't move. His wings appeared frozen in mid-flap. I focused my gaze. *Criminy!* This holy terror was no threat, merely another gilded adornment. I nudged Penelope whose raised fur stiffened on her back. "No worries, *ma chérie*. Look again." I nodded to the statue. "A pigeon doesn't poop on an eagle's head."

"And live to coo about it." Tension left her body. "You're so smart... and brave."

I lifted my chin and puffed my tail. "*Naturellement*, I'm a street cat. Seen and survived far worse. Stick with me, *chérie*."

"Speaking of life on the street, you haven't mentioned Bog's desire to make you his family pet. Rather an honor."

"*Oui*."

"Flattering to find a human who wants to adopt you."

"*Je sais*, I know."

"His little girl would smother you with cuddles and kisses."

"*Bien sûr*, Uh-huh."

"You don't seem very excited."

Words escaped me. To be honest, I had begun dreaming of a cozy hearth in a human home. Being wanted, even pampered, was wonderful. But the timing was terrible. I'd only started to explore the big, marvelous world. Such is the feline dilemma.

Penelope sighed. "I can appreciate your hesitation."

"You can?"

"Definitely. People don't understand. Cats adopt their human. Not the other way around."

I bobbed my head vigorously. She was quite right. Felines, picky by nature, reserved the right to choose their human.

"But," she added wistfully, "having said that, street cats don't enjoy many options."

My shoulders slumped. "Well, his family's stuck in Poland. No sense worrying now. Besides, we got a market to explore."

She smiled. "Indeed, we have."

Tails held high, we sauntered across the street. Unlike the wide-open parvis, leafy trees provided a natural canopy under which we strolled among the stalls. A few vendors I recognized from the daily market greeted me. Others tossed us scraps of meat and fish. Most, however, were strangers. Sellers, I presumed, who peddled solely at afternoon markets.

We kept watch for bootlegged perfume. Although Vaclav might lead us to Odysseus, he also meant danger. We risked capture by him and his band of traffickers. I motioned to the far side of the market where stalls offered wine, beer, and prepared foods. Spirited patrons bantered at tables. "Let's go over there."

Penelope furrowed her brow. "Aren't you interested in produce?"

I waved my paw in the air. "Seen it, eaten it. Blech! Who eats kale? 'The food stands. Those are the sights to behold,' Grumps says. 'Laughter, merriment. Alcohol makes humans kinder, more charitable especially toward four-legged beggars.'"

"Sensible."

"Grumps is very wise. If we're to hear any news about Odysseus, we'll find it among loose-lipped drinkers and foraging strays. Follow me."

Prowling among tables, we came upon revelers dining on a variety of mouth-watering dishes: Thai noodles, Chinese rice, fresh shellfish, Italian panini, and Moroccan delicacies. I turned to Penelope. "Odd. Where are the strays? Savory handouts should be a magnet for scavengers."

"Hey! You two." Turning toward the strange voice, we found ourselves staring at a one-eyed cat. His white fur had begun to yellow around the edges like the shaggy beards of chain-smoking camp people.

Penelope's head cocked. "Who? Us?"

"Yes you, Beauty..." The odd cat flashed a sneer at me. "And the Beast." I didn't waste my breath on a catty retort. He was clearly sight impaired. "Never seen you before. Lost?"

"I assure you, Monsieur..." I paused, waiting for him to offer up his name.

"Lucky. Call me Lucky."

Penelope and I strutted over to the enormous tree trunk among whose bulging roots the quirky feline sat. "I assure you, Lucky. We're not lost. We're exactly where we want to be."

"Have you seen a cat named Odysseus?" Penelope interjected, her voice rising with excitement. "He's my brother."

"Handsome fellow then," Lucky replied, ogling her too long for my liking. "Maybe, maybe not, *ma petite chou*. What's in it for me?"

His flirtations grew insufferable. With a leap, I pounced on his tail. My well-placed scratch drew a screech. "Hey," he cried. "What's that for?"

"Mind your manners or I'll put out your other eye."

"Okay, okay. Didn't mean no harm."

"Then answer the fair feline's question. Have you seen her brother?"

"No, but that's not unusual. The DeVilles don't take kindly to newcomers." He explained that the DeVilles were a gang of feral cats and mutts. In exchange for an exclusive foraging concession, the gang kept order for market vendors. "They'll run you two off soon enough. Won't pussy paw around it neither."

"Gee whiskers! We're not hurting anyone."

"Nothin' personal. Turf issue, that's all. You know how that goes."

I sighed. The unfairness of it all. "Answer our questions and we'll be on our way. You familiar with a Russian perfume peddler?"

Lucky flinched; his good eye widened. "Vodka guzzler? You friends of his?"

Penelope bristled. "No. Whatever gave you that idea?"

"That's a relief," Lucky replied. "Wouldn't talk to you if you were. Nasty chap even if he does smell good for a man."

"We were told he might have information," I said.

Lucky leered at Penelope. "About Beauty's brother? Makes sense he might. Shady operator. Even by human standards."

"Thought we might find him here," Penelope said.

Lucky laughed nervously. "DeVilles ran him off. They despise animal smugglers."

I scrutinized him. "You a DeVille?"

"Certainly not. How do you s'pose I lost my eye? No, I'm with Lucinda." He nodded toward a sultry woman with long black hair and dark eyes. She sold Italian specialties and wine out of a small caravan. "We travel from market to market. Calls me her good luck charm."

"So," I said, "the DeVilles leave you alone?"

"If they know what's good for them. Ever see a raging Italian woman?" Penelope and I shook our heads. "Not pretty. Recommend the same for you."

Penelope cocked her head. "An angry Italian?"

He laughed, revealing a gap-toothed smile. "No, silly, a vendor. Lots have adopted strays. Cats, dogs, bird or two. Pasta guy over there has a squirrel on a leash. We're one big happy family."

The arrangement was the best of all possible worlds. "You telling us that you travel from market to market *and* have a human home?"

"Pretty cozy deal, huh?"

Penelope shot me a look. I knew exactly what she was thinking. We adopt a vendor. One to transport us between markets. "Chances of finding Odie would soar," she whispered.

I winked. "Who knows? Your pampered dandy of a brother might have already hooked up with a fishmonger."

Penelope turned to Lucky. "Any leads? Vendors looking to adopt?"

Scrunching his face, he considered her question. "Might try the waffle lady. Or the old honey and quiche woman. Maybe the candy man." None of those appealed to me but I hid my disappointment. "There's…" Lucky hesitated. "Nah, nope, never mind."

Penelope pawed him. "Tell us."

I took two steps forward. "Don't hold out on us."

He lifted a paw. "Okay, okay. Was gonna say, *Le Roi de Poulet.*"

"And?"

"Remembered they hate strays. Last cat that got too close? Smack! Right in the kisser with a turkey leg."

Penelope shuddered but my imagination churned with possibilities. "A *King* of Chicken?" *A real authentic king like Grumps talked about.* "Winner, winner, chicken dinner. That's the one for us."

Penelope stammered, "B…but, what about Lucky's warning?"

I waved my paw in her face. "That's nothin'. Trust me."

Grumps' stories had fueled my fantasies. He called the palace, splendiferous. I figured that royalty stuck together. Like kings and queens on cards I'd seen up Bog's sleeves. Yep, *Le Roi de Poulet* was our key to the palace.

Lucky shook his head. "Your funerals. Don't say ole Lucky didn't warn you."

As he hobbled back to Lucinda's caravan on his three legs, I brushed his warnings from my head. I was a tiger, after all. "*Allons, ma chérie.* We have a command performance with the King of Chicken."

We marched through the market until we happened upon a large yellow truck emblazoned with *Le Roi de Poulet* in gold lettering. One side of the trailer opened into a service counter. Its glass display case featured a tempting assortment of side dishes and juicy meats. Behind the counter on a rotating rack, a flock of roasting chickens infused the air with delectable aromas. My heart beat in sync with the timpani of juices splattering into drip pans from golden brown roasters. I inferred from the presence of ginger-haired staff that le Roi de Poulet was a red king. Whether of diamonds or hearts I didn't yet know.

Penelope nudged me from my stupor. "Ahem…how do you suggest we ingratiate ourselves to these people?"

"Huh?"

"How do we entice them to adopt us?"

"Mama said that the surest way to befriend humans is to prove yourself useful."

"How do we do that?"

"Watch!" When we first approached the truck, I spotted three mice scurrying up its tires. They were our ticket in.

Penelope and I surprised the trio of chicken thieves. Without uttering a sound, I flung one by its tail. His two cohorts stared at me, their tiny bodies quivering. I lowered my chin and looked them in the eye. "Don't be afraid. Bit of show and tell, that's all." Scooping the pair into my mouth, I dropped one at Penelope's feet. "Pick him up and follow me."

Her eyes widened in horror. "A mouse?"

"Not just any mouse. He's what you might call *ingratiation*."

With a mouse fidgeting in each of our mouths, we paraded to the truck's open back door. After we climbed the few steps to the trailer floor, a redheaded boy pointed at us. "Look Aunty Marie, your favorite."

Her favorite. I puffed out my chest in anticipation of a hero's welcome. The short, round-faced woman, perhaps the Queen of Chicken herself, finished up with a customer before turning toward us. Lifting our tails in proud salute, we dropped the mice in tribute.

"Eek!"

I never heard such a shriek. Penelope and I froze in terror. The woman's face turned the same bright red color as her hair. Grabbing a broom, she began swatting us. Clutching onto the broom's straw, the mice catapulted themselves through the air. Fortunately for them, they landed in a box of organic lettuce and scurried to freedom.

Whack! The broom landed on my back. My legs splayed out under me. Bracing, I closed my eyes. Surely, her next thrust would pummel my head. No second whack came. I popped open an eye. Penelope hissed loudly, her back arched. The woman recoiled. The broom fell from her hands sending the two redheaded boys into fits of laughter. Jumping to my feet, I joined Penelope in fleeing the truck. We found refuge beneath a nearby caravan.

Penelope pawed my downcast head. "Don't feel bad. Maybe they weren't royalty at all."

Her words were small comfort. The experience dashed my hopes of seeing the palace. I should have listened to Grumps. A stray had no right to lofty dreams. Worse, we were no closer to finding Odysseus.

"May as well try the old quiche and honey woman," she added.

"May as well."

But the wrinkled purveyor of quiche shooshed us away as did the grimacing waffle lady, and the sourpuss candy man. The pasta-man's pet squirrel merely smirked at our ordeal. Exhausted and with heads lowered, we looked for a place to rest. No sooner had we set ourselves down beside a quiet stall selling organic fruit, than we found ourselves accosted by well-fed, ill-tempered, dogs and cats—the DeVilles!

A fat feline sized us up. "Scram if you know what's good for you."

A snarling mutt bit my tail. Still recovering from the painful notch inflicted by the rectory door, I cried out in pain. In no shape to counter attack, Penelope and I bolted from the market. We ran until we were out of breath. The rusty underbelly of a parked car provided refuge until the market closed. With our tails down and our backs to the market, we set out in search of a more comfortable, secure spot for the night.

Wandering into an overgrown back garden of an abandoned house, I dropped onto my stomach. "Not the best of starts to our adventure."

Penelope curled up beside me. "Street life doesn't suit me. I'm a parlor cat. Always will be. Can't understand why you prefer a dangerous life on the run to a warm hearth and cozy lap."

"You mean Bog? We went over all that back at the Town Hall."

"Before the Queen of Chicken tormented us and the DeVilles chased us from the market. Really Fluff, you nearly had your tail bit off. They might have killed you."

"Bit of an exaggeration, wouldn't you say? Why it was only—"

Penelope bristled at my attempt to downplay danger. My tail ached but to avoid upsetting her further, I stifled my distress. Arguing was pointless. The conflict between domesticity and wild abandon was something I had to resolve myself. My wanderlust was too new, too unquenched, to abandon. Fretting about our next adventure, I fell asleep.

Chapter 10
Châtelain

"Morning, drowsy eyes. Time to rise." Penelope's voice roused me from dreamland. She nuzzled me; my stubborn eyes squinted open. Radiating in mid-morning light, her pretty gray face made me grin. "Surprised you weren't up at dawn. Today we head to Châtelain."

"So."

"So? You've been drooling over Châtelain since we started our adventure."

With a dispassionate sigh, I shrugged. She was right of course. Of all markets, the one that took over a parking lot in the heart of Ixelles every Wednesday sat at the top of my list. I'd prattled on about it with childlike exuberance ever since hearing Grumps describe his visits—freshest produce, tastiest food, best-dressed customers—a carnival fueled by beer and wine. He called Châtelain, "the finest market in all of Brussels if not the entire world." What cat afflicted with wanderlust such as I wouldn't pounce at a chance to experience all that?

But as the day arrived to fulfill my dream, passion abandoned me. Instead of soaring, my spirit shriveled like the horns of a stale croissant. Our recent experience left me in a funk. Châtelain could be another disaster. More proof we were unwanted. My dream world didn't exist. Those lucky enough to savor the feast didn't make room for strays. Grumps was right; a dandelion needed to understand its place. So, it seems, did an uncultured street cat.

Penelope's expression turned stern. "Don't go all pity party on me."

"Wh…wha…who…me?"

"Yes, you."

"Our last adventure was a disaster." Defensiveness gave my tone an edge. But *my* dream, not *hers*, had shattered.

"Pish posh. Nobody gives up after a single misadventure, especially not one as brave, intelligent, and intrepid as you." I raised a single eyebrow. *Firing the heavy guns of pride and Ego, are you?* "Despite the drama," she added, "the market was still pretty nifty. Besides there's Odysseus to consider. Even if you're disheartened, we must find him. Might find Vaclav there."

I couldn't let disappointment derail our mission. Vaclav might, indeed, hold the key. "You're right, you're right. We can't forget Odysseus."

Penelope grinned. "That's my bold hero."

"I'm only going for your brother's sake. The market will be…what it will be. I've lowered my expectations."

"You're most adorable when you show determination. You strut like a tiger."

My fur hid the blush stoked by her compliment, echoes of my dear mother's very words. I lifted my chin and let out a mighty roar. *"Allons, ma chérie!* To Châtelain."

We zig-zagged along the sidewalks of a quiet residential neighborhood until we reached a busy intersection: Avenue Brugmann and Chaussée de Waterloo. A voice rose in my head. *"Follow Grumps' dream. Head south to Waterloo and Paris."* If I were alone and Odysseus wasn't our priority, I probably would have absconded. Unexplored paths intoxicate with unspoiled possibilities.

After several minutes of aimless walking, I grew agitated. Grumps' directions to Châtelain, a guide anchored by restaurants and trash receptacles, slipped from my mind—the likely consequence of discouragement and self-pity. Swallowing my pride, I was about to confess as much when Penelope stopped.

"I recognize that place." She gestured across the street to a four-story townhouse. "Least...I think I do. Let's take a closer look."

Trotting across narrow Rue Américaine, we stood before a gray stone house. The unique structure featured bold, curved lines and honey-colored wood trim around the front door and windows. Gold ironwork ornamented the façade. At its top, a balcony railing resembled the lacey wings of a gigantic dragonfly.

Penelope nodded toward a placard on the door. "This is it. Victor Horta Museum."

"Friend of yours?"

She giggled. Horta, she explained, was a long-deceased architect. The museum occupied his former home and studio dating to the turn of the prior century. "If you think the exterior is stunning," she added, "you should see inside. Mosaics, stained glass, and fancy wall decoration. A bounty of shiny objects to mesmerize the dourest of cats."

"How do you know all this?"

She nodded to a nearby townhouse. "Dear friend of Madame lived there." The elderly widow, she explained, looked after the Siamese siblings when their owner was away. "Took Odie and me to teas at the museum. Had to be on our best behavior. Valuable antiques you know."

I stared wide-eyed. Her pampered upbringing amazed me. "Why didn't the woman adopt you after your mistress died?"

"She and Madame had a falling out."

"About?"

"Us, as a matter of fact. Odie and me. Madame thought her friend took too many risks with us. We assumed she died. She was ancient... in people years. Penchant for teacakes and blackberry brandy as I recall."

"You're not sure? That she's dead, I mean. Would you recognize her name...on the doorbell or mailbox?"

"Of course. Fabiola, like Belgium's former queen."

Penelope led me to the house at Number 28. I scanned the name cards next to the series of apartment buzzers. "Only surnames. Wait! Here's an F. Severns. That your Fabiola?"

After a shrug, she glanced to the top floor. "Only knew her first name."

"We can wait here if you want. See if she comes out."

"And miss the market and a chance to find Odysseus? I think not. As I said, she's probably dead." Turning her back to the house, Penelope seemed desirous to distance herself, physically and emotionally, from a life she could no longer claim.

"Sorry. I only thought that well…maybe…"

"Fabiola could provide a home for Odie and me. Yes, that would have been lovely. But Odie is my priority. And I never would have met you. Let's go. I know the way to Châtelain from here." Raising her nose, she guided me with confidence.

Penelope's expression and tone softened. "Fabiola took us to Châtelain. For her weekly salon appointment. She had long fingernails and a whisker problem. Wrapped up her tower of hair every night with wads of toilet paper pulled from the roll."

My eyes bugged at the image. "Sounds positively feline."

She chuckled. "Probably why we became fast friends."

Resurfaced memories soon put Penelope in a pensive mood. We continued in silence, walking across the invisible boundary between Bohemian Saint-Gilles and upmarket Ixelles. From my whiskers to the black tip of my tail, excitement surged through my body. In my entire life, I'd never wandered farther from the cardboard box.

Penelope purred with satisfaction. "We're close." She nodded toward a church that anchored Rue Bailli, a busy stretch of specialty shops. "Fabiola always popped in to light a candle for her late husband…a diplomat. Tragic end. Crash of some sort."

Nearer the church, Penelope giggled like a kitten.

"What's so funny?"

"Odie always made a scene inside. Sneezed at the incense."

I sneered. "Father Pierre and his cohorts spoiled religion for me."

"Can't say I disagree. But the priest here at Saint Michel was sweet. Young, good looking. Tan and toned like a film star. Nothing like ancient, pasty-faced, Pierre. Father Jacques always had kind words for Fabiola and treats for Odie and me."

Her flowery praise drew my glare. Regardless of Father Jacques' star qualities, how could she forget that Father Pierre was sweetness and honey before brandishing a nasty stinger? Simple cardboard, my mother said, was sturdier than posh satin. Although Mama was referring to our home, the same truth applied to people, especially priests—fancy wasn't always better. A white-collared cleric sporting a tan in gray and gloomy Brussels aroused my suspicions.

"There's Father Jacques now. Isn't he dreamy?" At the door of the church, a tall handsome priest held a baby as he spoke with a young woman pushing a pram.

"He's purrrrrrfect." *But who or what does he have locked in his basement?* For the sake of our friendship, I kept my suspicions and further sarcasm to myself.

Fluffing her fur, Penelope preened for the priest's attention. But a crowded tram leading a parade of impatient cars obstructed our view. We had no time for such nonsense. I prodded her forward, leaving the flashy priest and his moldy old church behind. We soon came to an intersection anchored by four cafés. My nose twitched with exotic aromas. Motioning to our right, Penelope announced, "Châtelain Market."

I shrugged. My aloof façade, however, teetered with the first whiffs of waffles and custard tarts. Tottered at delectable aromas of cured meats and cheeses. And collapsed completely at the swirling scent of seafood and roast chicken. As if on autopilot, my legs trotted forward as Penelope huffed at my side.

We entered a smart, tree-lined square. In its center, tents, stalls, and mini caravans were arranged in a large oblong. Bisecting the loop, a single aisle of stalls offered hungry marketgoers an array of international cuisine. Shoppers' dress and demeanors suggested greater affluence than the market in Saint-Gilles. Patrons included professionals, nannies and mothers pushing expensive strollers, as well as an older, genteel clientele.

My eyes darted from one corner of the food carnival to another. "Get a load of the fancy haircuts, raised noses, and self-satisfied swaggers."

Penelope nodded. "Yes, the people are a bit more chic than Saint-Gilles and, I admit, infinitely more pretentious."

"I was talking about the pets." Well-groomed cats and dogs sporting jewel-encrusted collars pranced about with arrogance. All patrons in fact, two- and four-footed alike, were posh and aloof. "Can't understand why everyone acts so blasé. Especially in a place as fabulous as Châtelain."

Penelope snickered. "*Oui*, the Belgian stone face requires much practice to perfect. Madame considered enthusiasm middle-class, ebullience downright vulgar. 'Leave the idiotic grins to the Americans,' she always said with a raised eyebrow and sneer."

"Jeepers! Where's the fun in that?"

Ignoring my comment, Penelope scanned the market. Odysseus and Vaclav were her priorities. As we strolled among the well-heeled clientele, she became distracted, distant, surly. Her confident swagger vanished. Her shoulders drooped.

"Everyone's staring at us." I sensed embarrassment in her tone. "You were right, Fluff. We don't belong here. Not among these fancy cats."

"Don't let these pampered, perfumed pets intimidate you. Behind those lofty airs they're still tail sniffers who'd wallow in muck for a rotten one-eyed halibut. Not one could survive a single night on the streets. They'd wail a pitiful tune if their silky fur matted and lost its strawberry stink. Fooey!" I spat on the pavement. "They're no better than us. Matter-a-fact, we're better than all of 'em. Heck, Penelope, you're the prettiest darn thing at this market."

She offered a reluctant smile. "You haven't seen all of the market yet."

"Don't have to."

She purred. "You're an angel. Now let's find Odie and Vaclav."

"Oh no!"

Following my gaze, Penelope let out a high-pitched squeal.

I'd forgotten that *Le Roi de Poulet* was part of the afternoon market circuit. Although we hadn't seen the king's long yellow carriage, the two ginger-haired princes were walking directly toward us. Thankfully, the broom-toting queen was nowhere in sight. My backside throbbed just thinking about her.

Using shoppers as cover, we turned tail and ran. I led Penelope into a flower stall where we hid among buckets of fragrant blooms. Between serving customers, two pretty Flemish sisters arranged peonies, dragon lilies, roses, and other flowers into handsome bouquets. It came as no surprise that I didn't see a single dandelion.

The princes passed. With my stomach grumbling, we scavenged the market for food. My eyes kept getting bigger and bigger. Vats of olives, tubs of cheese, cases of cured meats—enough food to feed all of Brussels. Without realizing it, we found ourselves in front of the King of Chicken's royal coach. My stomach screamed for us to stop. Succulent aromas and the sight of juicy meats and crisp, golden skin tempted me. Survival instinct, however, pushed me past the temptation.

"Eek!" The shriek was unmistakably that of the Queen of Chicken.

One of the ginger princes shouted, "The two cats from Monday."

"Grab them," yelled the other prince.

"Bring them to me," commanded the queen.

The boys darted from the trailer. The hair on our backs stiffened. We circled the market until we lost them. Breathless, we came to a clearing. Under the branches of a large tree, people sat at tables drinking wine and dining on market fare. They chatted away like children. Out of the corner of my eye, I caught sight of a sultry woman with long black hair. She wore a flowing purple dress. I recognized her as Lucinda, purveyor of Italian specialties.

"Lucky!" My shout surprised the one-eyed, three-legged cat as he gobbled cheese from the pavement.

"*You*, it's *you*." His jaw dropped; terror flashed in his eye. He probably recalled the thrashing I gave him for flirting with Penelope. His expression softened when he caught sight of her. "Sorry about Saint-Gilles," he added. "Heard about your troubles. Warned you about the DeVilles and the chicken people."

To signal our peaceful intentions, I butted him gently. "No hard feelings."

We explained our current predicament and asked about food. Lucky hobbled toward Lucinda's caravan, returning a short time later pushing, with his nose, a plate of meat and pasta. "Best I can do. Sorry."

Penelope purred. "Looks delicious. You're a dear, and so handsome too."

"W…well maybe I can scrounge up some fresh clams."

"Before you go, any news on my brother?"

"Sorry, *ma petite chou*, but no. Châtelain is posher than Saint Gilles. Diplomats we got, strays not too much. Lousy tradeoff if you ask me." He laughed at his own joke. "Strays that do wander in don't stay very long. Police and animal control see to that." He nodded toward two men in blue-uniforms. "Best eat your meal out of sight and keep a low profile."

Lucky limped off in search of clams while Penelope and I retired to the edge of Lucinda's caravan. We slurped spaghetti as the vibrant scene entertained us. Four men caught my attention. Their serious expressions and intense conversation were out of place among carefree marketgoers. Two of the guys filled dark suits, one big and baggy, the other tailored and trim. A third man with shaggy blond hair sported khaki trousers and a blue sweater. The last guy, ruddy-faced and red-nosed, looked rumpled in baggy jeans and a stained denim jacket.

After studying them, I recognized Big Suit and the blond, Grabowski, as Pierre's dinner guests. They called the smaller man in a suit, Ivanovich, the name uttered in fear by Pierre. I quaked with rage. Before us sat the traffickers who kidnapped my family. Countless other strays too. Instinct urged me to pounce. Ivanovich's lifeless, ice-blue eyes were attractive targets.

Penelope placed her paw on mine. "A cat among pigeons is one thing, but a cat among wolves is quite another. In our present predicament, our ears are more valuable than our claws."

Big Suit nodded toward the blond. "Grabowski understands the urgency. Knows you're eager for the shipment."

Ivanovich sneered. "I wasn't happy having to fly to Brussels."

Grabowski turned white. Beer splattered to the ground from the glass in his shaking hand. "Never happened before. The animals were ready to cross the frontier. We're still trying to figure out why Polish Customs rejected the export certificate."

Ivanovich seethed. "Incompetence! Do you even know where those cats are?"

"Working on it," Grabowski stammered. "Hoping they're still in Poland. One source says they're in Brussels."

"Narrows it down, doesn't it?" Ivanovich's eyes flashed with rage. "To a thousand-mile stretch of road. Fool!"

"Sorry."

"Cheap word. Find them. Get them across the frontier."

Grabowski quivered. "Our Embassy contact is mining the diplomatic angle. Says we'll have an answer next week."

Ivanovich leaned forward, his glare icy. "Fix this by next week or I'll impose my own solution. Guaranteed it won't be pleasant. If the shipment is in Brussels, we'll have to fly the specimens to Moscow."

Grabowski scratched his temple. "Still don't understand why you're so concerned with three lousy cats. Say the word and I'll sweep the fish market and grab dozens of feral strays. I promise their fur is soft and plush."

Even at the distance we sat from the men, I could see Ivanovich seethe as Grabowski babbled. I half expected him to slap the Pole across the face. "Idiot!" Ivanovich snapped. "How many times do I have to tell you? I want…no I *need* that mother cat and her offspring. My reasoning is inconsequential and probably beyond your comprehension."

My heart raced at the mention of my family who, at that very moment, were somewhere between Belgium and Poland. Maybe even back in Brussels.

Big Suit gestured toward the fourth man "On the bright side, Vaclav here can get his hands on the male Siamese that Pierre let escape." Penelope and I exchanged a glance. Not only had we found the loose-lipped perfume peddler but we might learn Odysseus' location.

Vaclav swigged from a flask. "Close to nabbing that cat. He'll be on the end of a Russian leash soon enough."

"Poor Odie," Penelope muttered.

Ivanovich sneered. "What about the female Siamese and male tabby? They're valuable to me, especially the tabby."

"They're talking about us," I whispered. "They must really want my fur."

Vaclav shook his head. "Nothing yet. We're scouring Brussels. Another Pierre blunder. His close shave with my car should put the fear of God in him."

Ivanovich scoffed. "The priest may soon learn firsthand if there's a God." He glared at Grabowski and Vaclav. "Find the feline fugitives and I'll forget your screw ups." He turned to Big Suit. "And you, locate that missing shipment or you'll take its place in Moscow. If Claus and Saint Clovis move their business, you'll all pay. Do I make myself clear?"

Big Suit bobbed his head. "All will be set by next Wednesday."

Ivanovich motioned to approaching policemen. "Scatter. Update me Sunday. Flagey market."

The men casually rose from the table and parted company. Penelope turned to me, confusion on her face. "Flagey?"

"Another market," I replied, feeling my eyes widen. "We gotta be there Sunday."

Visions of a third afternoon market swirled in my head when Lucky returned. He pushed a plate of clams and shrimp in front of Penelope. Jealous of his attentiveness, I glared at him until, with a huff, he retreated to Lucinda's caravan.

I feigned a scowl. "How's this?"

Penelope flinched. "What's wrong? You angry with me?"

I winked. "Just practicing my sourest Belge face. Afterall, we're dining at chic Châtelain. Gotta act posh. What was it your Madame said? Enthusiasm is so very middle class."

"And ebullience downright vulgar." We rolled onto our backs in a laughing fit.

Our levity was short-lived. Vaclav and Grabowski returned for another drink. Reaching down to retrieve a dropped banknote, they spotted us. Time seemed to freeze; the four of us locked stares. With our hearts racing, Penelope and I bolted out from under Lucinda's caravan.

"Grab those cats," our pursuers shouted.

We serpentined through shoppers' legs. *We can't be caught.* The words repeated in my head. *Not now. Not when we finally have leads on Odysseus and my family.* We ran loops around the market until we lost them. Out of breath, I led Penelope up a short flight of stairs to rest. Familiar aromas jolted my memory as the door slammed shut behind us.

"Gotcha!"

The voice belonged to one of the ginger-haired princes. In a stroke of bad luck, I'd led us back to the King of Chicken. Like the king's succulent roasters, our goose was cooked. The queen, I feared, would soon appear brandishing her broom and commanding, "Off with their heads." Penelope and I paced back and forth between the princes, the words "*escape, escape,*" repeating in my head.

"We found them, Aunty," said one prince.

"Or rather, they found us," said the other.

The woman's chubby face and multiple chins matched the red hue of her hair. She flourished her broom. Penelope pressed against me.

"Ran right into our arms," added the first prince.

The woman wagged her finger at Penelope. "I'll not tolerate any more hissy fits."

"Please, Aunty," said the second prince, "you're scaring them. That's no way to get them to help us."

Help? Penelope and I looked at each other, puzzlement in our faces.

Setting her broom down, the old woman's expression softened. "I've been screeching at mice all day. Rodents aren't something we want advertised. Bad for business."

In a series of pantomimes and words, a prince explained that they needed to protect the trailer from vermin raiders. "Free room and board. And all the roast chicken you can eat." With a drumstick waving in our faces, Penelope and I became loyal subjects of the King of Chicken.

At evening's end with market closed and truck packed, Penelope and I reclined on comfy cushions. We had seven days to find our missing loved ones. In one short week, we'd be back at Châtelain for a final, decisive rendezvous. Until then, we could live like royalty.

I turned to Penelope. "We'll ride in style to every market. Come Sunday, we'll be delivered to Flagey to spy on Ivanovich." I heaved a sigh. "Full stomachs and free transport. Might say we're sitting in the catbird seat."

Chapter 11
Market Deal

With our bellies bloated by roast chicken, turkey sausage, and mashed potatoes, Penelope and I fought off drowsiness. By appointment to his majesty, the King of Chicken, we were commissioned as royal mousers, ratters, and all-around safe keepers of the crown's perishable provisions. Freed from threat of predators and sequestered inside the cozy confines of a warm truck filled with succulent aromas of comfort food, sleep pursued us. Our brains and bodies craved the deep and impenetrable slumber reserved for newborn kittens and pampered housecats. Our heavy heads dropped, and our fluttering eyelids drooped but we persevered. Our new responsibilities demanded vigilance, especially on the first night of the job.

After nudging me awake for a third time, Penelope suggested that we each rest with one eye open or sleep in shifts. Both options failed. Soon we were both asleep, our snores echoing through the dark trailer. How much time passed in peaceful repose, I couldn't say. High-pitched cries roused us. With sudden starts, we awoke to find ourselves whisker-to-whisker with a pair of trembling rats. Who was more surprised, the beady-eyed intruders or Penelope and me?

My tail stood at attention. "The king will have our heads."

"And the queen, our tails," added a distressed Penelope.

Upon interrogation, the rats spilled their guts, metaphorically speaking. Introducing themselves, brothers Benny and Clyde confessed to nightly raids. The pair routinely scoured the trailer for leftovers. They'd discovered a way into the refrigerator to nibble on poultry and side dishes. The royal family of chicken might have dismissed the pilfering of crumbs and scraps as a petty annoyance, but the disappearance of royal treasure was treasonous. Their plump roasters were the crown jewels of poultry.

Our royal house, the brothers confessed, was only one target. The rats made nocturnal raids on dozens of vendors. Their stories of undetected entry and brazen larceny were riveting, their intelligence and industriousness, impressive. I envied their flair for adventure and intrigue.

"Don't move," I roared, summoning my inner tiger. Even had they mustered the courage to run, they weren't going anywhere. Quite by accident, my paw pressed their thick rubbery tails to the trailer floor.

Penelope and I huddled, conversing in hushed meows. Raised on shredded meat, poached fish, and pâté, she found the notion of dining on creatures with whom she conversed unappetizing. With a look of revulsion, she dismissed the health and environmental benefits of consuming food that actually walked to one's table.

"Positively barbaric." She shot a furtive glance to our captives. "When there's no choice, well then, I can overcome my objection. But when we find ourselves surrounded by a bounty of savory edibles," she added with a scan of the trailer, "killing the poor dears seems gratuitous, indulgent, and quite immoral."

Her domesticated sensibilities had reasserted themselves. Grumps was right. You can take the cat out of the parlor, but you can't take the parlor out of the cat. Did a similar truth hold for strays? Were my dreams of domesticity mere fantasy? Was I deluding myself thinking I could be content living as a housecat? Answers had to wait. Penelope and I faced a showdown with two cunning rodents. Their raids of the royal pantry put our heads on the chopping block.

I turned to the rats, their chubby gray bodies quivering. "Don't you fret your pretty little heads. We got a proposal we think you boys will like."

Their trembling paused; they exchanged quizzical looks. Clyde, the plumper of the two, spoke. "What kind of proposal?"

I nudged his head. "The best kind. A real lifesaver...*literally*."

Neither rat joined me in laughter. Penelope shot me a disapproving look and muttered, "Incorrigible."

Considering it a win-win for cat and rat, I took a cue from the DeVilles. In exchange for regulated access to scraps, the brothers had to reveal their secret for gaining entry into the truck and refrigerator. They agreed also to share any leads regarding Odysseus and the animal smugglers. Benny and Clyde would live and eat in peace. And Penelope and I could sleep without fear of awakening to a looted trailer and an enraged royal family.

"Spread the word among the rodent community," I concluded. "The King of Chicken's loyal vassals now include two ferocious felines, knights-errant, who prefer mouse, rat, and all other vermin to poultry. Scavengers dine at their own peril."

Watching the brothers wobble away, their tummies bulging, I winked at Penelope. "They may be chubby rats, but we've become fat cats." Horror swept across her face; her paw glided over her flexed stomach. "Fat only in the proverbial sense, *ma chérie*. Cats who nap in the lap of luxury while their minions toil." We giggled ourselves back to sleep.

※

Next morning, we awakened bright-eyed and alert, a benefit of uninterrupted slumber. As locks turned and the trailer door opened, we sat at attention. The royal entourage entered without trumpet or fanfare. A bald man with a thick red beard boarded. We bowed our heads. No doubt, the esteemed King of Chicken himself. He lacked crown and regal attire, choosing common denim and flannel, a practical display, I thought, of royal prerogative.

Without as much as a "good morning" for us, the royals prepped for the day. As mere commoners, we accepted their brusque manner. Spurning his throne, the king threaded fresh, juicy chickens onto long roasting spits. The synchronized team of poultry peddlers was something to behold.

Sporting an uncharacteristic grin, the queen carried trays of side dishes from the refrigerator. Observing her good humor, I nudged Penelope. My voice blustered with pride. "She must have noticed that everything's accounted for. From giblet to drumstick."

The queen called to the ginger-haired princes, her tone giddy, "Lads, oh lads. Check out the refrigerator. Can't remember the last time I didn't find teeth marks on the chicken or footprints in the whipped carrots."

Penelope and I lifted our heads to await her praise, recognition for an admirable execution of our duties. Glancing at us with dimpled grins, the princes' faces glowed with appreciation. Inching toward the queen, I readied myself to sing purrs of joy. Surely, she'd baste us with compliments. Maybe even tap us on our shoulders with a roasting spit—arise Sir Fluff and Lady Penelope.

The queen lifted her chins and the royal bosom. "I'm brilliant, simply brilliant." Cooing her self-praise, she almost stepped on our tails. "Recruiting those cats was sheer genius on my part. Housing and feeding two grimy animals is a paltry price to pay to be rodent-free."

As she returned to the refrigerator, our heads dropped in disappointment. The younger prince burst out in laughter. "Don't mind her," he said. "Aunty thinks she invented roast chicken." Both princes praised our efforts, giving us robust head scratches, gentle belly rubs, and a generous chicken breakfast.

Throughout the day, a steady flow of shoppers kept the royals busy. The ginger princes had assigned us sentry duty. From our post beneath the trailer, we could ward off potential poultry pilferers and monitor the market for Odysseus and animal smugglers. But other than swatting away a few mice and hissing at an occasional stray, the day dragged. We didn't see a single animal smuggler nor were we any closer to finding Odysseus. Although proud of my service to the king, I found sentry duty dull and boring. A morning market, I also concluded, lacked the pageantry and majesty of an afternoon affair.

As my boredom peaked, a flash of red caught my attention. One of the princes, on his knees, poked his flaming red head under the trailer. "Earned an evening off." The king, apparently, had tired of audiences with his subjects. Instead, the royals spent Thursday afternoons cleaning the trailer and ovens, and provisioning for the week. "Back by midnight. Tonight, you earn your keep. The refrigerator will be loaded for the weekend. A juicy target. Remember, *midnight*. That's when we lock up."

Surprised by our unexpected holiday, Penelope and I eyed each other. As if reading our minds, the prince spoke, "Place Lux…Place du Luxembourg, or simply Plux. That's where you'd find me if I had a free Thursday."

We emerged from the trailer's underbelly when the other ginger prince seconded the recommendation. "Cafés, bars. Loads of journalists and EU hot shots: diplomats, politicians, paper-pushing bureaucrats."

"Huge street party," the first prince added. "Plenty of posh scraps and vermin. Paradise for strays. Hobnob with Parliamentarians, too, if you got the stomachs for it."

"Back by midnight!" The queen's imperial voice lifted the hairs on our backs. "Scat!" She didn't have to command us twice. We hightailed it in the direction pointed out by the princes.

When we were some distance from the trailer and its absolute monarch, Penelope turned to me. "What did they mean by bureaucat?"

I wrinkled my nose. "Heck if I know. Something about paper pushers. Or was it chasers? I got the impression bureacats don't do much."

"Probably because they swat everything off their desks."

Excited by another adventure, our pace quickened. The din of human voices and clanking of glass guided us the last few blocks to Place Lux. Neat whitewashed buildings of uniform height and style, 19th century according to Penelope, lined three sides of the formal square. On the fourth side, a handsome train station dating back to the start of the railroad age seemed poised for swallowing by the modern glass monolith of the European Parliament.

I gestured to the hulking structure. "Home of the chosen race called Parliamentarians."

Penelope cocked her head. "Chosen?"

I nodded. "By something called ballots."

Penelope scanned the well-dressed crowd. Alcohol-fueled chatter was louder than any afternoon market. "What do you think?"

Politicians and businesspeople strutted around in pinstriped finery. The throng spilled into cafés and bars. Blue clouds of cigarette smoke hung above packed terraces. A few stray cats lurked on the fringe as if afraid of being trampled. In the square's grassy center, a green-hued statue gave refuge to pigeons that roosted on the somber-faced man's head and shoulders. Loitering on the statue's pedestal were shaggy-haired humans with unshaven faces and rumpled clothes—two legged strays.

"You're asking me what I think? About a market that peddles only in people?" I feigned an exaggerated yawn. "Color me unimpressed."

Penelope swatted me with her paw. "Give it a chance. Think of Grumps."

Mention of my mentor, an eager explorer, reignited my spirit of adventure. With my chin up, I led us on a stroll among diplomats, politicians, and bureaucrats who, we learned, were not cats at all, but humans. Finicky tail chasers nonetheless. Overheard conversations included fishing quotas, advertising oversight, and food label regulations.

Flashing a smirk, I turned to Penelope. "And what do *you* think?"

She emitted an exasperated sigh. "Anyone who says cats lead

humdrum lives should spend an hour in Place Lux. *Boring!*"

"Now where's *your* sense of adventure?"

"Lost it a few droning conversations ago. Who gives a rat's rump about the proper curves of a banana or whether prunes actually make you poop?"

I stopped chuckling when my ears perked at the mention of animal rights. A heated exchange unfolded at a nearby table. I turned to find a youthful blond man with a handsome face and saggy socks. He shared a table with a stout woman with short hair, a deep voice, and frayed trouser cuffs. I led Penelope over for a listen.

"Question of ethics," said the young man who constantly pulled up his socks. "The committee must advocate for broader legislation. With hefty fines and prison time."

As the woman scoffed, her scuffed loafers tapped the pavement. "You must be joking, Hansen. The EU already has strong protections against animal exploitation."

"For products manufactured within the EU. I'm proposing a ban on all imports. Anything that harms animals. Stiff penalties for all profiteers."

"Such as?" The scuffed loafers tapped the pavement even faster.

"Breeders, traffickers, manufacturers. Corrupt officials who look the other way. The EU must stake the moral high ground. Otherwise, we're complicit in the exploitation."

"You'll have to prove your allegations. Won't get anywhere with the committee unless you do. Public's tired of frivolous legislation."

"Precisely why I need a smoking gun. EU-based enterprises that engage in illicit activity. I know they exist. Traffickers poach strays across Europe. Here in Brussels too. Animals are shipped east. Products exploiting them sold in the west. Prove that and I have my smoking gun."

The scuffed loafers stopped tapping; the heels grounded into the pavement. "May as well tip at windmills. You know I speak for a large bloc. Additional legislation is pointless."

The younger man's shoulders slumped. "Then if you'll excuse me, I have work to do." After tugging his socks, he rose from the table, lifted his chin, and strode away.

Penelope purred. "I love that man, saggy socks and all."

"Sounds outnumbered and outmaneuvered."

"Unless we give him that smoking gun."

"Yes! Father Pierre, Ivanovich, Vaclav, and Claus. The whole lot of traffickers would be a blazing cannon. In addition to our families, we can save animals throughout Europe."

We wanted to follow Hansen but the crowd grew dense. At ankle level, one pinstriped trouser looked pretty much like any other. But learning of a human ally in a position of power gave us renewed hope. Even though he was a bureaucrat.

As we emerged from under the table, two approaching figures stopped us. Joining Scuffed Loafers at her table were none other than Vaclav and Grabowski, the latter nearly unrecognizable in a pinstriped suit.

After lighting a cigarette, Vaclav ordered two vodkas. "Did the Great Dane of morality have anything important to say?"

Grabowski sneered. "Will he play nice?"

Scuffed Loafers spoke, "Hansen's a fool. Wants to change the world. And for what? Useless strays. Disease spreaders with IQs of a turnip. Unless he abandons this lunacy, we'll have to teach him what happens when you mess with the top of the food chain."

"You mean?"

"Yes, Vaclav, Plan B. Or rather, Plan BMW. You'll take another midnight drive through Brussels. This time, no near-miss. Now give me good news. I've got a dragon broiling my neck."

Grabowski downed his vodka. "We found the missing shipment. It's here in Brussels. Meeting our Embassy guy tomorrow to grease the customs angle. As for the slippery Siamese, we got him in a safe place." Penelope and I held our breath; we'd rescue Odysseus if we knew where he was. "He's—"

Scuffed Loafers interrupted him. "I don't care where you're holding that damn cat. Make sure you keep him this time. You can give Ivanovich the news at Flagey. And the other two?"

Vaclav cleared his throat; his hand thumped his thigh. "Still working on it."

Scuffed Loafers lowered her voice. "Ivanovich now says dead or alive. Just so he gets them next week at Châtelain."

"Dead?" Vaclav replied with a scoff. "Simplifies things. They're as good as in my clutches with or without a pulse. They'd make great seat covers for my car."

Penelope whimpered. I'm sure it was unintentional, but her cry gave us away. In an instant, three pairs of ice-cold eyes peered under the table.

I inhaled loudly. "Here we go again."

Vaclav and Grabowski lunged for us. Leading our pursuers on a mad dash through Place Lux, Penelope and I darted between legs, under tables, over planter boxes, and across laps of startled patrons. Thankfully, fleet-footed felines proved superior to plodding humans.

Running through deserted streets, we scampered aboard the royal trailer as a clock struck twelve. Slamming the door behind us, a frowning queen muttered four-letter royal decrees. Left alone and exhausted by our adventure, Penelope and I were fast asleep by the time Benny and Clyde arrived for scraps.

Chapter 12
Cataclysm

Passing the time in service to the royals, we counted down the days until the smugglers' appointed rendezvous. At Flagey we hoped to learn the whereabouts of Odysseus and my family. How we'd rescue them, we still didn't know.

Sunday arrived. After fitful sleep, we awakened and scurried out the trailer. Performing my morning stretches, I lifted my nose to breathe in fresh air. "Such a glorious day."

My search for family dovetailed with my thirst for adventure. Grumps touted Flagey's grand plaza and namesake market as 'cat-tastic.' Sharing the experience with Penelope was a bonus. A heated conversation between their majesties, however, pointed to disaster.

The queen's expression was stern, her puffy cheeks red. "Idiotic idea. One of your worst yet."

The king spat on the pavement. "Change is good."

Adopting a bulldog's stance, the queen glared at him. "What will our regular customers think?"

"That we've taken a well-deserved holiday. They'll appreciate us all the more next week. Place Jourdan might be a goldmine. Think of it as spreading our wings…and our thighs and drumsticks." The King of Chicken had spoken, adding a snorted laugh for effect.

The queen threw up her hands. "Sundays have always meant Flagey."

I stammered, "We're not at F...Flagey."

Penelope's fur fluffed in panic. The look of horror on her face likely matched my own. "Fine time for his majesty to assert his territorial ambitions. We must get to Flagey."

I bobbed my head in agreement. "But how? We don't know the way."

Despite the perks and prestige of a royal commission, circumstances left us no choice. Matters of life and death, called us elsewhere. We had to resign. I digested my disappointment with self-serving rationale. *More to life than poultry. Old chicken grease reeks. Never did get to the palace.*

As I contemplated our departure, the air swirled with an intoxicating mix of sweets and savories. I suggested we eat a hearty breakfast before leaving. The queen, however, thwarted our plans. Clutching her wood and straw scepter, she frowned as she gazed at the unfamiliar market. "Thinks he knows best. Some king. King of chicken sh—"

Her words trailed off as she caught us looking up at her. "As for you two: be alert. No slouching. No snoozing. It's a new market for us. God only knows what kind of scavengers we'll attract. Remember what happens to sentries who go AWOL." Using her finger, she sliced the air in front of her throat. "What's that?" she added. "Sniveling? *Enough!*" A stomp of her regal foot sheathed in white orthopedic leather, ended her decree. She abruptly turned, climbed the stairs, and disappeared into the trailer.

My paw caressed Penelope. "Escape's our only option."

Her eyes welled with tears. "We simply must find Ivanovich."

She was right. Eavesdropping on the traffickers was the best hope of finding our loved ones. The clock was ticking. In three days, the villains planned to pack up Odysseus for a one-way trip to a Russia. My family shared the same fate. Bog and Auguste were out of the picture. I assumed that they were wandering Eastern Europe unaware that Polish customs had returned Auguste's and my family to Brussels.

We prepared to abandon our posts when we found ourselves

cornered by the princes. Each ginger-haired boy brandished a collar and leash. The older freckle-faced boy spoke. "Hate to do this, but it's a command from on high. New market and all." With an apologetic expression, he nodded up to the queen who smirked over a tray of twice-baked potatoes.

Before we could react, the princes scooped us into their arms. We squirmed, twisted, and writhed but collars soon fastened around our necks. I bristled against the leather noose. To think that once I considered collars symbols of domesticity, a bond freely and mutually formed between human and pet. Robbed of my independence, I felt violated. Panic expressed itself in our chorus of frenzied yowls. One prince gripped Penelope in his arms. Managing to wriggle free from my captor's clutches, I dropped to the ground with a thud. My feet revved for flight. The taut leash, however, constrained my movement to a small circle.

Tugging me, the prince fastened my leash to the trailer's front bumper. "Now, now. This is only temporary. Aunty's worried about the new market."

The other prince attached Penelope's leash to the rear bumper. "She's thrilled with your work. Doesn't want you to desert your posts. Leashes will come off soon enough. We'll fetch you something to eat—"

"Unless you two expert mousers want to catch your own lunch," interrupted his brother. With trails of laughter, the ginger-haired princes hurried up the stairs and disappeared into the trailer.

Although they'd fastened our leashes to opposite ends of the truck, Penelope and I discovered that the leads were long enough to allow us to meet, nose-to-nose, under the trailer. With shoulders slumped, Penelope hung her head. "What do we do now?"

I stretched forward, the collar digging into my neck. There was enough slack to allow my nose to nuzzle the crown of her head. "Don't know, *ma chérie*. We'll figure something out."

"But Odie and your family..."

"I know, I know." Despite an equally deflated spirit, I spoke in a comforting tone. I flinched. "Wait! It's our *lucky* day."

Following my gaze, Penelope purred with delight. Not ten feet away stood our old pal Lucky. He and Lucinda were readying their caravan for market day. Chalking a menu board, the longhaired beauty sang a lilting Italian song. At her feet and purring in time to the music, Lucky appeared preoccupied with a small bird pecking breadcrumbs in front of the baker's stall.

I wrinkled my nose. "How to get his attention?"

Penelope winked. "My years in the litter box count for something. Stand aside." With a proud swagger, she turned her rear-end toward Lucky. Leaning forward, she used her hind legs to kick up a shower of gravel. Pellets flew through the air like bullets. "How am I doing?"

Mesmerized by her strong and shapely legs, I stammered my reply. "L…little b…bit farther. J…just a bit more to the left. No, *my* left… *your* right."

Lucky's humming stopped mid-purr. Cocking his head, he glanced in our direction. He recoiled. A volley hit him in his good eye—his only eye.

I leaped into the air. "Bull's eye!"

Lured by our hearty meows, Lucky inched forward. Once he stopped squinting, his face brightened into a closed-mouth grin.

Penelope purred loudly. "He's seen us."

"But can he help us?"

Lucky pranced across the pavement. "Friends, buddies, pals. Great to see you again. On second thought, maybe I shouldn't be so pleased. At Châtelain, you ran off without so much as a thank you for the clams." Lifting his nose, he started to turn.

"No!" Penelope shouted. "Be a dear. We need you. Please."

"We're sorry, Lucky, really we are," I added. "You've been a great pal."

After several more apologies and pleas to stay, he agreed to hear us out. We spoke of our harrowing escape from Vaclav and Grabowski. "A wrong turn, and voilà, we're vassals of the King of Chicken."

"First willingly, but now..." With a tug of her leash Penelope displayed our plight.

Lucky assumed a look of disdainful indifference, a feline's stock and trade. "Can't say I didn't warn you. Simply two more nose-in-the-air cats who won't listen."

Ignoring his sarcastic gibes, we plowed on with our story. We hoped to sow even the smallest seed of sympathy. I spoke of our excursion to Place du Luxembourg. We detailed the schemes of Vaclav, Grabowski, and Scuffed Loafers, the toe-tapping EU insider. Penelope mentioned Hansen, the young idealist and animal ally. All seemed to fall on deaf ears until I spoke of our being wanted *dead* or alive. Lucky gaped at us. Our tale of woe had become as mesmerizing as a shiny trinket.

Penelope batted her long eyelashes. "We fled Place Lux after another mad chase. Lost the villains in a maze of pinstripes. Been looking over our shoulders ever since."

I pawed Lucky. "You see, ole pal, we're in a heap of trouble. Sitting ducks. We gotta get out of these collars and hightail it to Flagey."

Slow to reply, Lucky interspersed his words with sighs. "Well...uh. Might be able to help...uh. With one of your problems...uh. But not the other...uh. No, definitely not the other."

I twitched my whiskers. "Whadda you mean?"

"Gotten out of collars before, plenty of times. But that was before a flying beer bottle claimed most of my teeth." He flashed a jack-o-lantern grin. "As for Flagey, never been. Lucinda spends Sundays here at Place Jourdan. 'More our style,' she says."

With somber expressions, Penelope and I stared at each other. She turned to Lucky. "Won't you try? Please. With what teeth you do have. But fast. The princes might return any moment with our breakfast."

Lucky couldn't resist. But Penelope's collar was fastened too tight. Tackling mine first, he gnawed enough to let me tear through the frayed leather with a forceful snap of my head. Freed, I turned my teeth onto Penelope's leash. Her collar would have to stay.

"What's all the blasted noise?" bellowed a gravel-voiced human.

I stopped chewing. Spitting out bits of ragged leather, I turned toward the sound. On his knees and with a cigarette dangling from his mouth, the red-bearded king squinted under the trailer. The three of us froze. Hair on our backs stood at attention.

Frowning, the king spat out his cigarette. "Her royal highness isn't amused by your caterwauling and tomfoolery. 'Wouldn't happen at Flagey,' she says. 'You and your grandiose schemes,' she gripes. Damn woman thinks she knows everything. A royal Queen B, that's what she is." With a huff, he grabbed Penelope's leash and pulled.

"Save yourself, Fluff."

Can't let this happen. I grabbed her tail. Our claws were useless on the gravel pavement. We both slid toward the king one terrifying inch at a time.

I called to her, "Listen. When I let go, run toward him."

"What?"

"It's our best hope. Run. Toward the king and then past him. Don't stop. Trust me."

"Nobody I trust more."

I released my grip. "Run! Fast as you can."

She stopped struggling and darted toward the king. Momentum could snap the last strands of stubborn leather. But the leash needed slack, plenty of it. She neared him; I held my breath. When she ran past the startled monarch, the leash loosened. It tightened again as she kept running.

Lucky leaped into the air. "It snapped. The leash snapped."

The king's face flashed with surprise. Lucky and I bolted from under the trailer to join Penelope in the shadow of Lucinda's caravan. A growing queue for the king's signature chicken proved a blessing. Customers kept the royals, already frazzled by a new market, too busy to bother us.

A stub of leash hung from the collar around Penelope's neck. "Now what?" she asked.

I turned toward Lucky. "Sure you don't know the way to Flagey?" He shook his head. "Anybody you can ask?" His head shook again. "What about strays? Ones you've never seen before?" He started to shake his head again but stopped. His single eye sparked.

"Yes, this very morning. A cat. Stranger around here."

I bobbed my head with excitement. "Promising."

Lucky fixed his eye on me. "Matter of fact. Looked a bit like you, only bigger."

Penelope scanned the market. "Where did you see him?"

"Let me think, let me think. Where did I see…" I wanted to swat him in the kisser. "That's right," he added after an aggravating pause. "Not a stray at all. A pet with a human."

My whiskers twitched. "What kinda human?"

"Brute of a man. Nasty looking fellow. Unshaven. Dark menacing eyes. Ask me, not the type of person to have a pet cat. More the Rottweiler type if you know what I mean."

Penelope looked at me, her voice dropped to a whisper. "You don't suppose—"

Lucky interrupted her. "There they are now."

Following his line of sight, I gasped. "Brother!"

"Bog!" Penelope exclaimed.

Emerging from a busy frites stand were Bog and Auguste. My heart raced with joy. A happy reunion was one thing, but we also needed their help. I made a move toward them.

Lucky grabbed my tail. "Wait! Best keep out of sight."

He was right. I'd lost count of our pursuers—Ivanovich, Grabowski, Vaclav, Father Pierre, and now, the royal family of chicken. Going out into the world wasn't for the meek. The cardboard box and squatters camp seemed dog years in my past. But nostalgia for that simpler life competed with adventure. The latter proved addictive.

Lucky facilitated a lowkey reunion behind Lucinda's caravan. After spirted hugs and customary pleasantries, Bog extracted Penelope from her collar. Sharing our story, I ended with an urgent request to sprint to Flagey. With everyone in agreement, Bog obtained directions.

We gave Lucky our undying gratitude. Bidding him farewell, we offered advice about, Benny and Clyde. "They're the ones raiding Lucinda's caravan at night. Now, Lucky, don't go getting all defensive. They're sly. I'm telling you this because they'll be wanting a new partner. For a few scraps, they'll leave you alone."

"Lucinda will think you're adorable *and* smart," Penelope said with a wink. "Tell Benny and Clyde that the royal family of chicken is fair game again." She ended with a catty meow.

Lucky thanked us, wished us success with our mission, and recommended the oysters at Flagey. "Never sampled them myself," he said, rubbing his tummy. "But customers and strays purr passionately about them. There's champagne too for celebrating."

"Ah," I said to my companions, "will we be celebrating or licking our wounds?"

Chapter 13
Sunday Rendezvous

"*Bonne chance, mes amies.*" Lucky's encouraging words faded in the air behind us as we set off on a new adventure. Flanking Bog shoulder to shin, Penelope, Auguste, and I trotted from Etterbeek. Pedestrian traffic, typical of Sunday mornings, was light. Our journey was short. We anticipated arriving at Flagey long before the market closed.

During our march to Ixelles, Bog and Auguste recalled their exploits. Tag-teaming their story with seamless ease, the pair shared a unique camaraderie, a friendship formed on their travels to Poland and back again aboard freight trains and soft-sided transport trucks. They understood each other in a manner, Penelope explained, typical of a pet and his or her human. Still, I wondered, had shared circumstances, two strays in desperate searches for family, forged their deep and incredible bond?

Auguste recounted their long, harrowing journey while Bog, his tone laced with resignation and regret, spoke above our heads, figuratively and literally. "He's got a need…to tell his story," Auguste explained. "Even if we're cats."

"Madame always said pets made the best therapists," Penelope said.

We felines fell silent as Bog began. He spoke of asking every refugee met along the trek to Poland if they'd seen his wife and daughter. "Each headshake, every 'no' broke my heart into pieces. I don't deserve to be called husband, father, or even son. I'm barely a man. And nationality? Meaningless when a country shatters into pieces and its people turn on each other.

"You know," he added. "Vilifying people is easy. Especially strangers. Those you fear or are taught to fear. I'm not as feral as people think. I trained to be a veterinarian, damn it." He gazed down at us. "Guess that's how I can communicate with you. Animal sense, they call it."

I didn't understand Penelope's meow of surprise until she explained to me the veterinary profession. She called the work, noble. However, when she detailed the poking, prodding, and pinching that happened during physical exams, my eyes widened. "They stick what? Where?" I shook my head. "I'll pass."

Bog sighed. "Can't change minds. People grasp for logic in an illogical world. Stick labels on things they don't understand. Good people, least those that consider themselves such, despise us because we seek to live somewhere decent. Want to give our families a future. Why scorn a person merely for wanting a better life?"

I expressed sympathy for his plight with a gentle headbutt to his shin before turning to Auguste. "Why'd you return to Brussels? Did you know our family was sent back?"

He gestured toward Bog. "His doing. Sending our family back."

Shocked, I almost stumbled. "Wh…what?"

Refugees they met in Poland, Auguste explained, knew of Bog's wife and daughter. His family, they said, had joined a group heading west to Belgium. The same refugees shared names of border guards and customs officials who took bribes. In exchange for Bog's money, corrupt officials revealed the Warsaw address where our feline family was being held.

"Bog didn't abandon me," Auguste added. "Says we're in this together to the very, and possibly bitter, end."

Reaching Warsaw, Auguste and Bog located the animal export office. Using his veterinary expertise, Bog informed officers that he'd been searching for the shipment. The three cats, he explained, carried a dangerous virus. A research lab had released them by mistake. Public health concerns required the shipment be returned to develop a vaccine. Their failure to comply would unleash a lethal pandemic across Europe.

Auguste chuckled. "All Bog needed to say. Oh, the horror on their faces. Couldn't release the shipment fast enough. Wouldn't give it to us though. Hazardous, unfit for export. Returned to shipper. So, we're indebted to Bog. Once we find our family, we gotta help him find his."

Jumping into Bog's arms, I licked his face in gratitude.

⇒‹‹◉››⇐

Pelting Auguste and Bog with more questions, we entered an open plain where a dozen streets converged. More trapezoid than square, Place Flagey buzzed with activity. Patrons packed café terraces. A large structure anchoring one side of the plaza drew my attention.

Penelope whispered in my ear. "Home of the Brussels Philharmonic. Fabiola said the building resembles a steamship. Art Deco."

I nodded. "Like Horta's work?"

She shook her head. "Horta's Art Nouveau." Responding to my quizzical look, she added, "One's flowery, the other's sleek. All in the lines."

"You're so smart."

"And you're adorable."

In addition to a Sunday market, the sprawling plaza contained a modern tram station and a fountain of water jets shooting skyward from stone pavers. Considering myself a market connoisseur, I formed an early impression. Flagey was sophisticated. More so than the weekend market on the parvis. But it lacked the elegance of Châtelain, the intimacy of Saint-Gilles Town Hall, and the cozy charm of Place Jourdan. I started to assess vendors and food offerings when I felt a nudge.

Penelope glared at me. "Hellooo! Where's your head?"

"Sorry, day dreaming."

She grimaced. "We need all eyes peeled for Ivanovich and the traffickers."

Bog nodded across the plaza. "My money's on the oyster stand. Where's there's champagne, there's probably vodka on ice. And where there's vodka—"

"There'll be Russians," replied Auguste.

"Especially Vaclav," I added.

As we strolled toward the stand, we tried to act nonchalant. Not easy for a burly Syrian and three cats in tow. As Bog predicted, the villains were dining on oysters. Attired in casual apparel, they blended in with the weekend crowd. Although he swapped out a tailored suit for beige trousers and wool sweater, Ivanovich was unmistakable. His eyes were as lifeless as ice-blue marbles. Vaclav, Grabowski, and Big Suit were there. Scuffed Loafers too, the nervous diplomat from Place Lux. Seeing the rogues made my stomach curdle while Penelope noted her discomfort with muted cries.

Bog turned to us. "Guessing they know you two? By sight I mean."

I sighed. He was right. Penelope and I were in great danger, helpless against five thugs who wanted us dead or alive.

Auguste pawed my shoulder. "Better let us take this one, li'l brother."

"Table's opening up," Bog said before rushing to claim a high-top near the conspirators.

Penelope and I hid beneath the skirted table of a waffle stall where a shower of powdered sugar caused us to sneeze. Peering through gaps in the cloth skirt, we observed Auguste stroll toward Bog. Jumping from his seat, Vaclav grabbed my brother by the scruff of his neck. Auguste squirmed. His cries caused my tail to fluff. Penelope's paw kept me from scampering to his defense. "They'll only grab you too."

Leaping to his feet, Bog shoved Vaclav. "What the hell are you doing to my cat?"

Vaclav's jaw dropped. "Your cat? Looks exactly like one we've been chasing."

Bog pushed his face closer to the startled perfume seller. "Chasing? Why?"

"F...for our Aunt Evangeline," Grabowski replied. The Pole stood beside Vaclav who gazed dumbfounded at the cat writhing in his hands. "Her precious pussy ran away."

"Poor dear's been out of her mind with worry," Ivanovich interjected. His silky tone and sugary smile chilled my spine. Taking Auguste from Vaclav, he scrutinized him before surrendering him to Bog. "Sincere apologies. As a peace offering may we offer you a drink? Perhaps a few oysters for your furry friend?"

Bog offered a polite nod. "Sure, don't see why not?"

Vaclav extended his hand. "Looking closer, I now see that your cat's chubbier than Aunty's. No hard feelings?"

"No hard feelings," Bog replied, shaking hands.

"See the danger you're in," Penelope whispered. "They thought Auguste was you."

We watched with growing concern as Bog accepted champagne refills poured by an over-attentive Ivanovich. The Russian's icy glare contrasted with his warm and obliging manner. Two rounds later, Bog almost slid off his chair.

Penelope gasped. I groaned. "Criminy! Hope Auguste's taking good notes."

No sooner had the words left my mouth when Vaclav, again, grabbed my brother. Hissing, Auguste scratched his captor's face. Payback, I presumed, for calling him chubby. Vaclav held on, shoving Auguste into a pet carrier that Grabowski must have procured when they plied Bog with alcohol. Bog tried to stand but fell back onto his chair. I felt helpless watching the villains spirit Auguste away. Penelope and I rushed to Bog, jumping onto his table.

Pulling a face, he slurred his words. "Do I know you two?"

Champagne, I assumed, triggered his confusion. Glancing to

Penelope, I realized that alcohol wasn't entirely to blame. An avalanche of powdered sugar had transformed us into albino cats.

Bog lowered his face into ours. He squinted. "Course I know you," he added with a hiccup. "And I know what you're thinking. Ole Bog let you down. Let my pal down too. Don't you worry though. Bog knows where they're going." My joyous meow prodded him to continue. "They're taking Auguste to join a prissy Siamese in the church." *Odysseus is back in Saint Gilles,* I thought. "Priest's got everything under control." *Father Pierre's back in their fold.* "Handing over both cats to Ivanovich at Châtelain. Flying to Moscow, Wednesday night. With the cats." He started to sob like a child. "Poor, poor kitties."

What about my mama and siblings?

As if reading my mind, Bog stopped crying. His eyes spun in his head. "Let me think. There's more. Something about a returned shipment. Yeah, yeah. Umm. Scuffed Loafers got them. Called in a favor with crooked customs agents."

Penelope turned to me. "At least we know who has them. But we don't know where."

Seeming to understand us again, Bog's head shot up. "Right! Scuffed Loafers told Vaclav and Grabowski to meet her in Place Lux. Tomorrow night. Same place as last Thursday. She'll turn over the three cats."

Despite an inebriated state, Bog had retained the most vital information. Before his head dropped onto the tabletop one last time, he vowed to save Auguste who he called, "furmily."

As Bog snored, Penelope and I stared at each other. Time was of the essence. We needed to hightail it back to Saint-Gilles and confront an old enemy.

Chapter 14
Faux Paws

"Auguste, Odysseus, Vanille, Licorice, Lily. So many abductions." Penelope ended her litany with a deep sigh.

"Countless others. Dognappings too, I imagine. Shudder to think how many strays have been taken for their fur. Least we've got a lead about our brothers."

Penelope's face flashed uncertainty. "But Father Pierre? I thought the Russians were through with him."

I gestured toward our snoozing friend. "You heard Bog. He distinctly said that they were taking Auguste to join that 'prissy Siamese' in the rectory."

"Were those his exact words?" As I nodded in reply, she shrugged. "Guess it makes sense. The rectory has all the supplies they need. But…"

"Course it makes sense. They're giving Pierre one last chance."

She shook her head. "They don't strike me as paragons of charity."

"Maybe it's the priest's final act rather than a last chance. You know, ship our brothers to Russia and shut down operations. There's also his debt to Claus to consider. Way I see things, we have no choice but to confront the rascal."

"Perhaps you're right. They are desperate. Take the fastest path to get what they want."

"Exactly what worries me. Ivanovich is jittery. Wants us dead or alive. How much patience does he have left for Odysseus and Auguste?" For that matter, Vaclav also concerned me. What revenge would he exact upon my brother for the nasty scratch to his face?

Penelope whimpered. "One not-so-minor detail stands, or should I say, sits in our way." She motioned toward Bog. His snoring had grown louder, drawing curious glances from nearby patrons. Stale odors of champagne and oysters wafted from his gaping mouth.

"Not much we can do." I pawed his forearm and tickled his nose with my whiskers. He didn't stir. "Hate to leave him here in this state."

"We can't wait. We must save Auguste and Odie."

"He's too big to move. Street smarts will have to protect him. If only we had a way let him know we're heading to the rectory. His brawn would come in handy."

Penelope's brow furrowed. "Got it! Wait here, Fluff."

"Where are you going?"

"Don't you fret your handsome little head. Back in two shakes of a cat's tail." Jumping to the ground, she vanished into the market maze as I contemplated her silky tail.

I tried to focus on a rescue plan but Bog's mouth sounded like a construction site. Ogling strangers proved equally distracting. To be fair, a cat coated in powdered sugar paired with a snoring Syrian were odd sights even for Flagey. When I caught someone's glare, I perked my ears, assumed an expression of innocence, and stared back with wide, adoring eyes. Most curious onlookers responded with soft sighs. Many commented on my irresistible cuteness and spectacular eyes of emerald green. Should anyone fail to succumb to my charm and good looks, I primed my inner tiger. Ready to hiss, scratch, and pounce.

Penelope soon sauntered back with purposeful stride. When a ray of sunlight caught her face, a shimmering object dangling from her mouth drew my curiosity. Leaping onto a chair and then up to the tabletop, she flashed a self-satisfied grin. Lowering my gaze to her clenched jaws, I studied the swaying gold chain and trinket. "What's that?"

Dropping her chin, she opened her mouth. The hidden treasure fell to the table. Always a sucker for anything shiny, I remained transfixed until she nudged me with her head. "Pretty," I said. "But really? Shopping at a time like this." I shook my head with disapproval.

She glared at me. "It's a crucifix."

I scoffed. "I know, smarty. Father Pierre wears an identical one around his neck."

"Yes! Exactly like this one, *exactly*."

Realizing her ingenuity, I meowed with delight. "Clever, clever girl."

"We burrow this into Bog's palm. When he wakes up, he should know where we've gone."

"To confront Pierre, Jean, Cook, and…Max," I added with a gulp. I nuzzled her to show my admiration before scooping up the cross. "I'll do the honors." I nosed the crucifix into his large palm. Instinctively, he clutched it. "No chance he'll lose that." My eyes widened. "Holy smokes!" Two uniformed policemen trudged toward us from the direction of the fountain.

"Can't let them see Bog," Penelope said. "They'll arrest him for public intoxication."

"Or send him home. He's a stray like me—no papers. Not a pedigree like you."

A look of horror swept across her face. "They'll find the crucifix. Brand him a thief. Throw him in prison if they don't deport him first."

Penelope and I leaped to the ground as fortune smiled upon us. A middle-aged couple with NYU emblazoned on their sports caps and T-shirts approached our table. They carried a plate of oysters, two glass flutes, and a bucket holding a bottle of champagne. The couple placed their refreshments on the table and settled into the chairs.

The man nodded matter-of-factly to the snoring Bog. "Feels like home."

To passersby, the scene looked like a cozy party of two boisterous Americans and their overserved friend. We had dodged the threat but wanted insurance. We darted straight for the policemen. "You go left," I shouted. "I'll go right."

When we grazed their ankles, the men flinched. They laughed off the encounter but soon, shouts trailed after us. "Damn pests." Looking back, I saw them inspect their powdered sugar-stained trousers. "Scram!" one policeman yelled. The other waved his fist in the air. "Kill shelter if we catch you." Instead of moving toward Bog, the policemen pursued us.

Despite our fear of water, we bolted toward the center of the plaza. Dozens of mini geysers shot skyward—ideal for cleansing powdered sugar. After a slight hesitation, I worked up my nerve. Tucking my chin, I raced into the fountain cringing at each step.

Reaching the other side, we shook our coats. Penelope scanned the plaza. "We lost them."

I chuckled. "They'll be looking for two albinos."

"Clever boy."

"Not clever enough. No clue how to find the Saint-Gilles parvis from here."

She pouted. "Neither do I."

Overwhelmed by options, we turned in circles. A dozen streets converged on Place Flagey. We knew our way to Place Jourdan but dismissed the idea of backtracking. By the time we made our way back, the market would be over. We didn't know how to get to Saint-Gilles from there anyway. Besides, cats never squandered a chance to explore an untrodden path.

Feeling as bedraggled as we looked, we lowered our heads and tucked our tails. Fate would decide our path. We wandered until chirrups and chatter of waterfowl aroused my interest. I pointed toward a patch of green at the far corner of the paved square. "That way!"

She cocked her head. "That the right direction?"

My whiskers twitched. "Beats me. I'm a sucker for ducks, geese, and small birds."

"What's that got to do with getting to Saint-Gilles?"

Puffing up my chest, I assumed an authoritative tone. Convincing required confidence and conviction. Even more so than knowledge and sound reasoning. "It's the complete opposite direction from Place Jourdan."

"So?"

"We know one thing for certain. Place Jourdan is *not* where we want to go."

"And?"

"We should pick the route that takes us as far away as possible from the place we don't want to be. That's this way." I motioned toward a stand of trees on the bank of a pond. "That, my pretty friend, is what's known as irre... irre... irrefootable logic. Perfect sense, right?"

She stared at me with glazed eyes. "I...I'm n...not sure I agree with your reasoning. But...um...what the heck, at this point any direction is as good as another."

"Maybe the birds can point us toward the parvis. As the crow flies so to speak."

"Natural drones."

"Yup, as well as a hearty meal," I added, licking my chops. "A fresh catch menu to please both of us."

"Raw food isn't my preference, but I am, if you pardon the expression, ravenous."

I smirked. "We'll ask the birds for directions *before* lunch."

A modern, ground-level tram station stood between us and our destination. I shouted above the whooshes and clickity clack noises, "Mind the trains."

Hustling across the tracks, I cleared two passing trains traveling in opposite directions. Penelope's high-pitched wail made my fur stand. Turning, I saw trams but no sign of her. Winded and with my heart racing, I crouched on the pavement. My eyes scanned under the carriages. My ears listened for cries, moans...any sign of life. *Nothing!*

Chapter 15
Unlikely Assistance

Penelope's cries echoed in my ears. My heart thumped like a frenzied drum. I dared not blink. Another train car passed. Merciless wheels rolled forward. The bitter odor of steel and fear hung in the air. Tram riders sat blank-faced, oblivious to the drama below.

Could I survive a sprint under the train? Did I have a choice? I inched forward, my mind calculating clearance and timing. Lowering myself into launch position, I lasered my eyes on my objective. *You can do this, Fluff. You must do this.* My tail dropped; my rump vibrated like a revving engine. Pressing my hind legs against the pavement, I prepared to pounce. *Count of three.* "One, two—"

"No, Fluff! Wait!" Penelope's disembodied voice came from under the passing train. "I'm okay." I exhaled into a deep sigh as her face popped into view beneath the moving carriage. "Train's almost passed."

Numbed and light-headed, my body quivered with spasms of relief. The train slowed before stopping at the station. Penelope emerged from behind the last car. My body surged with joy. I darted forward to embrace her. "Thought I lost you. Thank heavens you're all right." Edging backward, I gazed into her blue eyes. "You are all right?"

She purred softly. "I'm fine."

The sight of crimson droplets trailing on the ground behind her made my stomach sink. She responded to my visible agitation. "Single claw. Few licks and I'll be as good as new."

A fresh drop of blood fell to the pavement. "*Mon Dieu!* You're still bleeding."

"Nothing compared to your injuries." Gesturing to my twice-notched tail, she offered my cheek an affectionate lick before turning her tongue onto her wound.

"Tell me what happened, *ma chère.*"

Following her glance to the tracks, I flinched. Out from the tram's shadow stepped Rex. The Belgian Shepherd, a handsome chestnut brown and black, was our camp's Alpha dog. A small purse fastened to his collar spiked my curiosity but his razor-sharp teeth earned my undivided attention.

I stammered, "Wh… wha…what—"

He puffed out his muscular chest. "Nice to see you too, Adventure Boy."

Bristling at his barb, I assessed attack options. I arched my back and prepared to hiss when Penelope threw up a paw. "Calm down, boys. Both of you." She stroked my leg. "It's okay, Fluff. Rex saved me."

My neck stiffened. "He what? How?"

Rex basked in the praise as Penelope described the incident. "As I followed you in front of the tram, my paw lodged in the track. I stumbled. Thought I was done for. Rex grabbed my tail. Pulled me backward. If not for him, I don't know—"

Rex smirked. "*Enough* with the hero worship. I could say that anyone would have done the same," he added with a breathy sigh. "Then again, not everyone is Rex." He glared at me. "You're welcome."

"Y…yes, quite right." Jumbled with emotions, my head seemed to spin. "*Merci.* Thank you, Rex. We're in your debt. Both of us."

The ends of his mouth curled. "Yes, you are. So tell me, what brings you two vagabonds to Flagey, hmm?" Before we could reply, he lowered his snout into my face. His hot breath stunk of pizza and pear. "Tell you the truth, Fluff, thought you were all bluster and no muster. Wagered the pack you'd never leave camp." His eyes, as dark as black marbles, fixed on me.

As I debated whether to lower my head in shame or launch my claws into his smug snout, Penelope interjected. "Might surprise you, Rex, just how brave and adventurous Fluff is. He's not only shown me half of Brussels, he's outfoxed a band of—"

Clearing my throat, I shot her a cautionary look. For all we knew, he was in cahoots with Pierre and the Russians. He had strength, a cold-hearted core, and an aggressive personality that would benefit the most sinister of smugglers. In other words, if I were a villain I'd want Rex on my side.

Shifting his gaze, the hound stared down his long whiskered snout at Penelope. "Yes, my lovely. You were saying, hmm."

She swallowed hard; her eyes widened. "He outfoxed a band of... of feral strays. Yes, feral strays. That's who Fluff outfoxed. Have you ever been to the afternoon market in Saint-Gilles? Vicious dogs. Vile cats. Yes, cats can be mean too, the nasty brutes."

Rex sneered. "Vicious! Vile! Nasty, you say?" Penelope bobbed her head. "My brother Brutus runs with that outfit. One of its leaders, as a matter of fact. Call themselves the DeVilles."

Penelope's eyes widened; her tail lowered. "Oh. M...m...maybe I misunderstood their intentions. Perhaps not as vicious—"

Rex lifted his paw. I prepared to insert myself between them. His sneer, however, turned into a bona fide grin. "No need to sugar coat the truth, missy. You're quite right. They are a savage bunch. In our litter, Brutus was the mean one. Bullied me to no end. First out of the womb. No one ate till he ate. First dibs on cats to torment." Penelope's expression wavered between relief and bewilderment.

Rex turned to me, his expression a mix of respect and doubt. "If what missy here says is true, furball, I stand corrected."

"I should say so," Penelope said. "He's got the tail to prove it. Show him, Fluff. Show him your notched tail."

A look of revulsion swept across his face. "No need. Back to my question. What brings you two to Flagey? Something devilishly sinister I hope. Sightseeing is so mundane. Best left to pigeons and people."

I shrugged. "Actually, our business in Flagey is over."

"We want to get back to the parvis," Penelope added. "But neither of us knows the way."

He scanned our faces as if searching for our motive. "I can get you to Saint-Gilles."

My ears perked. "You'd help us?"

"Why the dubious look, hmm? Don't you trust me?"

I chose my words wisely. "It's just that…back at camp…you weren't so…so…"

"Kind, selfless, noble?" Penelope and I nodded; Rex chortled. "Simple case of keeping up appearances. Politics as humans say. Things said and done that we don't really mean. Said and done, nonetheless, because that's what our tribe expects. At camp, we're rivals, adversaries. Not supposed to get along. There's order in that setup. Keeps things neat, easy to understand. But we're not at camp, are we?" Penelope and I shook our heads. "No, out here in the wilds of humanity, we're…"

"Friends," Penelope replied, filling the silence as Rex grappled for a word.

He recoiled. "Wouldn't go that far. Compatriots is the word I was searching for."

I cocked my head. "Compatriots?"

"We come from the same squalid place. Breathe the same fetid air. Neighbors, birds of a feather so to speak. In short, it means I can help you."

"Gee whiskers, that's great."

"Then tell us the fastest way to Saint-Gilles," Penelope said.

Rex scrutinized her. "You are in a hurry. Even if you won't say why." His snout motioned toward the station. "Tram's the quickest way." Penelope shuddered. "Now missy, don't go worrying about steel wheels. We'll be riding up top."

My eyes widened. "With people? How?"

He lifted his chin; his tail stiffened. "You'll see. First, I need to run an errand. Back before you can say, 'Rex is great' ten times. Wait here."

It was more order than suggestion.

As he turned, his head jerked. The purse around his neck flew to the ground and burst open. Among the scattered contents were papers and shiny objects, gold coins big and small. They mesmerized me. Rex's darting eyes and quivering mouth betrayed his frazzled nerves. "*Merci*, thank you," he muttered as we helped him gather the loose articles. He nuzzled everything back into the purse. Scooping the black leather bag, again bulging, into his mouth, he dashed into the market.

"What do you suppose that was all about?" Penelope asked.

"Not sure we want to know. But I suspect, to use his own words, something devilishly sinister. Best we keep our rescue mission to ourselves."

Rex returned with the purse refastened to his neck. It bulged even more. His confidence, arrogance, and insufferable swagger had returned as well. "Follow me, missy and *Fluffy*."

I gritted my teeth. "Fluff. Just plain, Fluff."

"Whatever you say, Fluffy. To the trams."

Taking advantage of Bruxellois aloofness and concealed by legs of distracted passengers, the three of us scooted on board. We settled into an empty row in the back of the last car. Rex reclined on the floor. Penelope and I hopped onto a seat. I gazed wide-eyed out the window to my big, beautiful city, marveling at the mechanics that whisked us from Place Flagey. I turned to Penelope. "We have four legs, humans only two. Must be why they ride around in cars and trains all day."

She smiled. "Love your wonder at the world. Can't remember my first tram ride but I'm sure my face didn't exude excitement as yours does now."

"You've ridden on trains?"

She nodded. "And cars. Plenty of times. Fabiola often took Odie and me. One of the risky activities, Madame objected to. This tram goes to Châtelain. I'm sure of it."

Without having to take a single stride, we glided past fashionable apartment blocks and townhomes. The train stopped in the middle of broad, tree-lined Avenue Louise. Drizzle streaked the windows. A soft rhythm beat on the carriage roof. Despite the day's excitement and anticipation of the rescue, the rain's pitter-patter and train's rocking lulled me to sleep. I dreamed of my family. Together again, we snuggled in our cardboard home.

"Rue Bailli. Perfect!" Penelope's exuberant voice roused me from slumber. She gestured to a blue street sign. "Shops will be closed today but not the Irish pub. There it is. Fabioli loved the fish and chips. Don't know what she enjoyed more: televised football matches or the large pours of whiskey." Her eager gaze wandered out the train's front window. "Ahead, Saint Michel."

My ears perked up. "And your precious Father Jacques."

She giggled. "Calm down, jealous boy. We're not stopping."

"Not even to purr into the ear of your purrrr-fect priest?"

She rolled her eyes. "I'm simply excited," she added. "I know my way to the parvis from there. We're close."

"Thank heavens. By the way, I'm not jealous. Simply don't trust your priest."

Rex stood, his wolf-like head level with our perch. "Prepare to get off at the church."

"Why?" Penelope asked. "This tram goes closer to the parvis."

"I prefer that stop. Matter of a minute or two." Again, Rex's tone made it clear that this wasn't a debate.

My curiosity piqued. "Rex, you never did tell us why *you* were at Flagey."

"*Moi?*"

"*Oui! Vous.*"

After a flash of unease, he regained his composure. "No special reason. Brussels is my playground. I'm a veritable *bon vivant.*"

"Veritable something, all right," I muttered.

His ears pointed to attention. "What did you say?" Assuming a look of innocence, I shook my head.

Our exit from the train went unnoticed. After walking a short distance, Rex commanded us to wait. He bounded across the street to a shop where a tuxedo cat sat as sentry. After an exchange of pleasantries, the cat nudged open the door. Rex disappeared inside. A human hand pulled down a shade, obscuring our view.

I sighed. "Definitely up to no good. What is that place?"

"Grooming salon."

Responding to my quizzical stare, Penelope described the services offered. "Beauty parlor for animals. Trims, cuts, shampoos. Mostly dogs—"

"Figures. Cats know how to clean ourselves. Ain't no one touching my claws."

"They groom the occasional cat too. Odysseus insisted upon it."

"Bet he did."

"I knew of a rabbit who frequented a groomer. All part of the tamed, civilized world."

"Vets and grooming salons!" I scoffed. "Civility is for the birds." Her description, however, did get me wondering. A salon made a great cover for fur poachers.

"What are you two grumbling about now?" Rex's voice startled us. He'd exited the shop through its back door and stood over us. His leather purse looked empty. He deflected my questions about his visit with a nudge to my rump. "Let's get a move on."

The neighborhood and streets looked familiar. The parvis as well as Father Pierre's church and rectory were nearby. So was our former camp.

"Got you two here as promised. Now get lost." A grimace replaced the kind expression on Rex's face. "Gotta protect my reputation. Can't let my pack see me skippin' down the pavement, paw-in-paw, with two mangy felines." Penelope gasped. "Not that you're mangy. Least not you, missy. Simply gotta get back into character." Along with his demeanor, his grammar and appearance changed before our eyes. Our good-natured compatriot transformed into a tough, flea-bitten mutt.

After all Rex had done for us, I didn't want to cause him any trouble. "Understood. Politics as you say. Thanks again. You've been a real…"

"Purebred," Penelope interjected. "That's the word, Fluff is looking for."

"Don't mention it. I mean it. Don't tell anyone that you saw me today or you'll get a third notch in your tail." He let out a deep menacing growl. As Penelope and I raced up the sidewalk, I heard Rex laugh.

We stopped running when we reached the parvis. The weekend market was winding down. Catching our breath, we glanced to the church and rectory. We'd soon be reunited with our brothers. And then, harnessing our collective cat power we could rescue the rest of my family.

———◆———

It being Sunday, the church doors were wide open. At the altar wearing green robes trimmed in gold, Father Pierre celebrated mass for a few dozen people. We circled the rectory. The window through which we first gained entry was still boarded up.

Penelope fretted. "How are we going to get inside? Can't simply ring the doorbell."

"Why not?"

I didn't give her time to talk me out of my bold scheme. Marching up the front steps, I stood on my hind legs and rang the bell. Having spied Jean and Max on the parvis, I wasn't surprised not to hear barking. Cook opened the door and stared down at us. Her face went white.

"You. It's you." She pressed her hand to her chest. "Go away. Run before…" She pushed the door but her reflexes were no match for two determined felines. We dashed inside. The posh velvet décor and overpowering scent of incense and candlewax were all too familiar. Cook's expression was one of fear, not anger. "You really shouldn't be here."

Commotion in the kitchen drew our gasps and wide-eyed stares. Cook huffed. "It's Jean and Max. Into the basement, *quick*. I'll figure out what to do with you later."

Little did Cook know as she ushered us through the cellar door, that she'd played right into our hands. Our scheme to rescue Odysseus and Auguste was going as planned. The door shut behind us making my heart race. We descended the stairs in darkness.

"Odysseus," Penelope whispered.

My meow was slightly louder. "Brother!"

Gurgles from the ancient water heater were our only reply. We called louder. Our voices conveyed urgency and panic. No response. We searched the entire basement but found no trace of our brothers. We huddled in a corner. Our frets and anxiety surrendered to sleep, a result of an incredible day of escape, chases, close calls, and intrigue.

Feverish scratches at the cellar door awakened us. Max's deep, menacing growls sent chills down our spines. At the edge of the plywood-covered window, daylight snuck into the basement. We had slept through the night.

Panic in her eyes, Penelope turned to me. "Now what are we going to do?"

Chapter 16

A Fine Mess

Penelope paced back and forth. "Let's check again. Definitely what we should do. I'll start in the wine cellar. Maybe we missed—" Pained by her full-blown meltdown, I put my paw on her shoulder. She wasn't thinking clearly. We'd scoured the entire basement *twice*. Unlike our last extended stay, the various rooms were unlocked.

Upstairs, Cook dragged Max from the cellar door and scolded him for an overactive imagination. Could she keep the beast from betraying our hideout? Was she even an ally?

"We've searched every inch, *ma chérie*. They're not here."

"Perhaps we're too late?"

I shook my head and spoke in a sympathetic tone. "Said yourself that you couldn't pick up any scent of Odysseus or Auguste. Or any critter for that matter. Place has been cleared out. Looks like the Russians pulled the plug on Father Pierre after all. He's erasing every trace of evidence or he's preparing to flee. Maybe both."

Her whimpers softened. "Then where are our brothers? What were Bog's exact words? Try to remember."

I shut my eyes to focus. "Said the smugglers were taking Auguste to join the prissy Siamese in the rectory. 'Priest's got everything under control.'"

She nodded with a slight hesitation. "Obviously not *this* rectory... or *this* priest."

My eyes widened. "*Merde!*"

"What is it, Fluff?"

"Bog said, 'church,' not 'rectory.' I messed up, big time."

Penelope nuzzled me. "Don't blame yourself. You leaped to a logical conclusion. I'd have done the same."

I hung my head. "You tried to tell me the traffickers were finished with Pierre."

"How were either us to know? Perhaps they meant another rectory and church? Remember Pierre's dinner party, that horrible woman swimming in fur?"

"*Oui!* Claus was her name. Mentioned Saint Clovis. Probably the church. Thanks to me, we're trapped here while the clock's ticking. I'm an idiot."

Tackling me, Penelope rolled me onto my back and stared down. "Are you a tiger or a teacup poodle? No more apologies or self-pity. There's no time for that nonsense. The clock, as you said, is ticking. Scuffed Loafers is giving Vanille, Licorice, and Lily to Vaclav and Grabowski tonight. In two days, Odie and Auguste get handed to Ivanovich. Then a one-way trip to Russia for the entire lot. And don't think for one moment that we aren't in danger."

Her words sparked an epiphany. Pierre would use us to curry favor with Ivanovich. Even if the Russian wouldn't reconcile, we were still of considerable value to the priest. Hopefully, Ivanovich's 'dead or alive' edict hadn't gotten back to the rectory.

With a rush of adrenaline, I jumped to my paws. "*C'est vrai, ma chérie.* We need a plan."

Craning her neck, she scanned the basement. "Including another escape out of here."

I groaned. "Easier said than done. Cook's abandoned us."

"She did warn us. I bet she's terrified of Pierre. She should be. I keep hoping Bog will save us. Been nearly 24 hours since we left him at Flagey."

"Either he didn't connect the crucifix with Pierre or he bailed to save his own family. Wouldn't blame him."

Penelope pulled a face. "If he didn't want to help us, he'd have abandoned us long ago. Something's happened, I'm sure of it."

The basement light flickered on. We puffed our tails and waited. Tethered to a short leash, Max led the procession. The hound pulled Jean down the stairs two steps at a time. Muttering incoherent commands in Polish and French punctuated by nervous laughter, Jean tried to control the snarling animal. Penelope and I retreated to a shadowy corner.

With his nostrils flaring and chest muscles flexing, Max glared in our direction. I prayed that the stretching leash wouldn't snap. Max grew increasingly frustrated and irritable. "Sit down, boy," Jean bellowed. "You can hunt for mice later."

"Jean doesn't know we're here," Penelope whispered.

"But Max does."

Our attentions were drawn to another pair of legs descending the stairs. The person to whom they belonged moved erratically. His jerking movements and uneven thuds were soon explained. Behind him, a third pair of legs. These covered by black clerical trousers.

"Go on! Down with you." I recognized Pierre's voice. Not the sugary, affable pitch of his public persona but a colder, harsher tone hidden behind his false façade. "Don't try anything cute. I won't hesitate to kill you."

Our eyes darted from Jean and Max at the bottom of the stairs up to the men descending. Max was equally distracted. Penelope and I both mewled because the mystery man prodded down the steps was Bog. His hands were restrained behind him. A single lightbulb illuminated his battered face—dark bruises, fat lips, swollen eyes. Jean shoved Bog against the wall. The powerful thud concealed Penelope's cry.

"*Mon Dieu!* Seems our would-be rescuer needs rescuing himself."

Did this present an escape opportunity? Could Bog serve as a distraction to facilitate our flight to freedom? The upstairs door was shut but surely not locked—minor obstacle for one formidable feline let alone two. We could rescue Bog later. First help ourselves in order to, later, help our friend. The plan had merit. I started to share my idea when the drama intensified.

"One last time," Pierre said, his tone harsh and unpriestly. "Where are those cats? We know you're protecting them. Don't be a fool. They'd sooner cough up a furball than lift a paw to help you." His words stung my honor but didn't pierce my resolve to escape.

Bog squinted in our direction before turning back to the priest. "He's seen us," Penelope whispered. "He followed our clue. I knew it. Just as I knew he wouldn't betray us. He probably got caught trying to help us." Her words poked my conscience.

Pierre jabbed his finger at Bog's face. "Come on, refugee. Tell us where to find those damn cats." His spittle sprayed the air. "Perhaps you prefer Max find your tongue. See how many limbs you have left when we toss you into the canal." Pierre instructed Jean to loosen the leash. Max lunged forward; his jagged teeth snapped at Bog's thigh. My resolve wavered, torn between loyalty to our comrade and my nagging survival instincts. "Tell us where to find those cats and we'll let you go. Otherwise…" Pierre's words drifted off as he glanced down to Max. The dog continued to snap at Bog's leg.

We're in for, I thought. Bog only had to disclose our presence to save his own skin. With Pierre blocking the stairs, we were trapped. Penelope and I readied our claws. Cats didn't surrender without a fight.

Pierre slapped Bog's face so hard that the sound echoed off the walls. "Talk, damn it."

I held my breath. Bog spat in the priest's face. I gaped at him. Despite threat of injury, he didn't rat us out. How could I have considered abandoning him?

Pierre extracted a handkerchief from his pocket. Wiping his face, he kept his lifeless eyes trained on his prisoner. His stone-faced expression betrayed a slight sneer. My body shivered. He embodied evil. He ordered Jean to silence Max before pulling a shiny object from his pocket.

"A gun!" Penelope exclaimed. "We must do—"

Before she finished her sentence, Pierre thrust the silver barrel into Bog's mouth. My eyes focused on Pierre's hand. His palm cradled the pearl handle; his index finger toyed with the trigger. He intended to shoot. I knew it. And, he did...

The gun clicked. Penelope yowled before fainting to the floor. Thinking that our friend had been executed, I stifled a plaintive cry. But there was no explosion, no bullet, no blood. The room echoed with Pierre's macabre laughter and Jean's snickers. The commotion roused Penelope. Max seemed confused. He sat, head cocked, staring at the gun, which Pierre had extracted from Bog's mouth.

Bog seethed. "I knew you were a coward."

Pierre poked Bog's ribs with the gun. "Don't think I won't use it. Merely a taste of things to come." The priest fished bullets from his pocket and loaded them into the empty cylinder.

Bog's eyes flashed with anger. "Go on. Do it. Shoot."

Pierre grinned. "Why waste good bullets on someone who's no longer of any value?"

"Huh?" I muttered to Penelope. "No value? Why, a moment ago he needed Bog to tell—"

Pierre's shout interrupted me. "Lock him in the wine cellar, Jean. While you're at it, throw in his two friends." The caretaker looked confused until Pierre pointed the loaded gun at Penelope and me. "Didn't see you two at first, but here you are. All that's missing is wrapping paper and a bow." He prodded us toward Bog. "Enjoy your little reunion while you can. I'll return soon enough."

After instructing Jean to secure us inside the windowless room, Pierre ascended the stairs. He called back over his shoulder. "Tempting as it might be, Jean, don't kill the two cats. The same caution doesn't apply to the refugee."

Jean shoved Bog into the wine cellar. He ordered Max to shepherd us through the same door, promising him a bite of our tails if we disobeyed. "No kill doesn't mean no harm." He let out a burst of laughter and a malodorous belch. Max's gritting teeth, his hot moist breath, and the odor of sausage and onions from the dyspeptic caretaker nauseated me. At least we weren't facing a death sentence. But how long would our reprieve last? Once Pierre contacted Ivanovich, he'd learn we were as valuable to him dead as alive. He'd take great pleasure in exterminating us.

Jean pushed Bog onto the floor and ordered us into a corner. He tormented us with Max, loosening and tightening his grip on the leash. "Case you're thinking of escape, Max will be right outside." Bolts slid into place before his heavy feet plodded upstairs. Max pawed the door.

Penelope jumped into Bog's lap and licked his face. "What have they done to you?"

His animal intuition kicked in. "I'm okay. Not the first time I've been roughed up. You two should have fled the basement when you had the chance."

Penelope flinched. "What! And leave you. We'd never think of it, would we, Fluff?"

I swallowed hard. A knot formed in my stomach. "No, never. To even think that way…"

"Sorry about Flagey," Bog said. "There's really no excuse. Understood the crucifix at once. Ran to the parvis as soon as I could ditch the Americans. Told me their life stories and wanted mine. Even offered me a drink."

Bog explained that once he reached the parvis, he saw the open church. Searching it from basement to choir loft, he found nothing. He concluded that we were back in the rectory basement. Recalling our escape story, he located the boarded-up window.

"I squatted down," he continued. "Began pulling plywood. Then bam. Someone whacked me on the head. Woke up in Pierre's study. Grilled and beaten."

Penelope mewled. "Poor Bog."

"Only toughened my resolve to keep quiet. I feel sorry for Cook," he added. "Tried to stop the beating. Threatened to call the police.

Pierre knocked her to the floor. Ordered Jean to lock her in her room." Bog moved his arms, still bound behind his back. "Afraid I'm in no shape to help. Not in these handcuffs."

My eyes widened. "Do you still have the crucifix?"

"Yeah. In my pants pocket, why?"

"You'll see. Worth a try." I pawed his trousers, pushing the cross toward the pocket's opening. With a bit of effort, the chain appeared. "Grab that, Penelope. Your mouth's smaller." Her nose burrowed into the denim, her paws digging into the floor for leverage. "Good girl, almost there." A final, decisive yank sent her backwards onto her rump. But she had extracted the entire chain. And with it, the small silver cross.

She and Bog stared at me as I picked up the cross in my mouth. I mumbled for Bog to lean forward. Scurrying behind him, I went to work. The lock clicked open. "You did it, Fluff," Penelope shouted. "You're a magician."

With one hand freed of the cuff, Bog brought both of his hands in front of him. Taking the crucifix from me, he patted my head before freeing his other hand. He dangled the cross in the air. "Keeping this. It's a good luck charm."

We began to discuss escape when the sound of metal against metal came from outside the door. Grunts, groans, and growls accompanied the noises of a sliding bolt. Trembling with fear, Penelope pressed against me. "It's him."

Grabbing an empty bottle, Bog stood behind the door ready to pummel our captor. The final bolt cleared; we braced. The door creaked open. Bog lifted the bottle over his head. Penelope and I gazed up expecting to see Pierre's terrifying sneer. He wasn't there. No one was. Our eyes drifted down the doorframe. Penelope gasped.

I grinned. "About time you got here. Expected you hours ago."

Chapter 17
Unholy Alliance

"Fiend, ingrate, thief!" Rex shouted from the doorway.

In response to his explosive outburst, Penelope stammered, "W...well, I...I don't usually s...steal. It's only that we needed some signal to let Bog—"

I stopped her with a swat of my paw. Her confession was unnecessary and off the mark. "Rex isn't barking about the crucifix, *ma chérie. C'est moi.* I'm the thief he's growling about."

"Damn right, Fluffy. Fiend and ingrate too. Don't forget those. Least you're smart enough not to deny it." He craned his neck around the room. "Now, where is it? Not leaving till you give it back." He snarled, baring his big, jagged teeth.

I held up my paw. "Calm down. Never intended to keep your little treasure. Simply, shall we say, borrowed it. Bit of insurance. *Et voilà,* my little ruse worked. Here you are."

My words were greeted with bewildered stares. "First things first," I added. "Before I explain, where's Max?"

Rex smirked. "Do you take me for a mindless lapdog, hmm? The chubby janitor took Max outside to pee. At this moment, they're fertilizing the parvis."

"How'd you get in?" Penelope asked.

He snickered. "Where there's a will, missy, Rex always gets his way." He paused as if waiting for us to laugh or nod. When none of us did, he continued, "Pushed my way through the boarded-up window. A flimsy piece of wood couldn't keep out this fine specimen of doghood."

Penelope cocked her head. "Bog already loosen—"

I cleared my throat to interrupt her. Why deflate the blustering shepherd's Mastiff-sized ego before he helped us escape. "I never underestimated your abilities, Rex. Very brave of you to break-in."

"Don't sweet-talk me, furball. Paw over my coin or you'll be stiffer than a stuffed tiger."

"Never wanted to keep your coin." Rex tilted his head the way canines do when they're confused, which as it so happens, is quite often. "Knew you'd come looking for it. And if we were trapped, you'd be our ticket to freedom."

He frowned. "Certainly didn't break into this place to rescue you. Serves you right if I howled until the priest comes down."

Bog shook his head. "Not smart. We'd have to tell Father Pierre that you pried open the window. He'll offer you up to the traffickers as well."

"And keep your gold coin too, for the old collection plate," I said with a wink. "You'll get your coin. Then we can *all* get outta here in one piece."

Rex heaved a sigh. "Okay, okay. But it's the last time I mess with cats, hmm."

Penelope looked confused. "Will someone please explain what's happening?"

I motioned to the purse fastened to Rex's collar. "Remember *chérie?* Yesterday at Flagey? The leather pouch."

"*Oui.* It fell. Burst open."

"We helped him gather the spilled contents."

Rex bristled. "Devil! So that's when you stole. Sneaky, sneaky feline."

I rolled my eyes. "Please! *Borrowed,* not stole. Your canine carelessness gave me the chance to mouth your little coin."

Penelope scrutinized me. "That explains your recent bout of mumbling."

I grimaced. "It was horrible. The coin barely fit in my mouth. How do squirrels and chipmunks do it? My jaw ached for hours."

Rex cringed. "My precious coin...in a cat's mouth. I'll have you know, it's solid gold."

"Better it was chocolate or tuna fish. Gold is distasteful," I said, pulling a face.

He seethed. "Where is it? Where is it?"

In true feline fashion, I sashayed out of the wine cellar and into the main basement. Instructing them to wait, I ducked behind the hot water heater. Pawing the coin from its hiding place, I slid it across the floor. "Here Rex, here's your treasure. Fetch like a good boy."

He scrambled for the coin. "Careful! That's valuable. Can't have it slipping down a drain."

I scoffed. "Your pouch was loaded with them. Most, bigger than that. Makes one wonder. Yup, makes one wonder." My expression left no doubt that I believed Rex guilty of some misdeed.

Bog tucked the coin into the pouch. Rex looked uneasy, his pout suggesting hurt feelings. "It's not...um...not what you think."

Bog stomped his foot. "Hate to break up this happy reunion, but now that you've settled the matter of lost property, I suggest we get out of here. That fat fool and his mongrel will be back at any moment."

Penelope whimpered. "Bog's right. Max will tear us to shreds. Happy to do it too. And have you forgotten the priest...and his gun? He's still upstairs somewhere." Indeed, the occasional plodding of feet and strains of classical music seeping down through the floorboards informed us of Pierre's invisible presence.

I'd revisit Rex's unfinished story later. Till then, we busied ourselves with escape plans. Bog, we agreed, would lift Penelope and me through the window. Refusing assistance from man or cat, Rex boasted of his ability to clear the high ledge with a running leap. That left Bog, despite his injuries, to lift himself to freedom.

Trying his best to conceal his aches and pains, Bog lifted Penelope off the floor. "Come on pretty one. You first."

She scurried into his waiting hands. A commotion froze us in place. The basement door opened with a loud burst of music and raucous laughter. Jean bellowed in Polish and French. "You had your walk. Back to work. Guard our guests. Don't let them escape or there'll be hell to pay…for you and me." The door slammed shut behind Max.

"Quick," Rex said, "Back to the wine cellar. You too." He nudged a hesitant Bog.

I got into his face. "I'll stay. Help you."

Rex merely hoisted me by the scruff of my neck and deposited me into the wine cellar. "Don't overestimate your abilities, Fluffy. Never send in a cat…or a man for that matter…to do a dog's job." His snout pushed the wine cellar door closed as Max barreled down the stairs.

"*Bonne chance*, good luck." Penelope's words of encouragement, delivered through the closed door, were drowned out by blood-curdling growls, snapping jaws, and chomping teeth.

We huddled beside the door. Horrific images of the unseen canine battle flashed through my head. Two loud thuds rattled the door. No animal could survive such an ordeal. Loud music must have kept Jean and Pierre from rushing downstairs. Having picked up a large block of wood, Bog reached for the doorknob. We rushed over to block his exit.

"Rex knows what he's doing," Penelope said.

"Never seen a human come out a winner in a dogfight," I added.

"Can't let someone else fight my battle." Turning the doorknob, Bog pushed open the door. The basement fell eerily quiet.

"They've killed each other," Penelope cried. "I—"

Before she finished her sentence, chortles and guffaws reached our ears. Laughter from not one, but two dogs. I peered out the door. "Gee whiskers!" Rex and Max rolled around on the floor—snout to snout, tail to tail, paw in paw. A tumbling ball of fur. Infectious giggles informed us this that wasn't a fight to the finish as much as a playful romp between friends.

Penelope and I stuck close to Bog's shins as he approached the dogs. We waited for the mass of fur to come to rest. Max and Rex disengaged themselves, untangling paws and tails. Rising from the floor, lingering effects of dizziness showed in their wobbly gaits. Both hounds tried to focus on us but their heads rocked and their eyes rolled. Their faces wore crooked smiles.

Penelope stepped out from behind Bog. "I don't understand. Do you know each other? Friends?"

Rex butted Max's shoulder. "Not friends, missy, half-siblings. Brothers from different mothers."

Max returned Rex's headbutt but only harder. "Different litters, same misters." Max spoke with a Polish accent. Like his master, Jean, he even threw in an occasional Polish word among the French.

"Haven't seen each other since we were puppies," Rex explained. "Flabbergasted to make the connection."

Max nodded. "Me too. In the nick of time. I was an inch away from robbing him of his crown jewels," he said with rambunctious laughter.

Rex shot his half-brother an icy glare. "*I* had the advantage. Another second and you'd be peeing outta your—"

I shook my head in disbelief. "Boys, boys, how'd you recognize each other?"

After a nod from Rex, Max plopped down onto the floor and rolled over. His front paws reached for the rafters; his rear legs splayed to the sides. Exposed for all to see, his fully intact naughty bits. Rex lowered his snout toward Max's stomach. "Observe, my friends."

Bog leaned down as Penelope and I inched closer to the supine hound. Rex's snout pointed to a hairless patch on Max's stomach. Leaning closer, I saw a small pink mark outlined by dark fur.

Rex smirked. "Tell me what you see."

Bog shook his head, Penelope shrugged. "A blemish?" I asked.

Annoyance flashed across his face. "Blemish? It's a birthmark. And not just any birthmark. It's as plain as the nose on your face. The spittin' image of Mannequin Pis."

Penelope edged closer, doubt in her expression. "The little peeing boy?"

Rex lifted his chin higher. "The one and the same. Pride of Brussels."

I mustered an earnest tone. "If you say so." But there was no way that the tiny mark on Max's stomach resembled, in any manner or fashion, the iconic statue of the peeing boy that drew hordes of tourists to the city center. "You mean to say that the blem...er, birthmark informed you that Max was your brother."

Rex scoffed. "Of course. Get a load of this." He plopped down next to his brother and flipped over, his legs flailing in the air. "See, same birthmark. Papa's offspring all got them. The males anyway. Purebreds like Brutus and me as well as mixes like Max."

Although any resemblance to Mannequin Pis was questionable, the bellies of both dogs contained identical blotches. There was no denying that fact.

Max sneered at Penelope and me. "These your friends, Brother? Can't say I approve of your choice of...ass...ociates."

Rex snickered. "They're not half bad...for cats."

Max scoffed. "You la-di-da purebreds certainly have strange ideas. What do you suggest we do with them?"

I began to speak but Rex planted his gigantic paw on the crown of my head. "As a matter of fact, Brother, we were about to leave when you showed up."

Shaking his head, Max glanced up the stairs. "You're blood. That's one thing. But if I let them go, there'll be hell to pay. Besides, I loathe cats."

Rex made puppy-dog eyes. "Couldn't you...just this once...for the sake of family."

Max sighed. "Okay. But be quick about it. If you're lucky, they won't notice the escape for hours. Until my next walk. But those pesky cats better not show their ugly mugs around here again or there'll be trouble." He emphasized the threat with a snap of his jaw.

Taking a few steps backward, we offered our thanks and vowed never to return.

Rex and his half-brother hurried about staging the room to portray a daring escape and Max's valiant but unsuccessful resistance. After dragging the unused block of wood through a pool of Bog's blood, they placed it on the floor just outside the wine cellar. Dabbing his paw in the same blood, Rex stained Max's fur around his shoulders and neck. At the first sound of Jean or Pierre, Max would plop down and pretend to be unconscious. We hoped he was a good actor.

Before heading out the window, Rex offered his brother a hug, whispering something in his ear.

※

It was already late in the evening by the time we made it to the parvis. We'd never reach Place du Luxembourg in time for the meeting of Scuffed Loafers, Vaclav and Grabowski.

Penelope nuzzled my head. "I'm sorry, Fluff. I know you were counting on rescuing your family tonight. But all's not lost. There's still time. I suggest we hightail it to Châtelain."

"Châtelain? But the smugglers aren't meeting until Wednesday."

"Not the market, the church. Brussels has hundreds of them. But I know only one where we have an ally. Saint Michel and Father Jacques."

I groaned. "I don't know, *ma chérie*. Priests…"

She shook her head. "He's different, you'll see. We can ask him if he knows Saint Clovis. That's reason enough to visit. Besides, the church is warm and safe."

Bog shrugged. "A roof is a roof."

"And a meal a meal," said Rex, adding that he had business near Châtelain.

I could see my objections were futile. "Okay, okay. But on our walk, Rex, you'll have to finish your story."

He affected a blank expression. "Huh?"

"You know darn well. Your story about the gold coins and that pouch. Did you really think I'd forget about your mysterious business?"

Pointing his snout skyward, he sighed. "*Cats!*"

Chapter 18
Surprises

My feline instincts were on high alert. Was Father Jacques the savior that my infatuated friend believed or merely another false-faced cleric? I exerted self-control to keep my spine from arching, my tail from puffing, and my hair from standing on end. So, why did I agree to Penelope's pilgrimage to Saint Michel? Shame and embarrassment! My faulty guidance had led us back to Father Pierre's basement. The hours we wasted as his prisoners were precious minutes taken away from our desperate search for loved ones.

Why had I forgotten Saint Clovis and that scary Claus woman? She wasn't a priest and I didn't know her connection to the Saint Clovis parish, but her fur ensemble should have been my red flag. She was a walking billboard for animal exploitation. She wanted our fur. It was as plain as the whiskers on my face. Humans were complicated. Why couldn't they be as honest as animals, their motives as transparent? A snarling dog bites; a hissing cat scratches. No masks, smokescreens, blinders, or decoys. Pure and honest truth. Cats are wise to choose their human. For when it comes to people, a pet can't be too careful.

The route to Châtelain was a familiar one for all four of us. Although Max's bloody charade should have given us a lengthy head start, we stepped up our pace and kept our eyes focused forward. We dodged distracted drivers and zigzagged around unyielding legs of blank-faced pedestrians. Specks of drizzle were more annoyance than hindrance. Pizza, kebab, and frites shops announced their presence with savory aromas that stirred our grumbling stomachs.

As my travel companions chatted about the vagaries of Belgian weather, I pondered Rex's ulterior motives. Conditioned by my belief that a cantankerous canine eventually drew blood, his uncharacteristic behavior bewildered me. Why was he helping us? Were we walking into danger? The traffickers would reward him handsomely if he delivered us to them. Perhaps he intended to lure us back to the grooming salon where they'd rip the fur right off our backs? His prized pouch packed with gold proved his lust for money. His farewell whisper into Max's ear filled me with dread. What mischief and mayhem were the half-brothers cooking up?

That blood-curdling mix of curiosity and suspicion fueled my forward scurry. Adopting an air of aloofness, I sidled up beside Rex who led our little parade. "I'm impressed."

He shot me a sideways glance. "About?"

"You, of course. No worse for wear after your scuffle with Max. Head and tail held high. Robust stride."

"Got longer legs than you cats."

"Perhaps."

His eyes focused on me. "Perhaps? What's that supposed to mean?"

I shrugged. "It's almost as if…as if you're overly eager to reach Châtelain."

"Overly eager? Châtelain wasn't my idea, remember? Thought you and missy would be happy with my pace given your urgent business."

"Don't get me wrong, Rex. We're indeed pleased, very pleased. You've been a great help, a veritable Saint Bernard."

He snickered, baring what seemed to be dozens of razor-sharp teeth. "Why, Fluffy, you're trying your damnedest to be coy. Why don't you come right out and tell me that you don't trust me, hmm?"

I feigned a gasp. "I…I'd never say such a thing."

He glared at me. "But you'd think it. In the basement you stopped short of calling me a villain. But that look you shot me…wowee! Screamed guilty."

Oh boy! Careful Fluff. "Sorry you took offense. But…um…now that you mention it. Seeing that *you* brought it up. In the spirit of camaraderie and candor, you might consider—"

He cocked his head. "Consider what, hmm?"

"Finishing your story." I nodded to his neck. "About your pouch."

He let out a hearty laugh. "You're like a dog with a bone."

I scoffed. "At the risk of becoming yet another cliché, let's simply say that I'm curious."

"I'll say." He furrowed his brow. His words flowed slowly, deliberately. "First let me ask you a question. Seems you have it all figured out. What do you think I'm up to?"

You dog! He'd sniffed the bone but instead of savoring it, he flung it back at me. My mind churned to craft a tactful reply when Penelope appeared at my side huffing with excitement.

"I…I saw her, Fluff. She's alive."

"Who? Who's alive?"

"Fabiola, my late owner's friend. The sweet old lady I told you about. She just walked into the Horta Museum."

Engulfed in my conversation with Rex, I hadn't noticed our surroundings. A quick glance around informed me that we were, indeed, marching down Rue Américaine. Across the street stood the unique home and studio of the Art Nouveau architect. I recalled Penelope's stories of her beloved catsitter and their visits to the museum. "Are you sure, *ma chère?*"

She bobbed her head. "Recognized the hair and handbag. Shoes were her style."

Rex rolled his eyes. "Females!"

Wafting clouds of perfume, a stream of ladies flowed into the museum. The entourage was a rainbow parade: floral frocks, powdered and blushed faces, and teased hair in an array of pastels. We paused on the opposite curb to let Penelope explain her history with Fabiola to Rex and Bog.

When she finished, I gestured to the museum. "Do you want to wait? Go in after her?"

She became flustered, stammering her words and glancing back and forth between the museum and us. "Oh, I don't know. I'd love to see her again but no telling how long she'll be inside. Looks like a tea or lecture. Maybe a concert. Surely, they wouldn't allow you or me in." She nodded toward Bog. "Wouldn't let him in either. If they did, what would he say to Fabiola?"

Bog gave us a sheepish look. "I could pull a fire alarm."

"Or Fluffy and I could draw them all outside with a good old-fashioned street brawl." Rex sized me up as if I were a juicy veal chop. "Whadda ya say, ole sport? All for the greater good. You wouldn't have to sacrifice too much blood and guts."

Penelope gasped, saving me a reply. "Neither option appeals to me. We must get on with our mission." Lifting her backside from the sidewalk, she led us away. I observed her gazing wistfully to Fabiola's house before a final backward glance to the museum and her former life.

As we neared Châtelain, I still hadn't gotten Rex to tell me about his mysterious pouch. He cleared his throat. "Ahem. Pardon me my fine friends, but I must excuse myself. A quick pop in and out. Back before you can list all of my noble qualities."

"W…what…" My words trailed off as Rex dashed into the busy street. A young woman on a bicycle had to swerve to avoid hitting him. As on the prior day's pass through this neighborhood, Rex approached the door of the grooming salon. The same amber-eyed tuxedo cat sat outside the door. After a brief greeting, he nudged open the door. Rex disappeared inside. As before, a human hand pulled down the window shade.

"Won't get me inside. No sir, no way." Reacting to Bog's bewildered look, I told him about our prior visit and my observations of Rex's behavior. "All very odd. I don't think he's in cahoots with the traffickers. But I can't be certain, no I can't be certain."

Penelope scoffed. "You and your suspicions. If it's not Father Jacques, it's Rex. I don't know his business either, but he's been a great help to us."

"Helpful enough. Might be a clever front. Groomers know fur." I gazed up at Bog. "What do you think? You knew Rex at camp."

He shook his head. "No clue. Defended us at the rectory. Skirmish with Max seemed real enough. His wounds too."

Frustrated by their unwillingness to fan my suspicions, I heaved a sigh. "*Merde!* Then how about snooping inside the salon? Sniff around a bit?"

Penelope shot me a reproachful glare but Bog shrugged. "Couldn't hurt. Gotta use the toilet anyway."

A heartfelt meow signaled my satisfaction. "That's the spirit. I'll make a cat out of you yet."

He crossed the street, exchanged words with the feline sentry, and stepped inside. I couldn't contain my excitement. "Gee whiskers! His animal intuition makes him the perfect spy. Why, I bet—"

Penelope thrust her paw in my face and plopped down onto the curb. Side-by-side, we waited in awkward silence. Several minutes passed with me locking stares with the sphinxlike tuxedo cat. The salon door opened. Exiting onto the sidewalk, Bog and Rex looked as natural as a satisfied customer and his freshly-groomed pet. My eyes zeroed in on Rex's neck. The pouch was empty.

Penelope nudged me. "See that? The cat bowed to Rex. Very formal too."

I had, in fact, observed the gesture of respect. However, I saw no benefit in glorifying the arrogant shepherd. "Looked like an ordinary stretch. Must get stiff, sitting there all day." Penelope's snicker suggested that she recognized both my fib and envy.

As our companions waited on the opposite curb for cars to pass, I scrutinized Bog's face. What dirt had he discovered about the shady shepherd? Did he learn the truth about the groomers' lust for fur? I flinched. Bog smiled at Rex, actually smiled. The two bantered like old friends. Confused, I cocked my head. When he patted the shepherd's head, I cringed.

Penelope sighed. "Sweet. Man and his best friend. Don't you agree?"

I mustered every ounce of self-control to stifle a hiss. "We shall see."

All smiles and laughter, they crossed the street. I glared at them. "Before we take one more step, tell me why you two are so...so giddy?"

Rex gazed up at Bog. "Shall I?"

Bog replied with a friendly wink. "Fluff won't give us any peace till you do."

"Shut that mouth, Fluffy, or you'll swallow a fly." Rex flashed his teeth. The result something between a grin and smirk.

His account, corroborated by Bog, flabbergasted me. Penelope's deep purrs and teary eyes suggested that his tale of heroism and intrigue touched her. The self-anointed king of the canines, menace at large, and burr on my butt, was a bona fide hero, a veritable animalitarian.

"The tough-mutt act is a means to an end," Rex added by way of explanation. "Too many tail sniffers in my business as it is."

Although his brutish shell probably didn't stray far from his true personality, I better understood why he kept others at paw's length. He shuttled vast sums of money for a large network of animal rights activists that supported no-kill shelters and veterinary services in Brussels. Funds also aided cross-border rescues and sham adoptions. Many countries, he explained, banned "adoptions" used to move strays out of kill shelters in one country and into non-kill shelters in another. The group included grooming salons and market vendors. In addition to large donations, market vendors provided rescue leads and transportation.

Bog gazed at Rex. "He's saved many strays from the gas chamber. Dogs and cats."

"Not to mention the occasional ferret and squirrel," Rex added.

Scratching the soft underside of the shepherd's chin, Bog's tone sparked with excitement. "Might even be a role for me in their network."

Rex nodded. "Bog's veterinary background impressed them."

This encouraging news not only filled us with optimism, it gave me a pawsitively ingenious idea. Inspired by the parade of coiffed old ladies as well as our mishap at the Flagey waffle stand, I saw a trip inside the grooming salon as our salvation. I answered my companions' quizzical looks with a terse reply, "Humor me."

An hour later, we stepped out of the salon. Penelope and I were unrecognizable. Her fine fur of gray and black was dyed neon orange. My fluffy coat of black, tan, and gray was shaved, the remaining stubble dyed dandelion yellow. "Nobody will want our fur now." The groomers obliged my request for additional packets of dye for our loved ones, which a dubious Bog carried in his pocket.

We turned toward Saint Michel and the promise of a hearty meal and warm, dry beds for the night. As my paws traversed the wet pavement, I began to feel more hopeful about our future.

Chapter 19

Catbird Seat

Canvas awnings in an array of colors adorned dark storefronts that encircled Saint Michel. A Turkish and an Italian restaurant as well as a Chinese takeaway were the only signs of life. Their exotic mix of aromas loitered in the air taunting our empty stomachs. Trams slithered passed, fluorescent snakes flickering through the starless night. Their few riders stared ahead with somber faces and glazed eyes. Neither passengers nor the occasional passerby and stray took note of two brilliantly-colored cats, one dog, and a singular man trudging along the wet sidewalk.

I nudged Rex. "You see? No one's given Penelope and me a second look. You shoulda considered the groomers' rainbow dye. An ounce of prevention…"

He sneered down at me. "Isn't worth a pound of ridicule. Told you, I'm not dying my fur. Even if your hair-brained idea about fur poachers is true, it's cats they want, not dogs."

"First they came for the cats…"

His deep growl ended the conversation.

My cries of hunger went unnoticed, drowned out by Penelope's purrs of anticipation. Both reached crescendo as we neared the church. Adopting a blissful expression, Penelope appeared to glide above the sidewalk. "Saint Michel. Father Jacques. Sanctuary."

I squinted through unrelenting drizzle. "Looks closed."

"We'll find a way in. Father Jacques is always ready to tend to the needs of his flock. If you think the outside is spectacular, wait until you step inside." Her tone lilted with enthusiasm.

I wouldn't dream of bursting her kittenish delight. However, I found the façade of Saint Michel, drab, dirty, and dreadful. More prison or fortress than church, the soot-covered hulk brooded over the neighborhood. The stone monolith lacked a traditional steeple. Its flat face composed of three telescoping tiers resembled a giant mantle clock. Penelope's excitement and the promise of heat and food—mostly food—were the only things keeping me from hightailing it out of there.

"We should each light a candle. For lost family or…" Penelope turned to Rex. "Whatever it is *you* want help with. The gods of the humans always listen."

Rex scoffed. "I don't go in for religious hocus pocus. But give me a meaty bone and a dry bed and I'll worship whomever you want."

Bog's hushed laughter signaled agreement with the shepherd. But his lined face assumed a deeper, thoughtful expression that suggested a more complicated relationship with religion. Our harrowing experience with Father Pierre and my observations of churchgoers on the parvis left me cynical. However, the notion of gods who granted wishes piqued my interest.

Penelope must have seen the mix of confusion and wonderment on my face. She described her visits to the church with Fabiola. "You'll see for yourself. Marble gods. And in front of each, brass trenches filled with row upon row of candles. All lit by people with wishes and wants."

Her description reminded me of birthday rituals I observed among camp humans. "Who gets to blow out the candles?"

Penelope snickered. "Nobody, silly. These wishes are granted when you light the candles, not when you blow them out."

Rex furrowed his brow. "Who knew humans were more stupid than cats? What do they possibly hope to get from a big slab of plaster, hmm?"

Still light-hearted, Penelope replied, "Anything really. Don't know all the details."

"This magic work only for humans?" I asked. "Can animals make wishes too?"

"Don't see why not," she replied. "By the way, churchgoers don't say 'magic'. They call it faith."

Magic, faith, witchery. She could call it whatever she liked. With a promise of unlimited wishes, my eyes grew to the size of large emeralds. "Criminy! Food, warm bed, litter box. Our old pal Lucky should wish for a new eye and leg."

She twitched her whiskers. "Don't forget our families. Fabiola always lit a candle for her dead husband."

As I tried to make sense of a dead person's practical need of a candle, Rex lowered his snout into her face. "All this from a statue, missy? Well then, you suppose they'd crush my enemies, hmm?" A sinister sneer spread over his face.

Her eyes widened. "If that's what you really want. Never heard mention of restrictions."

Having silently observed us, Bog now shook his head. "Careful, Rexy boy. Think! If *you* can pray for those things, so can your foes."

Rex's sneer faded into a pout. "Damn! That's not fair."

Bog scoffed. "Every army in the history of mankind claims the moral high ground. The statues and languages may differ but the prayers are all the same."

I huffed with joy. "Got it! All we have to do is pick the biggest statue. Clever, huh?"

Penelope furrowed her brow. "Size doesn't matter. Except for baby Jesus. He's small but powerful. On the other hand, candles do come in small, medium, and large."

Grinning, I clapped my paws. "Hear that, Rex? Light the biggest candle you can lay your paws on. You'll pulverize your enemy."

Rex looked humbled. "But if they light a similar candle, it'll be a draw. Worse, they find an even bigger one. No, let's stick to wishes for finding your families."

Bog patted the shepherd's head. "Good idea."

I hadn't yet abandoned the idea of bigger candles when I observed Penelope's shoulders droop. "Why so glum, *ma chère?*"

She sighed. "We can't ask the statues for anything. Candles cost money. You'll see the little brass boxes. Rex emptied his purse at the groomers." In response to our expectant stares, Bog turned his empty trouser pockets inside out.

"I assume," Rex said, "that stealing a candle cancels its magical properties?" In reply, Penelope pulled a face and nodded.

"Holy smokes!" I exclaimed. "Who knew church magic, er…faith was only for the rich?"

Squatting down, Bog scratched Penelope and me under our chins. "Greedy statues may not listen to the poor. For that matter, maybe they don't listen to anybody. Let's pray that Father Jacques is more charitable to strays and penniless heathens like me."

With our expectations lowered, we reached the church. A rectangular window above the entry and the stained-glass along both sides were pitch black. The first two doors were locked. We sent up a collective sigh of delight when the third and final door surrendered to our push.

Once inside, my bones chilled. A consequence of poor heating and feline suspicion. The church, at least, provided refuge from the rain. Standing at the back, I surveyed the space. Flickering candles were set before statues as Penelope had described. Simple white tapers and others incased in red glass cast an eerie glow. The deathly silence unsettled me.

Penelope took charge. Only the priest, she warned, dared speak above a whisper. She chastised Rex for flicking water from his rain-soaked coat throughout the vestibule and swatted him when he drank from small bowls deemed holy. When Bog started to wash his face and hands, she hissed. The ornate sink, she explained, was a font reserved for washing babies. I sought to avoid incurring her glares, hisses, and swatted paw. But whereas the scent of melting wax only caused my nose to twitch, a more pungent odor made me sneeze in fits that echoed through the cavernous church.

I braced for a stinging rebuke. Instead, she merely mewled. A tear ran down her cheek. "Incense made Odie sneeze too. Oh, how I miss him."

A sound drew our attention to the front of the church. Light from a side door bathed the altar, illuminating a white tablecloth and silver candlesticks. A dark figure appeared. The tall, trim man dressed in black was Penelope's idol. With his hand poised to grab a candlestick, he paused to gaze through the darkness.

"Hello," he bellowed. "Anyone there?"

"A few cold and hungry—" Bog's reply was interrupted by Penelope's hearty meows and Rex's robust barks.

"I see. Creatures great and small," the priest added with a friendly laugh. "*Bienvenue* friends, welcome. Come closer so I can get a better look at you."

Penelope scampered ahead, reaching the altar before the rest of us began our slow march up the aisle. Bog strode forward without fear or apprehension. Perhaps chronic struggle had knocked those out of him. Rex motioned toward the priest. "I never trust 'em till I sniff 'em." Willing my spine not to arch, I observed the shepherd ogle our surroundings. Was he sizing up the silver and gold or identifying hiding places and escape routes?

Father Jacques stroked Penelope. "Almost didn't recognize you with that...colorful coat. But I'd know that adorable meow, pretty face, and those blue eyes anywhere. Always thrilled to greet a former parishioner." Purring loudly, she brushed up against his black trousers. I observed a flash of anger in the priest's dark eyes when he noticed strands of her neon orange fur clinging to his creased pants. "And you've brought friends," he added with a recovered smile.

When he gave me the once over, I swore he stifled giggles. Had he really never seen a shaved, dandelion yellow tabby before? Perhaps, priests did lead sheltered lives.

Offering an extended hand, Bog introduced himself. Father Jacques reciprocated with a firm handshake. "We're not set up for overnight guests. But you're all welcome. We've plenty of blankets and pillows for emergencies…and the occasional refugee. You did say cold *and* hungry, didn't you?" he added in response to Rex's barks and my plaintive meows.

The mention of food started our tails wagging. Using his mobile phone, Father Jacques instructed his housekeeper to fetch leftovers from the rectory. After he disconnected, he turned to us with a grin. "While we wait, tell me what brought the four of you together. I'm guessing it wasn't random chance." He directed Bog to the front pew and sat beside him.

"Before I begin," Bog said. "I know it sounds crazy, but could my animal friends light some candles? They think it will help. Problem is, we don't have any money."

Jacques studied Bog, barely hiding concerns about his sanity. "Of course. Happy to help the faithful of any ilk, stripe, and species. Your furry friends can light as many candles as they'd like. No charge." He wagged his finger playfully in our faces. "Don't burn down the church."

Rex whispered in my ear, "He didn't say anything about not peeing in his church." Our shared snickers drew a stern glare from Penelope.

After Bog assured us that he wouldn't omit any detail of our ordeal, Penelope, Rex, and I set out to explore the church and light candles. The bigger the taper, the better.

≈•《◉》•≈

The sound of a door opening behind the altar announced the housekeeper's arrival. Instructing us to wait in a pew, Father Jacques vowed to return with a feast fit for man and furry beast.

Bog nodded toward the retreating priest. "Had a nice chat. Jacques doesn't know any Claus. As for Saint Clovis, he claims that no church or parish exists by that name in the city."

"Very odd," Penelope said.

Bog raised an eyebrow. "What he says and what he knows may be two different things."

"Why didn't you challenge him?" I asked.

Bog raised both eyebrows. "Couldn't very well call the priest a liar in his own church, could I? Especially after he agreed to help us."

"Of course, he'll help. Isn't he wonderful?" Penelope sighed as she scanned our faces.

Bog shrugged. "Hasn't done anything to make me dislike him, *yet.*"

Rex bristled. "Don't look at me, missy. Haven't gotten a proper sniff. Probably won't with my singed whiskers." He had pushed his snout too close to the candles.

Penelope turned to me. "Didn't I tell you he was fabulous?" My expression must have betrayed misgivings because she snapped at me. "You're suspicious of everyone. First Bog, then Rex. Neither is the miserable, dishonest, malodorous brute you made them out to be, are they?"

My face warmed from glares directed at me by my companions. Maybe Penelope was right. Perhaps I was too judgmental. "Oh, um… did I say that? Well, I'm…I'm very fond of Bog and Rex. You know that, guys, right?" I shot a nervous smile at each. "As for Father Jacques, he seems very nice…"

The priest's return interrupted me. He lowered his chin to the platters of food in his arms. "Do not neglect to show hospitality to strangers, for thereby some have entertained angels unawares. Here you are, lady and gentlemen, a prodigal feast."

The sight and smell of roasted chicken caused my eyes to widen in anticipation. I glanced to the statue of a veiled lady and my flickering candle. "Wishes do come true!"

When the priest made us harness our appetites in order to cast a magic spell, I had an irresistible urge to swat him. He prayed for the meal and a hasty return of our families. He waited for our "Amens" before excusing himself to ready our accommodations. We dug into the heaping platters of food leaving only bones.

Perhaps Penelope was right. My full stomach certified the priest as a decent chap. But before I could share my revised opinion, my head drooped. I mustered only enough energy to jump into Bog's lap before my eyes shut. I fell asleep to his caresses and heavy breathing.

<hr />

"Get up, Fluff." I awoke to Rex's beef- and potato-laced breath puffing in my face.

I tried to focus on our surroundings. "W…where are we?" Penelope wheezed and Bog snored. Both slept on blankets spread across the concrete floor. "W…what happened?"

Rex snarled. "We're locked in the basement. Prisoners!"

I shook my head to shed lingering fatigue. "I don't remember a thing."

"We were drugged. I'm sure of it."

Before I replied, Penelope stirred, roused by boisterous sneezes. "Quiet, Fluff. Nothing above a whisper." Drowsiness garbled her words as her spinning eyes tried to focus on my face.

"Wasn't me, *ma chérie.*"

"*C'est moi, ma sœur.* It's me, dear sister, *ton frère*—your handsome brother. You know that incense makes me sneeze."

Our eyes widened; we turned toward the familiar voice. Standing in the room's shadows was Odysseus. And beside him, my brother Auguste.

Chapter 20

All Cats Go to Heaven

Penelope sprinted through the darkness. Squealing with joy, she almost knocked over Odysseus. Equally elated with our reunion, Auguste and I rolled on the floor in playful rapture, nipping each other's ears and necks. For all their faults, foibles, and failings, family provided constancy, a comforting reminder of home and shared history.

Rex licked Bog's face to rouse him but was swatted away. Dog licks and hand swats grew in tit-for-tat intensity. Bog's nose, tickled by Rex's charred whiskers, twitched. He opened his eyes. Mission accomplished, Rex inched backwards.

Squinting his swollen and bloodshot eyes in the darkness that tested human vision, Bog shimmied himself into a sitting position. He held his head, rocking back and forth and muttering in Arabic what sounded like expletives. The rest of us observed in silence.

"What the hell?" Bog seethed with anger as Auguste and Odysseus confirmed our imprisonment in the basement of Saint Michel. Forming a fist, he thrust his pulsing hand toward the timbered ceiling. "Damn you, priest." Taking a deep breath, he addressed his wide-eyed audience. "For a non-believer, I've spent far too much time in churches."

Visibly distraught, Penelope fretted. She'd put her full faith in Father Jacques and encouraged us to trust him. "I'm so ashamed. We're in this mess because of me. Please forgive me."

Recalling her compassion after I erred in leading us back into captivity with Pierre, I nuzzled her head. "No more apologies or self-pity." I intentionally parroted her words of understanding. "We've no time for that nonsense. The clock is ticking."

"He's right, missy. Plenty of time to dole out blame later. And don't you fret. You'll be high on that list, believe you me. Right below Fluffy, hmm."

Bog glared at Rex before patting Penelope's head. "You're not at fault, princess. You aren't the first, and certainly won't be the last, to mistake a serpent for a saint."

Indeed, the venomous priest had tricked us all. My mother's cautionary words about demons hiding behind dimpled smiles echoed in my ears.

Strutting forward, Auguste brushed up against Bog's tattered trousers. He added soft purrs of comfort. Bog choked back tears. "I'm so sorry, little buddy. Should have protected you. It's my fault the smugglers nabbed you. Did they hurt you?"

Auguste lifted his chin. "Ask Grabowski and Vaclav that question. I scratched those scoundrels something silly. Almost bit off their fingers too. They took a vial of my blood, though. Guess it was their way of getting back at me for drawing theirs. Don't give it another thought. I'm no worse for wear." Placing his paws on Bog's thigh, he began to knead and coo in a steady rhythm.

Caressing my brother's back, Bog calmed. "Tell us what happened. You too," he added with a nod to Odysseus.

Odysseus puffed out his chest. "Mine is a breathtaking adventure, a harrowing tale worthy of stage and cinema. That I'm alive to share it is nothing short of a miracle. I can't begin to count how many of my lives were lost since I absconded from the parvis, skillfully escaping the evil clutches of Father Pierre and his gang of murderous rogues."

Turning to me, Rex groaned. "Is he for real?"

"You'll get used to his bluster," I whispered. "Loves to hear himself talk, that's all." I didn't mention that my affection for Penelope fueled my patience for her narcissistic and annoying brother.

Odysseus heaved an exaggerated sigh. "I don't know where to begin."

"At the very end...*please*," Rex muttered under his breath.

Bog extended his palm toward Odysseus. "Let Auguste start. Most of us witnessed his abduction. We already know a lot of the details."

Huffing his disappointment, Odysseus glared at my brother. "Try not to bore them."

Stifling a chuckle, Auguste bowed his head. "I'll save that honor for you, friend."

We clustered around my brother. "After spiriting me away, Vaclav, Grabowksi, and Ivanovich ducked into a nearby bar." Adopting a smirk, Auguste turned to Bog. "Thought you'd follow them. You terrify them."

"I'll do more than terrify them. If I ever lay my hands on them..."

Auguste continued, "They placed my carrier atop a pub chair. Perfect perch to eavesdrop. Ivanovich punched a number into his mobile and said, 'father' and 'church.' I assumed he was talking to our old nemesis, Pierre. Told the person to expect Vaclav and Grabowski with a special delivery—me—for safekeeping. Said I'd keep the prissy Siame...I mean, Odysseus, company."

Penelope nodded. "We also thought they meant Father Pierre."

"Well, you can appreciate my surprise when they brought me to Saint Michel. Dumped me here in the basement. Found Odysseus cowering in a corner."

Odysseus scoffed. "Meditating, *not* cowering."

"I stand corrected."

"They say anything else?" I asked. "About our mother and Licorice and Lily?"

"Only what you already knew. Vaclav and Grabowski were to collect our family, Monday evening, from someone connected to the EU."

Penelope gasped. "Scuffed Loafers. She's a nasty bureaucat."

I sighed. "She handed them over, last night, in Place Luxembourg."

"We didn't escape the rectory in time," Penelope added. "Our last chance comes tomorrow at Châtelain. They're meeting Ivanovich at the market."

Confusion swept over Auguste's face. "You're both wrong."

I scrunched my face. "Whadda you mean?"

"You've mixed up days. You're one off."

I couldn't make sense of his reply when Bog interjected. "Are you telling us that yesterday wasn't Monday?"

Odysseus chuckled. "Course not. Yesterday was Tuesday. Assumed you knew. Every week follows the same pattern. Tuesday comes after Monday and before Wednesday. Except, of course, leap year. Oh my, maybe I got that wrong."

My jaw dropped. "Can't be."

Odysseus scoffed. "I assure you, I know my calen—"

Auguste cut him off. "Today is Wednesday all right. And from the organ music you hear coming down through the beams, I'm guessing eight o'clock mass has just begun."

Penelope, Bog, Rex, and I looked at each other. Our faces registered shock and panic. "B…b…but that means we slept through Tuesday," I stammered.

Rex seethed. "Told you we were drugged."

Bog sighed. "We've no time to lose. Ivanovich gets all the cats this afternoon. Means the four of you too, I'm afraid."

Penelope's head drooped. "Then tonight, we all fly to Moscow."

"Not necessarily," I said, waving my yellow tail. "They might take a pass when they see our colored fur. Now all we have to do is dye our brothers. I'm thinking indigo for Auguste and purple for Odysseus."

"If my fine gray fur must be defaced," Odysseus replied, "I prefer you call it fuchsia. Purple is the color of cartoon characters."

"Then fuchsia it is," I replied. "Can't do anything until we have water."

Auguste groaned. "I'm with Rex. No dying my fur either. We don't even know that's what they want. Besides, they can always dye it back.

Did you think of that?" He brushed against Bog's trousers. "You know, they'll do something to you too."

Bog lifted himself off the floor. "We must find a way out of here... *now.*"

A plaintive cry caught our attention. Plopping onto a blanket, Odysseus pouted. "I knew I should have gone first. Doesn't anyone wish to hear my harrowing story of abduction?"

Rex rolled his eyes. "I'll wait for the movie."

Penelope scurried to her brother's side. "We all want to hear your story. It's just that well...um...we don't have time. Not now. You understand." She licked his head.

He heaved a sigh. "Okay. I'm nothing if not a team player."

Handicapped by darkness, Bog sought the help of Auguste and Odysseus. Both had spent several days and nights as prisoners. "No one explores like a cat. Tell us what you boys found. Any way out of here?"

"Only one door and it's bolted shut," Auguste replied. "Walls are solid stone. No windows, air vents, or secret tunnels that we could find. A mouse or rat might be able to squeeze through but that's about it."

Although my ears perked at the prospect of a fresh, warm meal with whiskers, another idea popped into my head. "Say, Rex, any chance you got another half or whole brother who belongs to this parish? Maybe a cousin?"

"My family aren't what you'd call regular churchgoers. But, anything's possible. Shouldn't count on it though."

Odysseus coughed with exaggeration. "May I speak?"

"Of course," said Bog.

"Keep it short," barked Rex.

Taking in a deep breath, Odysseus strutted to the center of our circle. "My esteemed friend has missed something. One must look skyward for salvation. Especially in a church."

Rex groaned. "Oh brother! More religious mumbo jumbo."

"Are you speaking about statues?" Penelope asked sweetly. "Prayers and miracles?"

Odysseus adopted a smug expression. "Hardly. No, something more practical. From my previous prowl-abouts, while Fabiola lit candles and flirted with Father Jacques, I made a discovery. Floor grates in the side chapels. For circulation, I guess."

Penelope looked surprised. "I never saw any grates."

"You weren't as curious as I. That, or the same tan priest who bamboozled Fabiola, charmed you."

She struggled to control her claws. "I don't see how any of that matters, dear brother."

Bog patted Odysseus' head. "You're absolutely brilliant. Let's find those grates."

Auguste looked up to the ceiling. "You really think we can raise ourselves to freedom? Seems mighty high, even by human standards."

Bog shrugged. "We can try. Might need to hoist Rex onto my shoulders. Even if one of us reaches freedom, he can seek help from his grooming friends."

The prospect of escape excited me. "How about a man, dog, cat pyramid? Bog, Rex, and me."

"Swell," the shepherd replied. "That gets us what? Another foot at best, hmm. No, if the grates are out of reach or won't budge, I'll simply bark for help."

Penelope sighed. "Nobody would hear us, even if Bog shouted at the top of his lungs. The side chapels aren't used. Except for a few candles, they're dark and isolated."

Bog squinted up to the timbered beams. "First things first. How do we find the grates?"

Odysseus purred. "*Moi* to the rescue once again, *mes amies*. Grates provided a convenient place to...to relieve myself."

Penelope recoiled with disgust. "You didn't? Inside a church?"

He flashed a fiendish grin. "It was either there or under the main altar. You should be thanking me. We need only track my scent. A grate will be directly above. Shall we?"

I winced. "Be our guest."

He scoffed. "Must I do everything?"

With his nose to the floor, Odysseus identified two spots that retained telltale odors. Gazing up to the timbered beams, I discerned a grate and beyond that, the church's painted ceiling. Gold stars and haloed angels floated in a celestial blue sky. *Heaven? But where are the cats?* Regardless, the distance to salvation seemed insurmountable.

Bog groaned. "Too high. We need something. A chair, table, even a box."

Auguste nodded to a door. "There's some furniture in there."

Successive trips into the adjacent room garnered Bog two tables, a stool, and several chairs. He mocked up different combinations, each wobblier than the first. "Opening's still several feet above my head. Can't reach the grate even if I lift one of you."

"What about the ladder?"

I glared at Odysseus. "What ladder?"

He pointed to a dark alcove. "There. Found it when I had to pee."

Rex rolled his eyes. "Who knew cat pee had so many benefits?"

—◦《◉》◦—

Bog positioned the step-ladder atop two stacked tables. "There's enough height to push a cat through the grate. Only question is who."

Auguste pawed Bog's shin. "I'll do it."

I swatted his other shin. "I'll go. I'm skinnier."

"No, I'm the smallest. The logical choice," Penelope declared.

"If you didn't raise your paw, missy," Rex said, "I'd have voted for your brother, hmm."

"*Moi?*" Odysseus stammered. "You want to be rid of me. Admit it."

Rex shrugged. "The thought did cross my mind. But no, pee pee boy. You're the most familiar with the grate and the church. Said so yourself."

"So I did. But I'm terrible with heights. Cirque du Soleil made me puke. Penelope can tell you. I'm also as slow as a tortoise and have no idea how to find your groomer friends."

Bog nodded to Penelope. "Smaller and faster settles it."

I kissed her cheek. "Careful, *ma chérie*, careful."

Bog raised himself onto the first table where Penelope joined him. Next, he lifted her onto the second table before climbing up himself. The two stood side-by-side. The trickiest part remained. Mounting the ladder together then raising her over his head.

When Bog scooped her into his arms, I cringed. Pressing her to his chest, he stepped onto the ladder. The makeshift tower wobbled. Odysseus whimpered but his sister remained calm. I swelled with admiration. With each step, Bog rebalanced his weight. He repeated the slow, deliberate process, rung by rung.

Reaching the top, Bog gazed down at us. "This should work." He turned his attention back to the grate. He lifted Penelope slowly, stopping frequently to maintain balance. Penelope's hind claws grasped his thick hair. Although light-headed, I forced myself to watch. I willed her through the grate. Inching her nose toward the bars, she said something but her words were muffled.

I called up. "What'd she say?"

"She can't quite reach it," Bog replied. "I need to step on the very top."

"Too risky," Auguste said.

"Come down," I shouted.

Neither of our heroes uttered a sound. We held our breaths. Bog lifted one foot then the other. Penelope wriggled her head between bars. Odysseus began to swoon but Rex whacked him.

Bog groaned. "Opening's not big enough."

He began to lower his arms when Penelope shouted, "Wait! I see Fabiola. She's lighting a candle."

Penelope meowed loudly and Bog shouted up to the grate. But the pipe organ smothered their calls for help. Loud fanfares and flourishes reverberated through the church.

I shouted to our comrades. "Does she hear you?" Bog and Penelope shook their heads.

Odysseus whined. "Fabiola never had the best of hearing."

Penelope whimpered. "She's walking away."

Odysseus leaped onto the first table then the second. After a brief pause, he hopped up the ladder, rung by rung. Reaching the top, he clutched Bog's shoe laces. From their lofty perch, the Siamese siblings let out a chorus of ear-piercing shrieks.

A shadow fell over the grate. Then a face. "Penelope? Odysseus? I'd know those voices anywhere. What in heaven's name...?"

Against the loud din of the organ, Bog attempted to explain our predicament. Fabiola interrupted him. "Locked in the basement? Sillies! Can't make out a word you're saying. Stay right there. I'll get Father Jacques."

The organ drowned out our screams.

Chapter 21
Old Friends

"My, my." Odysseus wallowed in lament after descending to the cellar floor. "My death-defying climb was all for naught. All is lost, all is lost. Poor, poor Fabiola. What shall become of her?"

"I'm in a terrible fright," Penelope said through sobs. "It's our fault that she's involved at all. Oh, the beast."

I rubbed my head into her fur. I too suspected the worst from Father Jacques but hid my concerns behind smiles and a comforting tone. "Don't you fret, *ma chérie*. The priest's too smart to hurt an old woman. He'll charm but not harm her."

"Fluff has a point," said Bog. "I'm guessing your friend has deep pockets. I've not met a cleric yet who'd mess with his collection plate."

"Hmm," Rex added, twitching his whiskers. "Unless…"

"Unless what?" asked Odysseus.

"Perhaps Jacques has already sweet-talked his way into Fabiola's purse. Talked her into leaving her fortune to Saint Michel. In that case, she's a goner. Already as stiff as a statue."

Penelope mewled; Odysseus swooned.

Rex whacked Odysseus again. "Relax, we don't know nothin' for sure. Maybe the ole gal sucker-punched the priest and put him in a chokehold. Save your pity for ole Rexy. I didn't exactly sign up for this all-inclusive catacomb, Inquisition, and Russia tour. Don't get me wrong, you're all nice critters. Simply proves that no good comes to dogs who play pawsies with cats."

Penelope caressed his snout. "Poor dear. You're right. You're only in this mess because of us. I'm so sorry."

Visibly touched by her compassion, Rex sighed. "Don't think nothin' of it, missy. If I wasn't here with you furballs, I'd be shivering on the cold, windswept parvis."

Minutes dragged like hours. We speculated what Jacques might do when Fabiola spoke of seeing cats and an exotic stranger in the bowels of Saint Michel. Would he affect an air of artificial sweetness and call her story absurd? Maybe he'd insinuate that she'd lost her grip on reality. Perhaps he'd take a harsher approach and throw her into the basement with us.

Concern for her welfare jumbled with our other priority. We needed to escape and get to Châtelain in order to rescue my family from Ivanovich. Our sense of dread intensified with each passing minute. A great weight seemed to push against my chest, squeezing the air out of me. A cat, especially an adventurous stray like me, becomes anxious when caged or cornered. Had pride unleashed the wrath of fate? Perhaps I deserved my predicament—the fall of a dandelion that aspired to be a daffodil.

"It's Plan B." Odysseus's pronouncement shook me from my trance. All eyes turned to him.

Penelope spoke for all. "Plan B?"

He bobbed his head as if the scheme were common knowledge. "*Bien sûr!* Of course, dear Penny. When Father Jacques collects us for the handoff at Châtelain, Bog, Rex, Auguste, and Fluff pounce. *Et voilà*, we flee à pied, on foot."

Auguste glared at him. "Aren't you forgetting someone?"

His face lit up. "*Sacré bleu.* How silly of me. Indeed, I forget. Penny will act as bait, a clever distraction." He detailed a ruse in which his sister lay lifeless on the floor. When the priest opened the door, the rest of us would wail our despair. "The priest will drop his guard. Fall to his knees to check on her. When he does? *Blam*, you attack. *Frère Jacques,*

Frère Jacques, dormez vous! Lights out for Father Jacques. Simple? *Oui!* Ingenious? *Oui! De rien*, you're welcome."

My turn to whack his head. "Foolhardy? Most definitely, *oui!*"

Auguste pushed his face into Odysseus's. "I meant *you*. What's your role?"

Raising his chin, Odysseus pressed his paw to his puffed chest. "*Moi?* Surely you jest. Haven't I done enough? I not only scaled the ladder but am now taxing myself to plot our escape. Have you no sensitivity for my battle fatigue?" An exaggerated yawn ended his protest.

"Definitely more ham than cat," Rex mumbled under his breath.

Bog shook his head slowly. "First off, we can't be sure Jacques will enter the basement by himself or even come at all. Perhaps he'll send in a gang of thugs. A man who used drugs to imprison us isn't somebody to take a risk with our removal. He's too clever and sinister not to neutralize his prisoners."

Odysseus' eyes widened. "Neutralize?"

Rex shot him a sideways glance. "Don't you know nothin'? Means snip, snip. Off with your balls." Flashing a mischievous grin, he sliced the air with an imaginary knife.

A look of horror swept across Odysseus' face. He emitted a high-pitched cry. "Ghastly. You must be joking."

Rex smirked. "Dead serious. In fact, until I observed your backend sashay up the ladder, I assumed from all your preening and la di da lingo that you'd already been neutralized."

Odysseus recoiled. "Why, why…I never…. Next you'll tell me that humans rip our claws right from our paws."

Bog patted Odysseus. "I said 'neutralized.' Rex is talking about neutering, which is a common practice and humane procedure. Happens to the best of pets from the poshest of homes. As a veterinarian, I've performed a number of the procedures."

Odysseus sneered. "Well then, do tell. If it's as common and as humane as you say, I assume that you yourself have…"

"Hold it right there." Rex stuck his snout, as dogs are wont to do, into Bog's crotch. "Nope," he replied, removing his nose. "He's all there. Every last bit of him."

Penelope scoffed. "Regardless of breed or species, boys are all the same."

Bog let out a hearty laugh. "Now that we've settled everyone's parts inventory, let me clarify." He explained that Father Jacques, being neither naïve nor stupid, wouldn't move us without precautions. "Especially if Fabiola tells him that we're awake and plotting an escape."

Mention of Fabiola prompted a resurgent chorus of whimpers from Penelope and Odysseus. In reply to their downcast heads, he added, "I'm telling you this so you don't get your hopes up, that's all. I haven't given up nor should any of you."

Odysseus's head perked up. "So, Plan B is still an option?"

Bog shrugged. "It's not perfect. But unless we can figure out some other way out of this dungeon it may be our only option. I didn't survive the bombing of my village, a thousand-mile trek, and separation from my family to be defeated by a fiendish cleric. Especially one who preys on the meek and downtrodden…of the two- and four-legged variety."

My ears twitched. From the looks on my companions' faces, they too heard odd noises. Pointing toward a small crevice in the wall, Rex's nose quivered. He silently mouthed the word, "Rodents." The thought of sweet, warm, juicy vermin triggered hunger pangs in my empty stomach. Other tummies rumbled too.

"Rodents!" Odysseus exclaimed. Shaking our heads and shooting him glares, we implored him to be quiet. "Whaaat? I'm ravenous," he replied. "This might be our last supper. Did you forget that I scaled the ladder?"

Rex whacked his head. "And plotted our escape. Blah, blah, blah. You mentioned all of that in nauseating detail. Now, be quiet or you'll scare away our supper."

My heart thumped in my chest, my breathing slowed, and my whiskers twitched as we stared at the door. Squeaks and shuffles grew louder. There was more than one trespasser. Auguste pressed against the wall to one side of the crevice and directed me to the other. "Quiet," he whispered. "Once the vermin squeeze into our lair, we'll block their escape." Backing away from the wall, the others prepared to pounce.

"All share in the spoils," whispered Auguste.

Bog held up his palm. "Thank you all the same. But no."

Whiskers emerged from the wall. Then a nose and an entire head with black eyes and pink ears. After a slight hesitation, the first rat was through. He made a hushed series of squeaks. A signal of some sort. A second rat appeared. Auguste and I joined shoulders to thwart their escape. The rodents seemed familiar. But then again, to a cat all rats look pretty much the same.

Odysseus launched into the air.

"Stop!" Penelope wailed. Jolted by her shout, Odysseus splat-landed on his belly, his four legs outstretched. He groaned.

Startled, the rats pivoted on their heels to retrace their steps. I dropped my nose into their frightened faces. I flinched before extending my paw to restrain Auguste. "Wait!"

Penelope reached my side. Acting as a buffer between the trembling rats and our starving companions, we greeted our old friends, Benny and Clyde.

Clyde, the chubbier of the two, stammered, "F…Fluff and—"

"Penelope." added Benny. "Different colors but same faces."

"Sharp memories for names," I said. "Impressive. How've you boys been?"

"Great, great! Since you and the missus left the market circuit, we're—"

"Fat and happy."

Penelope and I blushed at their false assumption regarding our relationship. But try as we might, we couldn't get a word in to correct them. Our heads ping-ponged between the gabby brothers. Their habit of finishing each other's sentences seemed more pronounced than I recalled. Perhaps, a result of their agitated state.

"How's our old pal Lucky?" I wondered if he'd heeded our advice and partnered with the rats to safeguard Lucinda's caravan from rodent raiders.

Benny shrugged. "About the same. Still has only the one eye and only—"

"The three legs," added Clyde. "He told us that you were the ones who—"

"Suggested our partnership. So far, it's—"

"Been a win-win. Benny and I are back to dining on the best of—"

"The King of Chicken. Such juicy—"

"Goodness. My tummy's grumbling—"

"Just thinking about it," concluded Benny, rubbing his round little belly.

Rex, Odysseus, and Auguste stared at us with wide eyes. "Don't tell us," said Odysseus. "These two morsels of savory goodness are your friends?" When Penelope and I nodded, he heaved a sigh. "I presume that takes feasting on them off the table?"

"Afraid so, dear brother," Penelope replied over the rats' agitated gasps.

Odysseus glared at us. "Then ask your friends to refrain from describing in graphic detail the joys of roasted chicken. It's cruel. Their audience is ravenous and our patience thin."

Penelope and I explained our history with the brothers. Although Odysseus bemoaned the friendship, Bog and Auguste extended warm greetings. Rex shrugged. "Not much meat on those bones anyway. More trouble than they're worth."

Clyde bowed as low as his chubby frame allowed. "Thank you—"

"Very much," added Benny, bowing even lower. "Much obliged."

Forcing a smile, Rex muttered, "Cats, now rats. How the mighty Alpha dog has fallen."

As we explained our predicament to the rats, muffled voices outside the door silenced us. One bolt, then a second slid open. A key turned in the lock.

Grabbing a chair, Bog raised it over his head. "Positions, everyone."

The knob turned. Lights flickered on. The door opened. Fabiola. Her powdered and rouged face assumed an expression of great shock. Behind her towered Father Jacques. Gripping her shoulder, he pushed. She stumbled forward. "Join your friends. I'll give you time to get reacquainted. By the way," he added, snapping a photo of Penelope and me. "Can't wait to show Ivanovich and Claus your vibrant transformations. They'll each have a good laugh. Might even make you more valuable." He slammed the door and refastened the bolts before we could attack.

"Hmm," I muttered as my companions glared at me. "Not the reaction I was hoping for."

The Siamese siblings scurried to greet their old friend. With an inscrutable expression, Fabiola stared at Penelope. "My compliments. You're rocking that neon orange." Crouching down, she lavished them with caresses. "My precious darlings. I thought you were lost to me forever." After learning of her estranged friend's death, she explained, she visited the flat looking for the cats. "Landlord said he gave you to a nice expat family. I was heartbroken."

Benny and Clyde ended the poignant moment. At the first sound of the door being opened, they'd scurried into the shadows. Once Jacques left and they witnessed the cozy reunion, they trotted back into our presence. Their grins faded when Fabiola swatted them with her purse. Had Penelope not intervened, she would have batted them against the wall. After Bog explained things, Fabiola offered an apology. However, she kept her eyes trained on them.

With the tearful reunion and introductions behind us, Fabiola informed us that we only had an hour before Jacques' return. Huddled around her, we nibbled mints pulled from her purse. Translating among canine, feline, human, and a smattering of rat, Bog described the priest's nasty scheme.

Fabiola's face turned bright red. "All this villainy under our very noses. I feel betrayed. To think, I confessed *my* sins to that devil."

Because her late husband had been an EU diplomat, she was intrigued by the woman we called Scuffed Loafers as well as the compassionate young bureaucrat. Our account of their conversation in Place Luxembourg riveted her. "And operating with impunity inside the institutions of the EU. I still have many friends with the Commission. I'll unleash a rage of Biblical proportions on those scoundrels."

Bog mentioned Jacques' upcoming meeting at Châtelain with the Russian traffickers. "Unfortunately, our four feline friends here along with the boys' family will be on a plane to Moscow tonight. Maybe even Rex. As for us, dear lady, I don't know what nastiness he has in store. Want to be honest with you."

Fabiola lifted her chin. "Father Jacques has messed with the wrong woman. I may be ancient but I still have a lot of fight left in me. I hope you'll allow me to join your resistance." All of us, even Benny and Clyde, nodded our assent.

Despite Fabiola's resolve and our bold rhetoric, our situation seemed hopeless. But even if the others felt the same, none of us let the conversation drift toward death and doom. Rex began to tell an off-color joke about a priest, a rabbi, and a cat when Jacques returned. Waving a gun in our faces, he hurled two pet carriers into the center of the room. "Two cats per crate. The dog, refugee, and old lady stay…for now. Move it or I shoot." Penelope hopped into the carrier with me. With a huff, Odysseus joined Auguste. "Zip them shut."

Fabiola and Bog started to close the carriers when faint high-pitched squeals caught my attention. Two flashes of gray darted across the floor. In the excitement, I completely forgot about Benny and Clyde. Pausing for a moment on top of the priest's polished wingtips, the brothers exchanged words and an affectionate nod. Benny disappeared into one trouser leg and Clyde vanished inside the other. Shocked and horrified, Father Jacques' eyes practically bugged out of his head. Benny and Clyde burrowed up his trousers. First wriggling and writhing, the priest progressed to giggles, groans, and grimaces. He pointed the gun toward his crotch. For a split second, I thought he might even neutralize himself. He dropped the gun to the floor and began to swat feverishly at the bulges advancing up his trousers.

Scrambling out of our carrier, Penelope and I joined our brothers who had done the same. Gritting his teeth, Rex backed the hysterical priest into a corner.

"Go," urged Fabiola. "Get to the market." She brandished a long hatpin extracted from her purse. "I'll be fine."

Picking up the gun, Bog shouted to Rex. "Lock Jacques in. Benny and Clyde can escape through the wall. Help Fabiola to safety. If the priest tries anything—"

Rex pointed his snout toward Father Jacques' groin. "I'll neutralize him."

Chapter 22

Châtelain Again

"C'mon, Fluff. We have to go." Penelope's nudge didn't budge me.

"Doesn't feel right. Abandoning our pals. Aren't you concerned about leaving Fabiola? You only just found each other. If I get to see my mama again, I'll hold onto her forever."

A tear-stained cheek betrayed her brave front. "Odie and I know where she lives. She said we're family, a forever bond. The most important thing, now, is to save *your* family."

"I'm torn."

"You heard Fabiola," added Odysseus. "She wants us to escape."

Auguste nudged my rear end. "Rex said the same."

Bog patted my head. "Not ideal, little guy. But my money's on Benny and Clyde's teeth, Rex's bite, and Fabiola's hat pin."

Auguste lifted my chin. "Our friends got this, li'l brother. We must get to Châtelain or Mama Vanille, Licorice, and Lily will be lost forever."

I despaired until noises from our former cell soothed my conscience. Snarls, snapping jaws, and shrill reprimands drowned out the priest's cries for mercy. I must confess, I grinned at the sounds. "*Allons*, let's go!"

We scurried through a long, narrow corridor. Pungent odors of wax and incense sent Odysseus into a sneezing fit. Although we feared the noise might alert unknown accomplices to our escape, no one responded. We came to a staircase, which we climbed. It brought us to a hallway behind the altar.

"Wait here," Bog said. "I got an idea." He hustled back downstairs and up again. He held the two pet carriers. "Fabiola says she's pricked the priest so many times that he'll spout altar wine like a champagne fountain."

Only Odysseus didn't giggle. He looked frightened as he nodded toward Bog's hands. "W…wh…what do you want with those?"

Bog chuckled. "One might think your gray fur is the result of constant worry."

He scoffed. "I'll have you know that I'm the very picture of calmness. A stuffed cat is more skittish than I."

Bog stifled a laugh. "Don't you fret, my little friend. I'll explain everything on the way to the market. But before we leave, I have one more detour."

"We've got time," Penelope replied. "The church bells just tolled noon and the market doesn't open until two."

"And for all we know," said Odysseus, "the smugglers won't rendezvous until later. They'll blend in better among the *apéro* crowd. You know, afterwork cocktail goers," he added in reply to our blank stares.

Dropping the cases to the floor, Bog opened several doors before disappearing through one. Behind the closed door, cupboards, closets, and drawers opened and shut.

Penelope's heavy sigh drew my attention. "My fond memories of Saint Michel have soured. I shall never return."

I twitched my whiskers up toward the yellowed ceiling, down to the dulled wooden floor, and sideways to walls covered with ghastly portraits of saints writhing in agony. "Good thing, *ma chérie*. This place gives me the creeps."

Auguste nodded. "*Moi aussi*, me too. Those who hurt innocents are the worst kind of predator. Collar or no collar."

Odysseus stopped sniffing the carriers. "I tell you what gives me the creeps. These fancy...*cages*. For that's precisely what they are, cages. What do you think Bog has in mind? Suppose he'll barter us for his wife and daughter? The Russians probably know exactly where they are. Desperate times and measures you know. I'd steer clear of these death traps if I were you. You're welcome!"

The very picture of calmness, indeed! The rest of us dismissed his wild speculation. Auguste offered the sharpest rebuke. "Quiet. He's a good man. A loyal and brave friend."

His raised eyebrows and pursed mouth, however, suggested that Odysseus hadn't abandoned his suspicions. When the organ roared to life, he gasped. "Bach! The next mass. What'll we do? They'll search for Father Jacques. Where's Bog? We mustn't tarry. Good heavens!"

When he concluded his rant, the door flew open. Our mouths fell open. Bog had exchanged the clothes of a homeless refugee for trousers, shirt, jacket, and overcoat, all black. A stiff white clerical collar made his transformation almost complete. His appearance, however, remained untamed—a mad, homeless priest.

"Good thing the priest's my size," Bog said, lifting the carriers from the floor. "I'll explain the costume change but have one more stop if we're to pull this off."

Whatever his plan, I didn't know. I was simply glad that Bog, a man of integrity and intelligence, had one. Despite that fact, Odysseus kept peddling his own hair-brained scheme. In it, he explained, once we reached Châtelain, Penelope would feign a dramatic death in front of the smugglers. The rest of us were to overpower the catnappers and free my family. Each of us had an assigned role except, of course, himself.

With his tail and chin raised high, he defended both his plan and passive role. "You're amateurs. Someone needs to direct. Simple? *Oui!* Ingenious? *Oui! De rien*, you're welcome."

I whacked his head. "Another pawsitively dreadful scheme. Might even call it a cat-astrophe."

As the organist stretched out the opening hymn, we exited down the main aisle. For two dozen ogling worshippers scattered among the pews, we presented quite the spectacle: four cats of assorted colors and a dark, bearded, wild-haired priest. Bog joked about leading the congregation in chants of, Allahu Akbar. The rest of us were relieved, however, when we reached the door without his doing so.

Pausing in the doorway, we scanned the Ixelles horizon. Heavy, lead-colored clouds and gusty winds ruffled awnings and bowed tree tops. Raindrops plunked to the pavement. Inclement weather didn't bode well for an afternoon market and our daring rescue.

"We've no choice," Bog said. "Can't stay here. They'll find Jacques sooner or later."

Auguste dismissed the weather with a wave of his paw. "Little rain never hurt anyone. Least of all a seasoned street cat. This is Brussels, not the Côte d'Azur."

Taking his cue, I strolled onto the stone porch. Cool rain pelted me. Based on Jacques' reaction to my colorful coat, I hoped the rain might fade the bright yellow dye. I faced the others. "*Allons, mes amies.* Let's go."

Odysseus eyed the rain. "W...well, um, maybe it would be prudent for me to...um, you know, um, alight into one of those cozy carriers. If you're carting them around anyway. Seems silly for you to...um, go to all that trouble for...um, nothing. Don't you agree?"

Bog snickered. "You mean where it's warm and dry."

With a sheepish grin, Odysseus looked up at him. "Oh yes, that too. I do have a delicate disposition. It's only of late, you understand, that Penny and I find ourselves cavorting among common street cats, *les chats de rue*. Right, sister dear?"

A mix of anger and embarrassment registered in her face. "Dearet Odie," she said with a simmering sigh. "I'm of the opinion that our recent adventures with these fine creatures have transformed—better yet *elevated*—us into street cats. A breed that's admirable, courageous, and kind. About as uncommon as they come. I'm proud to call myself *une chat de rue.* That is," she added with a glance to my brother and me, "if our uncommonly kind companions consent to confer that honor upon me."

We responded with robust nods. "*Certainement!* The honor is all ours."

When she blew us a kiss, my insides warmed in a way they never had. "*Je t'aime, ma chérie.*" The words flew from my mouth. Had I really uttered them? My racing heart and smirking companions provided the answer—a resounding, *oui!* Fearing her response, I trembled.

Her demure giggle and batting eyes melted me. "*Moi aussi, cher* Fluff. Me too. You're such a sweet dear." She licked my cheek.

"Fine, fine," whined Odysseus. "Now that we've settled who loves whom, how about my conveyance?"

Bog lowered both cases onto the ground. "Be my guests. *All* of you. No need for anyone but me to get wet."

A look of horror swept over Penelope's face. "Wait!"

Odysseus scoffed. "Please! It's perfectly safe. I trust Bog and so should all of you."

"No," she replied. "The rain. If it doesn't let up, the traffickers might skip the market."

Bog scratched his beard. "Don't worry just yet. Let's see what the next hour brings. But first, that stop I mentioned."

He motioned us inside the cases. I shouldered Odysseus in order to cozy up to Penelope. Zipping us in, Bog grabbed the leather handles, hoisted us, and marched down Rue du Bailli. Despite the rain, the high street bustled. Viewed through the hatched screen of a pet carrier, the city looked different. Where I placed my paws and dangers lurking in doorways or around blind corners didn't concern me. I simply enjoyed the journey, bumpy as it was. Pedestrians who ordinarily strolled with repellant faces showed curiosity in a priest toting cats. As passersby glanced into our carrier at two brightly colored cats, Penelope and I made faces, even sticking out our tongues at the most prune-faced among them.

I cooed. "Boy oh boy. Bet Grumps never traveled like this. If this is what he meant by the pampered life of a posh parlor cat, sign me up."

Giggling at my wide-eyed wonder, Penelope likened our journey to cinema experiences that she and Odie enjoyed with Fabiola. "No popcorn or subtitles, but a show just the same."

Lying side-by-side with our faces pressed to the soft mesh, I spoke about our futures. "If we come out of this okay, are you thinking that you and Odie will live with Fabiola?"

She purred loudly. "Prr...prrobably. Called us her babies. But time will tell. You? Fabiola would make room. I'd like that. Odie too. If not, I'm sure Bog's offer is still open."

"I dunno, *ma chérie*. I need to find my family first."

She nuzzled my head. "I understand. I also know that there's a lot of pent-up adventure still inside you. Whatever happens, our time together has been magical. I'll cling to these precious weeks as I'm holding onto you now."

I purred as our paws locked in embrace. "*Moi aussi, ma chérie*, me too..."

⏤«◉»⏤

"What's going on over there?" shouted Odysseus. "Such savage noises. Is he hurting you, dearest Penny? I swear I'll—"

"Never mind him," bellowed Auguste. "Carry on, lovebirds. I'll try to explain to him, the birds, bees, and the place from where kittens come. He may not be neutered but the poor dandy has led a sheltered life."

Bog whistled. "Congratulations! Been wondering when the two of you would finally get around to...*cementing* your relationship. Such adorable kittens you'll have."

Their banter was mere background noise. Penelope and I stared into each other's eyes. I'd never felt more connected to another creature or so removed from everything and everyone else. Our embrace filled me with safety, security, confidence, joy. My human friends Peter and Sarah came to mind. They had a word that described how I felt at that moment, *Heaven*!

A loud, high-pitched squeal from Odysseus jerked Penelope and me from our blissful trance. "What? Barbaric! You must be joking."

Bog lifted our brothers' carrier. "Shoosh. Behave when we're inside."

Penelope and I glanced out the mesh. "Hair salon," she whispered. "Human groomers."

Bog used his clerical collar to appeal to the salon owners, scamming a haircut and shave. A modern style and whisker-free face made him nearly unrecognizable. The homeless refugee looked more respectable than the villainous priests. Penelope declared him, "Irresistibly cute."

A masterful stroke of genius brought extra doses of charity from salon staff including cookies and cash. Bog told them that his cats were a pilot program that provided shelter pets to resettled refugees. "The collar opens hearts and wallets," he said when we left the shop.

The bells of Saint Michel tolled two when we found ourselves at the edge of the market. The rain had let up and the sky cleared. The intoxicating sights, sounds, and scents of Châtelain were familiar. Sensory delight soothed the memory of our prior visit—a narrow escape from Vaclav and Grabowski and our service to the royal family of chicken. A cat's life, I pondered, is simply a series of chases—as pursued and pursuer.

Circling the market in our cozy carriers, I luxuriated in aromas of steamed mussels, savory meats, and roast chicken. With no sign of the villains, Bog used his recent gain to buy bread, cheese, and olives. My gentle whimper prodded him to add chicken although Penelope and I huddled in the shadows of our carrier before the ginger-haired royals. They probably wouldn't have recognized the neon orange and dandelion yellow cats as their old subjects anyway.

Bog spotted a bench near the Flemish flower vendor for our picnic. Setting us down on either side of him, he unzipped the cases. "Now, here's my plan to outfox the wolves."

Chapter 23
Tiger, Tiger

Bog's scheme exhilarated and terrified us. Hair-raising details churned our stomachs and threatened our appetites. Feline practicality, however, prevailed. The plate of roast chicken was simply too delectable to let anxiety and anticipation spoil. We chewed the bones clean.

Bog stashed the empty carriers behind a dense hedge. With time on our paws until the traffickers arrived, curiosity nagged at us. Reconnaissance and a promise of more nibbles—sweet and savory—inspired a walkabout. Before we set off, Bog cautioned us to avoid police patrols and steer clear of the royals' greasy clutches. "Remain as inconspicuous as a bright yellow and orange cat can," he added with a chuckle.

Concealing ourselves as well as a quartet of cats could, we prowled behind tents and under skirted stalls. Our mission, we agreed, was too risky to reveal ourselves to Lucky. We'd seen our old pal and savior on our loops through the market. Standing outside Lucinda's caravan, he mingled with customers. Part of me envied his simple life. He traveled from market to market without worry of food, shelter, or companionship. Lucky indeed!

Penelope and I roamed shoulder to shoulder. Our brothers followed behind. We caught occasional glimpses of Bog, outside the market. He turned up the collar of his black overcoat and burrowed his hands in its pockets as he watched for the traffickers. The tolling of each passing hour reminded us of our friends at Saint Michel. Had they neutralized Jacques, or would the infuriated and battered priest turn up at Châtelain? In his eye-for-an-eye, tail-for-a-tail thinking, he'd relish helping the smugglers whisk us off to Moscow…dead or alive.

Church bells rang six times. Still no sign of the traffickers. Pausing beside a caravan selling cheese, Auguste gathered us around him. "Most of the afterwork crowd are here. But not the villains. The earlier downpour probably doused their plans."

My head drooped. "They gotta show. They just gotta. We don't have another plan."

Odysseus plopped onto the pavement. "My paws are utterly exhausted."

"He's got a point," Penelope added. "I'm tired myself. Sorry Fluff, but if—" She stopped in mid-sentence and her eyes grew to the size of saucers.

I followed her gaze. But my relief was short-lived. Grabowski and Vaclav were empty-handed. Where was my family? Auguste draped his paw around my shoulder. "Don't worry, li'l brother. Plenty of reasons why they wouldn't bring them."

"B…but—"

Penelope nuzzled my head. "Auguste is right. They're probably nearby. In a car or van. Maybe in a shop for safekeeping. What other reason would the smugglers have for keeping their rendezvous?"

I could think of plenty. But I yearned to believe her explanations that I swept the nightmarish scenarios from my head.

Odysseus pushed his face into mine. "You forgetting your inner cat? What about the tiger you aspired to be? Use your nose, Fluff. As unpleasant and unsavory as the experience promises to be, sniff the smugglers. If they've been around your family, you'll know."

"Sometimes, you're brilliant."

He smirked. "Sometimes?"

We scampered for cover in a tent that sold Portuguese tarts. From under a skirted table, we observed the blond, shaggy-haired Grabowski and swarthy Vaclav. Approaching a stall that sold alcohol and seafood savories, they began to flirt with the young petite purveyor.

"Let's hope they guzzle like English or Russian sailors," Auguste whispered. "Our odds are better if they do."

Odysseus hissed. "May the ruffian and scallywag quaff a case of bubbly."

Penelope snickered. "They don't strike me as champagne connoisseurs, dear Odie."

"My money's on beer and vodka," I said with a wink. No sooner had the words left my mouth than the young woman handed the men two beer bottles and two tumblers of chilled vodka. "Yippee! Double-fisted drinkers."

Auguste nudged Odysseus who was slurping custard from a fallen tart. "Keep your eyes on them while Fluff gets in a few sniffs. I'll tell Bog that the rats—no disrespect to Benny and Clyde—have arrived."

I observed him dart away. He scooted under a pram and scampered through the legs of marketgoers. His unflinching bravery and willingness to pounce headfirst into any situation swelled my pride. Were his courage and confidence consequences of birth or, as I suspected, garnered from a life of adventure? Whatever its source, heroism clung to him as handsomely as did his coat of black, tan, and gray fur.

"You're so much like him." At the sound of Penelope's voice, I turned. Her eyes sparkled with affection. "I know you don't believe it, but you are. As brave and courageous...and cuter. Don't forget cuter. Even as you currently look. A yellow dandy...lion."

I averted my gaze. "If only I had a smidgen of his courage, *ma chérie*."

She nuzzled my head. "You have that and more. You're simply too modest to see it. You also have something he'll never have."

I cocked my head. "What's that?"

"My love." She licked my head when a familiar voice surprised us.

"What's this? Brazen display of affection. And at Châtelain of all places. I knew you'd get all sappy sweet. Probably knew it before you did. I expect you to name one of your kittens after—"

"Lucky!" Penelope shouted.

"The very same," our old friend replied. "Don't think for one minute that I didn't see you prowling around the market all afternoon. Did you really think that a clowder…cluster…clutter, or whatever you call a crowd of cats would go unnoticed? And your new avant-garde colors didn't fool me for one second. I may have only a single eye, but I still possess the instincts of a shrewd and cunning feline."

"In that case," I replied, "you might consider pawing away that strand of spaghetti dangling from your chin."

Giggling, the three of us fell into a furry scrimmage of friendly nibbles and paw whacks. But Odysseus cut short our joyous reunion with exaggerated coughs that suggested a grapefruit-sized furball. We stared up at him. "About time I got your attention," he said. "Are good manners and breeding relics of the past? Are you not going to introduce me to your… um…strong and strapping friend?"

Rising to our paws, Penelope and I made introductions.

Licking a stubborn dollop of custard from his mouth, Odysseus grinned. "So, this is the intrepid Lucky. You failed to mention how handsome your erstwhile hero is. Heard you lost your teeth in a barfight and your eye and leg in a rumble with the DeVilles. A brooding romantic figure if there ever was one. Pure tiger."

Flustered by the rare and unexpected compliment, Lucky stammered his thank you. "You got most everything correct. A beer bottle did take out my teeth and the DeVilles got my eye. But they're not to blame for my missing leg."

"Oh," I said. "When you told us about the eye, I just assumed the leg…"

"Easy mistake. Lost the leg escaping from a trap. Traffickers caught me and a tabby in the same snare. I was lucky to get away. Not so the poor tabby. Sent off to a research lab, I heard. But enough of my boring history. What brought you back to Châtelain?"

"I gotta get a whiff of those two guys." Lucky's gaze followed my nose as I motioned toward Grabowski and Vaclav. Advancing to their third drink, they'd taken a seat at a table. "I don't want them to see me."

Lucky scrutinized me, an odd expression on his face. "O…kay!"

"Sounds strange, we know. It will make sense. Really. Will you help us?" Penelope enhanced her plea with a gentle lick to his cheek. He replied with a sheepish nod.

I slapped his shoulder. "Attaboy! Create a diversion, typical cat stuff. I'll sneak under the table for a quick sniff."

Moving in a slow, wide arc, I led Lucky toward our targets. They'd already downed drink number three and moved onto round four. With surprising agility, my three-legged friend jumped onto the table. He didn't upset a single bottle or glass. Having used the diversion to scurry under the table, I couldn't see the men's reaction. But I heard it—bursts of laughter followed by curses at the "damn cat." Lucky dawdled as planned while, below, I avoided kicks and foot stomps.

Pressing my nose against Grabowski's denim shin and Vaclav's threadbare tweed, I cooed with satisfaction. My head spun with memories of our cardboard home, nights snuggling with littermates in a mass of fur, and Mama's soft caresses and wise counsel. I hadn't smelled them for months, but I recognized my beloved family's scent instantly.

How long did I linger, dreaming of home, my first taste of heaven? A third man's arrival jarred me from the pleasant memory. His polished shoes smelled of expensive leather; fine wool trousers sported razor-sharp pleats. Before he uttered one word, I knew it was Ivanovich. The sound of his voice made me seethe. I wanted to sink my teeth into his fat calf.

Suppressing my tiger-like ferocity, I told myself that Bog's plan was still our best option. Overjoyed that my family was near, I ran to my comrades, arriving as Bog and Auguste returned. We cautioned Lucky to keep his distance. After his tabletop antics, we didn't want him getting hurt. We'd already involved too many innocents in our risky mission. Wishing us success, he sulked away disappointed at being excluded.

Bog led us back to the dense hedge to retrieve the carriers. When he motioned us inside, Odysseus inched forward. "My, my, my. Don't know if I have it in me."

Auguste chuckled. "You got it in you. Might say, you're full of it."

"Don't worry," I said choosing a different tactic. "You only have to sit still and look handsome. Nobody does that better than you."

Penelope nudged his rump. "I'll be right beside you, Odie. Bog wouldn't ask us to do anything that wasn't absolutely necessary and completely safe."

No one else saw the flash of concern that knitted Bog's brow at the mention of safety. He hadn't sugar-coated the risks. He'd cautioned us of the danger. Should one of us slip up or the slightest detail not go as expected, every single feline would face unspeakable horror in Russia. For Bog, failure likely meant deportation, indefinite separation from his family, and maybe even death. To risk so much to help those in no position to reciprocate spoke volumes about his character. His compassion touched me. So much so that I warmed to the idea of his adopting me. He represented my best hope for a home. However, I doubted whether I'd ever be able to suppress my insatiable hunger for adventure.

Bog zipped up the bag containing Penelope and Odysseus. Sensing my anxiety or maybe simply guessing my state of mind, he reassured me. "She's only in a different case, not a different country. This should be over soon. Now, hop on in with your brother."

I understood his rationale. Presenting two pairs of littermates would excite the traffickers—the juiciest worm on the hook. From the chatter at Pierre's dinner party, we knew that Claus, Saint Clovis, and the Russians placed huge premiums on cats from the same litter. Although my initial assumption about their wanting matching fur had been debunked, their true reason for hunting us remained a mystery.

"We need every advantage," Bog had explained. "Greed is magical. Animals live and die by physical truths and natural instinct. Humans, on the other hand, see and believe what they want. Money is true north on their moral compass. I'm counting on greed to blind the traffickers to our scheme's sloppy details."

Among the sloppy details, none was more pivotal to our success than Bog's cover. Would the traffickers buy the story that he was acting on behalf of an indisposed Father Jacques? Or would they see through his priestly disguise, recognize him as the refugee they duped at Flagey? We also assumed that Vaclav and Grabowski had my mama and siblings in their physical possession to hand off to Ivanovich. But if those arrangements had changed, might not Bog simply be delivering four more feline victims?

Auguste voiced strong support. "Won't know until we try. I trust Bog with my life."

With the Siamese siblings secured, Bog turned to my brother and me. Scratching our chins, he nudged us into the second bag and zipped it shut. Adjusting his coat and collar, he took a deep breath before marching us toward an uncertain rendezvous.

⸺ ◈ ⸺

"Monsieurs Vaclav, Grabowski, and Ivanovich I presume." Bog's voice quivered.

Vaclav looked up, his glassy eyes trying to place the stranger. "You're not Jacques."

"Who the hell are you?" Alcohol fueled Grabowski's sharp tone and loud voice.

"The guy who'd like to buy Father Jacques' friends another round." Bog's soft laugh, I imagined, was designed to calm the men and himself. "Then, you'll see the finest of felines." He lifted the cases. "You'll be pleased, very pleased."

I heard Penelope hush a hissing Odysseus but even I trembled at the men's icy glares. Auguste pressed his body to mine. "Easy, sport. Easy."

Ivanovich cleared his throat. "You still haven't answered the question. Nor for that matter have you shared your name." His voice was as cold as a tombstone.

"A thousand pardons. Father Ephrem." Bog now spoke with confidence. He placed the cases on empty chairs and extended his hand. "Syrian. Recently assigned to Saint Michel. To help with the refugee crisis. Terrible thing. Human tragedy."

"So it is," Ivanovich replied matter-of-factly as he shook Bog's extended hand. "But tragedy breeds opportunity. Father Jacques, where is he?"

"Sends his apologies. Last-minute request from the Cardinal."

Vaclav raised his empty glass. "Now, those drinks. Vodka for me."

Ivanovich shot him a stern look. "You've had enough."

"Indulge me with one," said Bog. "A Brussels welcome for me and a farewell for you and the felines." Not waiting for an answer, he moved to the bar. In his absence, we eavesdropped.

"Some...thing about that guy looks f...familiar." Grabowski slurred his words.

Vaclav snickered. "Maybe you've seen him at Sunday mass."

Ivanovich dropped his voice to a whisper. "I don't know if we can trust him."

Vaclav glanced at us through the mesh screen. "He brought the cats. Even the yellow and orange ones from Jacques' photo. Besides, there's three of us and only one of him."

Bog returned with a tray of drinks. A fifth round of the same for Vaclav and Grabowski, and champagne for Ivanovich and him. Relocating the carriers to the ground at his feet, he sat and raised his glass. "Santé!" After they drank, he added, "Jacques said there'd be other cats."

"Safe in our van. White one over there," Grabowski said, drawing a kick from Vaclav.

"That's not your concern," added Ivanovich.

Bog held up his hands. "Only small talk. You leave tonight for Moscow. Everyone or just you?" He nodded at Ivanovich who extracted a phone from his trouser pocket.

"You ask a lot of questions for an assistant. Why don't we get your boss on the phone? You can badger Jacques with your queries." Vaclav and Grabowski shifted their chairs, boxing in Bog with their shoulders.

Were we all doomed? I heard only one side of the phone conversation. As Ivanovich spoke, he grew irritable. He shouted into the phone before disconnecting.

"What's wrong?" asked Vaclav. "This guy an imposter?"

Ivanovich seethed. "No! Not according to the old lady who answered the priest's phone. Said they were dealing with rats. Said she had better things to do than answer silly questions from some old foreign fool! Exasperating woman."

Auguste and I mouthed, "Fabiola." Bog's cover was secure...for now.

"Almost forgot," Ivanovich said to his men. "Before you drop me at the airport, we have to swing by Saint-Gilles. Pierre's got more cats. Ferals he's used to round up other strays."

"Scratch and Ollie, I bet," Auguste whispered. "Serves them right."

"Not sure if he's tired of them," Ivanovich added, "or he's simply trying to get back into my good graces. Tried to peddle an old cat too." His sinister laugh made me shudder.

I gasped. "Grumps."

"What do you want with an old cat?" asked Vaclav.

"Not a single thing. Told Pierre to wring the mangy coot's neck. Wouldn't fetch a single euro from a shady butcher."

"Hope he waits for us," replied Grabowski. "I'd love to watch."

"I'll even do the honors myself," added Vaclav.

"Drink up," said Bog. "You don't want to miss the flight."

After emptying his champagne glass, Ivanovich told Bog to leave.

They were waiting for colleagues with export certificates, he explained, and didn't have time for any more small talk.

"Guessing he means, Scuffed Loafers and Big Suit," I said to Auguste.

"All the two-legged rats will be in one place," he replied.

Bog stood. "Been a real pleasure. Hate to drink and dash. I must insist, however, on taking my furry friends with me."

Ivanovich reached for the bags. He tried to shout but his words slurred. Vaclav and Grabowski's heads drooped; their chins rested on their chests. Ivanovich tried to stand but sank onto his chair. "You! Flagey..." He reached for Bog but his arm dropped onto the table.

"Little trick I learned from you chaps. Jacques' happy pills mean good night for the bad guys." Bog snickered as he fished in Vaclav and Grabowski's pockets and produced a key fob.

Shouts drew our attention. "You there. *Attends*! Wait!"

"*Arrêt!* Stop!"

Big Suit and Scuffed Loafers.

Bog grabbed both pet carriers. "Come on kiddos. Reunion time."

As if reading my mind, Penelope yowled. "First stop, Saint-Gilles. Grumps needs us."

Chapter 24
Operation Grumps

Pursued by Big Suit and Scuffed Loafers, we fled the market bracing for a wild ride. Bog's feline-laden arms swung at his side. A shower of curses erupted from his lips in French, Flemish, and Arabic. In addition to the pet carriers, he also held the key fob. He kept pressing a button in our frantic search for the van. The vehicle not only held my family, it meant freedom.

Flashing lights and a blaring horn pinpointed our target. After a final sprint and only seconds ahead of our pursuers, Bog scooted into the vehicle, pitched the two cases onto the seat beside him, and pushed the ignition. Panting, he pulled away from the curb as explosive fists pounded the van's rear door. We accelerated. Auguste and I sighed, our relief turning into purr-packed joy. Among odors of vodka, nicotine, cheap perfume, and pine, was our family's scent.

Bog managed to drive and free us from the leather and mesh bags. Sweeping the empty cases onto the floor, he turned to Auguste and me with an affectionate grin. "Go! Check your family. I'll open the crate when we get to Saint-Gilles. Right now, we simply gotta get outta here. Won't surprise me to have company on the road."

"Floor it, Buster! Shake the tail." Odysseus delivered the terse command with his paws on the dashboard and his nose pressed to the windshield.

As his artificially deep voice and strange accent echoed through the van, my head jerked and my claws dug into the upholstery. Eyeing him from the passenger seat, Penelope seemed most surprised by the outburst. "What on earth! An American accent? Where'd you learn that?"

He flashed a self-satisfied grin. "Vintage cinema. Black and white films Fabiola watched after midnight. American gangsters loved that stale line. Seemed apropos."

Penelope and I chuckled but Auguste seethed. "Bog can manage without your screeches."

"It's fine," Bog replied. "Except, there's no GPS. I could use help with directions." Never having driven through the maze of Brussels' narrow streets, he clutched the wheel. The veins on his hands bulged. He planned to navigate to Saint-Gilles to save Grumps. The parked van, however, pointed away from our desired destination. We were driving in the wrong direction.

My brother leaped forward, shouldering Odysseus aside. "*Voilà*, CPS. Cat Positioning Service." Auguste instructed Bog to turn the van and maneuver us onto Avenue Louise toward the city center.

With Auguste otherwise occupied, Penelope assisted me in the cargo compartment. Among boxes of Vaclav's perfume sat an empty crate, its door ajar. The sight sent shivers down my spine. The smugglers, I presumed, intended to use the box to transport the four of us to Moscow. A second crate secured with a padlock, commanded our attention. We scratched the wood door but our efforts were in vain.

Small holes along the upper edges were the crate's only openings. They were too tiny and the interior was too dark to reveal anything. Frustrated and frightened, we yowled. Although my family's scent was unmistakable, their deathly silence distressed me. I pressed my ear to the holes, relieved by sounds of wheezing and light snoring.

Penelope caressed my cheek. "Don't worry, Fluff. The traffickers probably drugged them for the flight. Picture your mama, Licorice, and Lily curled up together dreaming of cream, salmon pâté, and soft human laps."

She was probably right about the drugs. However, worry wouldn't leave me until I set eyes on them. I shouted our discovery up to the front seat but Auguste was too busy giving directions and gesturing out the windshield. I recognized Place Stéphanie. Floodlights bathed the whitewashed facades of its handsome 19th century buildings. We neared the parvis.

"Look!" Penelope pointed to a floodlit billboard atop a building. "Isn't that—"

Indeed, it was. Staring down at us was the unmistakable face and long golden mane of Claus, the fur-trimmed femme fatale from Pierre's dinner party. Her giant red-glossy lips blew a kiss at a bottle of amber perfume. The name on the bottle? Saint Clovis. The tagline, "Become a Legend."

I gasped. "Claus isn't associated with any church and Saint Clovis isn't a parish."

"We're not being hunted for our fur," Penelope said.

"No," Bog added. "She and Ivanovich are using animals to make better lipstick, perfume, and shampoo. Explains their desire for littermates. Science stuff, control groups."

Odysseus whimpered. "We were to be their lab rats and guinea pigs."

"Might be the reason they took my blood at Flagey," said Auguste.

"Most likely," replied Bog. "But I can't help thinking they had another reason."

"We must stop them," I said. "They're evil."

"First things first," Auguste shouted. "Gets tricky, here," he added, waving his paw out the window. "Just after the Steigenberger Hotel, follow the circle to the left. That'll put us onto the Chausée de Charleroi."

Odysseus stammered, "W...watch the t...trams."

"And the pedestrians," Penelope added.

"Keep an eye out for cyclists," said Auguste.

"And strays," I added.

Bog heaved a sigh. "Okay, okay! If one of you would rather drive, I'll be more than happy to turn over the wheel. Fair warning. Your paws won't reach the pedals."

After a few wrong turns, a couple of dead ends, and a hair-raising excursion down a one-way street *in the wrong direction*, we arrived at the parvis. Although Bog didn't think we were followed, we faced a different problem. Auguste had guided us to the wrong side of the square. The expansive pedestrian zone separated us from the church and rectory. Heavy chains attached to concrete posts prevented vehicular access. Bog could try to navigate the van through the dark maze of unfamiliar streets or detour around the concrete and chain barriers. The latter scheme required careening onto the sidewalk and serpentining over an obstacle course of outdoor cafés and their patrons, a not-so-subtle advance on the church.

Fatigued and frustrated by his motoring adventure, Bog voiced his concerns. "Simple case of not being able to get there from here. We'd only get lost if I kept driving. I say we park and proceed to the rectory on foot and paw."

Auguste nudged his shoulder. "Where's your sense of adventure?"

Bog groaned. "Typical cat perspective."

"It's not as if I'm asking you to climb down a tree."

Bog heaved a sigh. "B...but the pedestrians."

Penelope scoffed. "So?"

Bog shook his head. "Cyclists?"

Odysseus shrugged. "Inconsequential!"

"Strays? Surely you're concerned about strays."

I swatted his head. "Honk. They'll move...if they're smart."

Bog motioned to a quartet of blue-uniforms. "And the police? Clerical collar or not, a Syrian refugee driving a van down a Brussels sidewalk doesn't strike me as prudent."

Auguste shrugged. "He's got a point. Paws it is."

I whimpered. "Time's running out for Grumps."

"And your family," added Penelope. "We have to break into the crate to rescue them."

I hated to admit it, but any effort to break the lock would take time we didn't have. Grumps' life dangled by a thread. Besides, if my family were drugged for the flight to Moscow, they'd be asleep for some time. "They're as safe and secure as they can be," I said. "One of us needs to stay with them in case..." I didn't mention that those of us invading the rectory might not return. Max had threatened to tear us to pieces if we dared return.

Odysseus turned to Bog. "Enlighten me. What's your fiendishly clever plan this time? I'm sure you've devised a thorough and flawless scheme to extricate our feline friend without harm coming to a single one of our fine hairs."

Bog shrugged. "Haven't got a plan."

Odysseus bristled, his expression one of surprise and disappointment. "Well, remain calm and carry on as English felines say. I could proffer that...uh, no plan is a plan of sorts. As a rule, we cats have no patience for them. We set our eyes on one thing and in the very next moment we're distracted by some other shiny object." He offered a polite haughty laugh. "Let's simply hope for the best, shall we."

For her safety, I wanted Penelope to remain behind. But she had other ideas. "Odie will stay. Suits him best." She was already grooming herself in the rearview mirror.

Odysseus couldn't contain his joy. "Of course, of course. Despite the harrowing and heightened risk involved, I'll be honored to defend and protect your family. And being the selfless cat that I am, I'd sacrifice one of my lives if need be. But leave the heat on. Mind you, I'm only thinking of the poor kitties in back. Classical music too, if you please. *Bonne chance, mes amies, bonne chance.* Don't forget to close the van door behind you."

After tuning the radio, cranking up the heat, and cracking open a window to give him an emergency exit, we wished the eager sentry a fond farewell. After several headbutts and Penelope's affectionate lick to his head, we exited the van. From its open window, Odysseus shouted to us in his deepest American-accented voice, "Give the dirty rats hell."

With an occasional glance back to the idling vehicle, we zig-zagged through cafés. We felines would have preferred hopscotching across tabletops. But grounded by our non-agile human friend, we plodded over the cobblestones. For some of the colorful bohemian patrons, a cat of bright yellow and another in neon orange would have made ideal accessories. Few bystanders shot us a single glance. Disguised as a priest, however, Bog received several reverential nods.

He verbalized his thoughts for his own benefit, I assumed, as much as ours. "We know the rectory layout as well as the characters we're dealing with. Huge advantage. And there's the element of surprise. They'll be shocked to see us again. How to get in...front door, kitchen? There's that basement window Rex used. That's where all this trouble started for you two," he added with a wink toward Penelope and me. "We'll case the place. That's what we'll do. Walk around a couple of times then decide what's best."

Weaving through a café, we happened upon a young couple preoccupied with each other's lips and naughty bits—the human equivalent of tail sniffing. From the back of the amorous pair's metal chairs, Bog snatched umbrellas. After inspecting the pointed tips, he flourished the umbrellas in the air. "Bit of insurance should we face resistance. Pierre and his jolly caretaker will make ideal shish kebabs."

I giggled. "Tons more meat on Jean."

"What happened to Auguste?" Penelope asked.

"Dunno. He was here a second ago." I joined my companions in scanning the square.

Bog pointed across the parvis. "There. That's him, isn't it?"

Indeed, my brother was exiting a butcher shop, his tail and chin lowered. His mouth held a shopping bag. Scampering to rejoin us, he dropped the parcel at Bog's feet. "Insurance of my own." Replying to our quizzical looks, he added, "Beef. To butter up ole Max." He mimicked the hound's exaggerated jaw snap.

Bog patted his head. "Atta boy. Rex may have convinced him to help us last time, but Max isn't fond of cats or refugees. I'll use Jacques' knockout pills is necessary."

Auguste shot an anxious look back to the butcher shop. "Better hurry. Won't be long before the hairy-legged shopper figures out that this adorable kitty pilfered her tenderloin tips."

Hightailing it to the rectory, we didn't wait for Jean to take Max for a walk. The threat to Grumps required quick, decisive action. We agreed to an attack plan. Auguste would ring the front bell. When the door opened, he'd bolt inside and create as much chaos as one cat could. Under cover of that distraction and armed with umbrellas, Bog would push his way through the kitchen door. At the same time, Penelope and I would sneak in through the basement window. Grumps along with Scratch and Ollie, we assumed, were imprisoned in that dark dungeon.

Bog forced a smile. "We'll cause such a ruckus they'll think they're being invaded by a small army. We'll save ole Grumps...one way or another."

Auguste turned to Penelope and me, a grimace on his face. "What about Scratch and Ollie? Those scoundrels tricked you into Pierre's evil clutches."

I huffed with anger. "Probably sent scores of strays to their deaths. Love to see them turned into Russian lipstick and perfume."

Penelope scoffed. "Silly boy. Labs don't turn animals into cosmetics, they test the products on them."

Auguste howled with laughter. "Picture Scratch and Ollie parading around the parvis wearing pink lipstick and blue eyeliner, and smelling like roses."

Penelope's expression and tone turned serious. "Those labs mean cruelty and torture. As vile as Scratch and Ollie are, not to mention the harm they've done to other strays including our pal Lucky, we'd be no better if we didn't help them."

Bog sighed. "And I wouldn't be much of a veterinarian to let any animal suffer."

Scurrying into position, Penelope and I waited outside the basement window. The doorbell rang; our adrenaline surged. Operation Grumps commenced.

Chapter 25

Rectory Ruckus

"Jump, *ma chérie.*"

"*Quoi?* What?" Peering over the window ledge, Penelope turned her ears toward me.

The ruckus above was louder than either of us anticipated. From one end of the basement to the other, the ceiling shook with unbridled mayhem. Shattered glass, heavy thuds, soft clatters, and discordant plunks from the grand piano sounded as if a battalion of feral cats were attacking the rectory. In the kitchen, a shower of broken china and the harsh din of clamoring pots and pans suggested an intense scuffle, a knock-down, drag-out brawl.

I roared up to Penelope. "Ça *va.* It's fine. Aim for the pillows."

Despite twisting a paw on my descent, I'd managed to stack a couple of cushions on the concrete floor. The satin leftovers from our first captivity would soften Penelope's landing. I held my breath as she dived through the void. Retracting her claws and rolling off the pillows, she sidled up to me. "Are you all right? You took a nasty tumble."

I managed a slight smile. "Got the wind knocked out of me that's all."

"You are a tiger," she said before glancing around. "Any sign of Grumps? The others?"

I gestured toward the workroom. "In there, I presume. The only closed door." Images of my first foray into that room flashed through my head—shipping crates, Russian address labels, matted fur, and a blood-splattered floor. "Humans must be upstairs. It's pitch black."

"We've not a second to spare." Penelope trotted toward the door. "Not sure how long Bog and Auguste will be able to fend off Pierre and his staff. They may require our assistance." The sound of a loud crash caused her to cringe. "And Max? Haven't heard a single bark."

"Maybe my brother got the better of him."

"Or Bog slipped him the drowsy pills."

I hoped for one or the other. My twisted paw compromised my defenses. The workroom door opened with a push of our heads. When we were last inside, we found the room cleared and cleansed. However, it now looked as it did on my first visit. Crates, cages, and boxes filled the floor and shelves. Muzzles, leashes, prods, and other ghastly devices rested on the work table.

"Will you look at what the cat dragged in?"

"Another cat. Funny-looking too. Even in the dark, that yellow and orange are blinding."

The disembodied voices made my ears perk. Cage bars obscured their faces but I recognized the crass meows of Scratch and Ollie. Placing her paw on my shoulder, Penelope stopped me from hissing my disdain. She whispered in my ear, "You're ten, no, one hundred times the cat they are."

"No more wisecracks about our looks." My tone was brusque.

"All kidding aside, we're glad to see you two," said Ollie.

"Get us outta here before the priest and caretaker come back," added Scratch

Stifling my anger, I called up to the rascals. "Where's Grumps?"

"First, get us out," Ollie said.

"Then we help," added Scratch.

"You'll get out when we're good and ready," I replied. "Where is he?"

Scratch sighed. "And here I thought you had smarts. Four heads and sixteen paws are better than two dithering amateurs."

"Dithering?" Jumping up to the shelf, Penelope pressed her face to the cage. "You're in no position to barter. Tell us where to find Grumps. Then, we can talk about your release."

Surging anger twisted my tongue. "Your f…friends b…better not have h…harmed him."

"Friends?" replied Scratch, his tone laced with false outrage. "You got us mixed up with someone else. We're victims here, bud."

"Save it," Penelope replied. "What about Grumps?"

"Jean was pretty rough with the ole coot," replied Ollie. "Have a heart. Show us mercy."

I bristled. "Mercy?"

"Then as camp comrades," said Scratch. "After all, you're to blame for our predicament."

"What?" Penelope snapped in reply. "You must be joking."

"If only you'd accepted your fate in the first place," added Ollie. "The two-timing priest swapped us for you. Imagine that. After all we—" Scratch's exaggerated cough stopped his co-conspirator's accidental confession.

Penelope shook her head. "*Incroyable*! Your audacity is unbelievable."

"As a matter of fact," Scratch replied, brushing aside her remark, "we're also stuck in these damn cages on account of you. Pierre said it was necessary because you two and Sissy Boy kept escaping. Gotta admit, never thought you had it in you, Adventure Boy."

His former taunt stung afresh. I seethed. "For the last time, where's Grumps?"

"Okay, okay," he replied. "Down there on the floor. Big crate."

Penelope jumped down to help me investigate. Her ears turned toward the far wall. "Over there. I hear wheezing."

The noise came from a crate resembling the one containing my family. Tiny airholes ran along its top edges. Labored breathing gave us hope that our old friend was alive. Standing on my hind legs, I yowled through the small openings. "Grumps, Grumps."

"Lower your voice," Penelope said. "Don't scare him. He's been through a lot."

A single fastener secured the door. We worked in synchronized precision. After several tries, we flipped the latch. *Catproof indeed!*

Cracking open the door, I offered a hushed meow. "It's your old pals, Fluff and—"

"The Siamese newbie you called a posh parlor kitty," Penelope added over my shoulder.

"What the…" My heart pounded; my hair stood on end. "Quick! Shut the door." Hopping backward, I helped her butt the door.

Her eyes raced between me and the crate. "What is it? What's the matter?"

"It's n…not Gr…Grumps. It's M…Max. Just inside the d…d… door. Nostrils the size of grapefruits, mouth like a wolf, and those teeth. Millions of 'em as sharp as razors."

"Heavens. Whatever will we do?"

"For starters, pray he doesn't wake up. Then? Who knows?"

She inspected the latch. "We'll never be able to re-secure the door. Not without a human finger and thumb. And we certainly can't sit here all day with our rumps against the door. Would that even do any good? Max must have 60 pounds on us, combined."

I scanned the other boxes and crates. We couldn't abandon Grumps. "Let me think, let me think." Snickers from above startled me. My shocking discovery had driven the caged scoundrels from my head.

"Our bad," Scratch said. "Shoulda warned you about the hound."

"Yes," Penelope replied. "That would have been the polite thing to do. Perhaps you boys really want to go to Moscow?"

"Our deepest apologies, madame," added Ollie. "Scratch tried to tell you that we could be of value—six heads and fourteen paws. Can't say he didn't. Nope, can't say he didn't."

As I wrinkled my nose at Ollie's fuzzy math, Scratch heaved a sigh. "If only you woulda listened. But all's not lost. Hop on up here while the beast sleeps. Free us. We'll keep Max inside while you two tend to

Grumps. Way I see it, you're in a terrible fix. And I always say, when a cat's in a terrible fix, ole Scratch is the guy for the job."

I whispered to Penelope, "Hate to admit it, but he's right. We're in a horrible mess."

"You were going to free them anyway. You know you were."

"Come on, come on," Scratch added. "What's taking so long? Don't dither like at camp, Adventure Boy. Max might wake up any moment. Then, where will you two be?"

"Out the door," I replied without thinking. "And you'll still be caged. Soon to be perfume and lipstick. Eau d'Ollie and Scarlet Scratch lip gloss have nice rings, wouldn't you say?"

Ollie snickered. "Aren't you forgetting one little detail? Your beloved Grumps."

"Damn! We have no choice, *ma chérie*. We must free them to save our friend."

She caressed my cheek before we leaped up to the shelf. The pain in my twisted paw had eased but not disappeared. Their cages were secured with simple clasps. On a count of *un, deux, trois*, our paws flipped the latches. Both doors flew open almost sweeping Penelope and me from the shelf. Jumping to the floor, Scratch and Ollie gazed up and smirked at us. We waited, but no *merci* came. I grumbled out of frustration.

Penelope scoffed. "Terriers have better manners."

My leap to the floor made me wince. I motioned to Max's crate. "Quick! Press your rumps against the door. We'll search for Grumps."

"Go on," Penelope added. "What are you waiting for, treats?"

Scratch turned to Ollie. "They talking to us?"

Ollie shrugged. "I didn't hear nothing."

"Well, if they were talking to us, they must be mistaken. I don't take orders from a ne'er-do-well braggart and a stuck-up housecat especially ones who look ridiculous. Do you?"

I pushed my nose into Scratch's face. "We had a deal."

"Ollie," Scratch said. "Did you see paws shaken?"

"No!"

Scratch flashed a smug grin. "Well then, guess you're mistaken. No paw, no deal."

Penelope bristled. "Haven't you heard of a gentleman's agreement?"

Scratch smirked. "Case you haven't noticed, Miss Prima Donna, we're no gentlemen."

"Damn proud of the fact, too," Ollie said before nodding to the door. "Shall we?"

Scratch swept a path forward with his paw. "After you." He offered us a parting wink.

"You double-crossing snake. I'll—"

Before I had a chance to bowl him over, whimpers and cries froze me in place. "Fluff? That you, my boy?"

Penelope and I dashed toward the sound of our old friend's moans and faltering meows. The crate door wasn't closed. Grumps was too feeble to move and too weak to notice our colorful transformation. Sprawled over the metal grate, he looked like a heap of old rags. His once-proud and alert eyes were mere slits. He could barely lift his head. Huddling in the cramped quarters the best we could, we caressed him.

Penelope shuddered. "Poor dear, what have they done to you?"

He extended his paw toward my face. "Fluff, my dear boy. I'd love to see the parvis and maybe even the palace one last time before I..." A wheezing fit cut him off.

"We'll get you outta here, Grumps."

Penelope's knitted brow suggested doubts with our ability to move him. We didn't even have an escape plan for ourselves. And there was Max. Once the beast awakened, we'd be trapped with a raging maniac.

I nodded toward the door. "Follow those double-crossers, *ma chérie*. If we're stuck down here, so are they. Unless—"

Following my train of thought, she grinned. "Unless the snakes know of another exit. Of course, as Pierre's accomplices they must know a secret way in and out of the basement."

She peered around the doorframe. As she played spy, I set myself down beside Grumps. Offering a faint smile, he struggled to meow. He dismissed my plea to save his strength. "I must speak," he said. "Always had my eye on you. You weren't like other strays."

"Because I yearned to wander? Follow in your footsteps?"

He tried to shake his head. "No, dear boy. Because you had a pure heart. Made me feel special. Listened with wide-eyes to this old fool's silly stories—"

"You're not an old fool. Your stories are anything but silly. They're magical."

"Maybe, maybe not. Sweet of you to say. What's more, you befriended the two Siamese strangers when everyone scorned them. Even I dismissed them as pampered and posh." He pawed my head.

"Guess I did. B…but you considered *me* foolish. For aspiring to be better, grander than was my right. A dandelion must know its place, you said, to survive. I shoulda listened. Since leaving the parvis, it's been one nasty scrape after another."

A tear welled in his eye. "I was wrong, dear boy. Forgive me. You're no ordinary weed at all."

"No?"

"You're the noblest of all blooms."

I flinched. "More noble than the bestest rose in the royal palace garden?"

His chuckle aggravated his breathing but he continued, "Nobler than the King's most splendiforous roses, orchids, and gardenias."

"Gee whiskers! What's more nobler than all those?"

"A wildflower, my young friend, a wildflower."

"What's that?"

Under fluttering eyelids, he gazed at me with affection. "Untitled royalty, my boy. Tenacious, colorful, simple, and pure. Heroes of hillsides, meadows, gardens, and city plots. Wherever the winds carry them. Seeking the sun, they flourish anywhere and bow to no one. I'd like to think I was such an untamed flower…"

"Oh, but you are. The wildest, bravest, and most colorful of them all."

He tried to smile. "I'm just an old blustering fool. But you, Fluff, you are a wildflower." Spoken by my role model, mentor, and hero, his words filled me with pride.

His expression turned serene. "Now, my handsome boy, enthrall me with your adventures."

His face radiated joy as I described the afternoon markets—his idea of heaven. Gushing with exuberance over Châtelain, I stroked his cheek. He didn't move. "Grumps. Grumps…"

My caresses and whispers didn't stir him. Tears welled in my eyes. Lowering my head onto his still, lifeless shoulder, I wept into his fur.

"Is he…" Penelope stood on the threshold of the cage.

"Afraid so, *ma chérie*."

"I'm so sorry. I know how much he meant to you." She licked my head, tears flowing from her eyes. She never looked more beautiful.

"Seek the sun, bow to no one," I muttered. With a final kiss for Grumps, I lifted myself up. "*Allons, ma chérie*. We must honor his legacy and escape. Did you see where Ollie and—"

Her puffed tail silenced me. "Someone's coming."

A human figure appeared in the doorway. We braced for an attack. The light flickered on—Bog. At his feet, Auguste. Swaying above the floor, Scratch and Ollie who Bog held by the scruff of their necks.

"Heavens!" Penelope exclaimed. "We thought—"

"That Pierre and Jean got the best of us," Bog replied with a hearty laugh. "We got the better of them."

Auguste flashed a mischievous grin. "The rectory is a disaster."

Bog hoisted Scratch and Ollie. "Grabbed these two by the tail. They had a secret tunnel."

"Go ahead, Adventure Boy," Scratch said. "Tell this brute that we're buds, old pals."

"Yeah," added Ollie. "We're all victims of Pierre. All for one, one for…"

From the expressions on Penelope's and my face, Bog and Auguste understood the truth. I was tempted to feed the traitors to Max. But Bog, I knew, wouldn't have the stomach for it. Besides, they weren't responsible for Grumps' death. Not directly. I told Bog to set them down. But not before Auguste shut the door to prevent their escape.

Auguste and Bog grieved for Grumps. His death hardened their resolve to bring the smugglers to justice. With our rumps planted firmly against the door of the crate, Penelope and I warned them about the sleeping beast. They astonished us by dismissing our concerns.

"Pierre considers Max a traitor," Bog explained. "Saw through his story about our escape. Matter of fact, Max was going to Moscow. If Ivanovich would have him. Otherwise, the canal."

My heart filled with sympathy for our nemesis. "Rex will be pleased that we saved his half-brother from such a horrible fate."

Penelope nodded toward the ceiling. "Upstairs sounded like a battle field."

Bog and Auguste exchanged glances and burst into laughter. They delivered their account employing the same tag-team approach used when they had recounted their journey east. "The front bell was answered by Pierre," Auguste said. "Shoulda seen him as I trashed his precious rectory. Curtains, canvases, and chintz pillows clawed to shreds. Thought his head would explode. Kept shouting for Jean and Cook."

"Who I kept busy in the kitchen," Bog added.

"B...but there's not a scratch on you," Penelope said. "I swear I heard two people getting boxed and battered."

"You did. Simply wasn't me." Our dropped jaws made Bog laugh.

He described the incident. Barging through the kitchen door, he found Jean and Cook having tea. When he flourished the umbrellas, Cook screamed and Jean disappeared. "I assured Cook that I meant her no harm. When Jean returned with a gun, she flew into a fit of hysterics. Grabbed a frying pan off the stove and chased him around the table. He hurled dishes at her. Quite a sight," Bog said. "Turns out

Grabowski is Cook's nephew. She's furious that Jean got him mixed up with the traffickers. She hates Russians."

I gazed to the ceiling. "Where is everyone?"

"Frying pan got Jean. He's sprawled out on the kitchen floor. Cook's sobbing on the phone with her sister in Warsaw. Pierre locked himself in the powder room."

Auguste cackled. "Priest's gone stark-raving mad. Kept screaming, 'devil!' Hope he knows a good exorcist."

"We're not sure he's even a priest," said Scratch.

"Heard he has a wife and seaside villa in the Crimea," added Ollie.

Bog opened the workroom door and Scratch and Ollie bolted. Although grateful that we let them go *again*, they weren't thrilled with the terms—banishment from Brussels.

Bog looked down at the three of us. "Back to the van. Odysseus is either beside himself with worry or bored. High time we got your family out of that box, too. After that, off to Saint Michel to check on Fabiola, Rex, and the rat brothers."

As we cowered behind him, Bog awakened Max who thanked us with slobbering licks.

Bog cradled Grumps' lifeless body in his arms. "He'll get his wish. After we get all this sordid business behind us, we'll give him a dignified burial near the parvis."

I paused at the bottom of the stairs. "I don't ever want to see a rectory, priest, or Russian again." The others sang a chorus of "amens."

Ascending the stairs, we heard the front door open followed by Cook's shout. "Pierre! He's trying to escape."

"Can't let that happen," Bog said.

"Careful," she added. "He's got a gun."

Placing Grumps' body onto a chair, Bog rushed to the front door. Auguste, Penelope, and Max scampered after him. Limping behind, I reached their side as Pierre turned. Waving the gun, he shouted something. Pushing us aside, Max bolted out the door. With his teeth bared, he forced Pierre off the curb. A dark BMW veered toward the priest. This time, Vaclav didn't miss.

We rushed to Pierre's side and Bog checked his pulse. He confirmed that the priest was dead just as a second dark sedan screeched to a stop. The plates of the Mercedes carried the CD designator, Corps Diplomatique. The passenger door swung open. Out jumped Big Suit brandishing a gun. "Get in. Everyone but the mongrel."

Bog, Penelope, Auguste and I packed into the back seat. Seated beside Big Suit at the wheel was another familiar face, Scuffed Loafers.

Chapter 26
Herding Cats

"Enough with the chatty catties. Shut them up or I will."
Rude! The nerve of the loud-mouthed goon. We weren't the ones who snatched innocent bystanders from a city street and crammed them into the backseat of a strange sedan. A car, mind you, littered with greasy food wrappers and reeking of onions, hamburgers, and cigarettes. The late-model dumpster, an affront to its Corps Diplomatique license plates, reverberated with the ear-grating sound of Russian pop music. *Annoying indeed!* Penelope's and Auguste's faces registered similar shock and dismay.

Big Suit's verbal threats and insults were one thing. The gun he thrust into Bog's face was quite another. From his perch in Bog's lap, Auguste shot a piercing look at Penelope and me as we huddled against the door. His message was clear. Keep quiet! At least until we hatched an escape plan.

Bog scoffed. "All gun and no guts." *Careful, Bog!* Unfazed by the danger, he continued to bait. "You must feel like a big man to threaten defenseless animals."

Big Suit smirked. "Animals? Eh, not so much. No challenge. Don't even need a gun. Wring one neck, wring another, then another. Twist-off bottle caps." His sinister laugh made my tail puff. "Guys on the other hand, especially big ones like you are another matter." His eyes lasered on Bog. "Watching tough types squirm with a gun in their face makes me feel good, damn good. More fun even than pulling the trigger." Snorts peppered his hideous cackle.

Bog smirked. "So, where are you taking us? Dinner and the theater?"

Better yet, I thought, *a carwash!*

Scuffed Loafers glanced back from the wheel. "Patience. All in good time. Sit back. Relax. Enjoy the fine German engineering. Smooth ride, yes?"

Bog continued to speak but our abductors raised the volume of the music. Except for some chatter about directions and timetables, they kept silent. Puffing on pungent cigarettes, they shrouded the car in a noxious haze of blue smoke.

Despite the nicotine fog, I noticed that we were traveling under Place Louise. Motorists, pedestrians, and trams traveled across the overpass. Boutique windows showcased eye-catching glitter and sparkle, Tiffany's glistening silver no exception.

Penelope giggled. "*Fais-tu du lèche-vitrine?* Window shopping again?"

"*Oui, chérie.* My eyes devour the shiny displays."

Truth was, I wanted to do more than lick shopwindows, the literal meaning of, *lèche-vitrine.* Like Grumps, I yearned to move behind the glass and feast on life itself. But great adventure, I had learned, came at a steep price. More costly than designer clothes, shimmering jewels, and silver teapots. Adventure had robbed me of freedom, a nightmare I hoped was only temporary. My exploits, however, had brought Penelope into my life. Our shared struggle forged a deep bond. We loved each other.

Rejecting the allure of shop displays, I forced my gaze to the windshield. We were following Vaclav, not as predator and prey but as a marauding pack. I scanned his car's interior, Grabowski, Cook's fair-haired nephew, its only other occupant. Where was Ivanovich, the ruthless leader of the traffickers?

Vaclav signaled a right turn. Scuffed Loafers guided our car onto the exit ramp behind him. At the stoplight, a costumed street performer juggled balls while a boy in colorful face-paint approached idling cars, hat in hand. Perhaps if I had learned some carnival trick, market vendors would have rewarded me with more than shrimp tails and grizzled scraps of meat. The beggar boy peered into our window but the light turned green before I could yowl our distress.

We trailed the BMW through a cavernous valley of glass when Auguste whispered, "The airport."

My stomach soured. They were driving us to Zaventem for a flight to Moscow. Penelope shimmied her trembling body against mine. "At least Odie and your family are safe."

Offering a reassuring smile, I hid my concern that Odysseus might not secure help to free my family in time. With my future looking bleak, I wanted to believe that Mama, Licorice, and Lily would be saved. If they lived, any sacrifice on my part would be worth it.

Bog broke his silence. "Would you mind giving me a cigarette?"

"Cigarette?" I muttered. "All you gotta do is breathe. This heap's a smoldering ashtray."

He brushed off my comments with a wink. "A condemned man gets a last smoke," he added, continuing to address the humans in the front seat.

Big Suit produced a pack with a single raised cigarette. "Good strong Russian tobacco." Clarification wasn't necessary. Bog took it and Big Suit extended a lit match. With his lips pursed around the dangling cigarette, Bog mumbled his thanks. Although he appeared to relax with each drag, I questioned his ulterior motive. Would he jab the hot tip into Big Suit's neck and snatch his gun? Perhaps he'd blow a gust of smoke into Scuffed Loafers' eyes causing her to crash the car. Despite my fantasies, the cigarette burned down without incident. The car kept speeding toward our dreadful fate.

I whispered to Penelope, "Guess he only wanted to smoke."

She began to reply when Big Suit spoke during a lull in the music. "I'll text the warehouse. Let them know we're near."

"Text Vaclav to drive ahead," added Scuffed Loafers. "I have to stop for gas."

"Perfect," Bog mumbled under his breath. The car turned into a nearly-empty petrol station. "When the doors open, run. Don't look back."

Pleased with the prospect of escape, I observed Bog. He blew on the cigarette. Lowering it to the floor, he pressed its glowing tip into grease-stained food wrappers. He pushed flaming paper under the front seats before kicking more rubbish, of which there was plenty, to fuel the fire. Smoke engulfed the car.

"What the…" Swearing in Russian, our two abductors threw open their doors. The outside air was ripe with petrol fumes.

Bog bellowed, "Go!"

"B…but what about—"

"*Now!*" he shouted.

Penelope and I bolted into the front seat and out the door. Assuming the others would follow, we scurried across the street. Reaching a safe distance, we turned. Scuffed Loafers had my brother by the tail. I should have guessed that he wouldn't abandon his friend. With Auguste hoisted in one hand, Scuffed Loafers pointed a gun at Bog. Having used the station's fire extinguisher to douse the flames, Big Suit directed Bog toward the open trunk. Raising his pistol, he brought it down on Bog's head before pushing his slumping body into the trunk. Scuffed Loafers threw in Auguste and slammed the lid. Standing behind the car, Big Suit aimed his gun at the closed trunk. Penelope and I shuddered. But he only pretended to shoot before getting back into the car. As they drove off, hideous laughter from the car's open windows befouled the night.

"We've no choice, *ma chérie*."

She nodded, tears running down her cheek. "I know, dear Fluff."

We sprinted after the car, keeping its red tail lights in our sights. From their prior exchange, we knew the rendezvous point was nearby. Assuming that they notified their cohorts of our escape, we kept watch for Vaclav's BMW. Every oncoming car sent us into the soggy gulley that ran alongside the roadway. Our journey wasn't long. Only a quarter mile up the desolate road, the car turned into an air cargo facility. The sprawling complex had signage in French, English, and Russian. Pressing our noses through the chain-link fence that surrounded the property, we watched the Mercedes pull inside the warehouse. A steel door closed behind it.

Penelope whimpered. "What are we going to do?"

"We gotta get inside."

"And then?"

"We'll think of something."

Feline instinct, I hoped, would kick-in. A cat could find its way into and out of most places. Bog was another matter. Searching the perimeter, we spotted a broken window on an upper floor. I persuaded Penelope to let me test the ascent and inspect the window. If safe, I'd signal to her. Feline agility and well-placed shipping containers allowed me to reach the window. Access inside, however, meant an upward leap of several feet. The jump was one thing, but what was on the other side? An empty room, a table filled with villains, or perhaps a lethal fall?

I called down, "Risky but not impossible."

"Consider it a blind leap of faith, my brave tiger." She blew me a kiss.

"*Attends!* Remember, wait till you hear my signal." Her smile faded as her gaze wandered over my shoulder to the high window and void beyond.

I took a deep breath and felt my beating heart. "I leaped through the missing pane. Crossing into darkness, I searched for a landing pad. My paws found a conference table. Except for chairs and stacks of papers, which I instinctively swatted to the floor, the room was empty. Signaling

Penelope with a mewl, I awaited her graceful dive. She didn't come. My meows and yowls went unanswered. Something or someone, I reasoned, probably scared her off. I trusted she could take care of herself while I tried to save Bog and Auguste. Loud, angry voices drew my attention. I strutted toward the noise coming from the ground floor.

"Get him down here or we start shooting." Vaclav addressed Bog who sat in a chair, his face battered. Grabowski held a gun to a pet carrier. To my horror, Penelope was inside. A second bag at Bog's feet contained Auguste. A third, its flap open, was empty.

Big Suit cackled with laughter. "Animals always get caught by security cameras. The dummies never see us coming."

"You heard Vaclav." Scuffed Loafers thrust her gun into Bog's face. "Call the other cat down here or we start shooting. The pretty Siamese first, I think."

Claws and sharp teeth were no match for guns. Lifting my chin and tail, I descended the stairs. I strolled toward the empty carrier as if it were my own idea. After zipping me in, Grabowski kicked the soft-sided case. *Stupid animal!*

Looking down at the three cases, Big Suit spoke to Scuffed Loafers. "They'll be put inside a cargo container closer to depar—"

A loud crash followed by the shuffle of feet stunned us all.

"Stop!"

"Don't move."

"Drop your weapons."

The voices conveyed urgency and authority—people not to mess with. Another, more measured, speaker perked my ears. "That's her, officers. These others must be accomplices." I recognized the voice but couldn't place it. The man was beyond my line of sight. I glanced to the other carriers. Penelope's tail puffed with excitement. "Saggy Socks! Place Lux. Remember?"

Of course, Hansen, the young animal rights activist who argued with Scuffed Loafers about traffickers. At last, he'd found his smoking gun.

"Officers, lock up these dregs of humanity. Throw away the key."

At the sound of the voice, Penelope squealed, "Fabiola!"

Stepping into my field of vision, Fabiola squeezed Bog's shoulder. "Are you okay?" After he nodded, she dropped her eyes to the floor. "Now let me see my furry friends."

Fabiola and Hansen's appearance dumbfounded me. How had they combined forces and tracked us to this warehouse? *That's it!* I recalled our conversation in the dungeon of Saint Michel. After hearing about our experience in Place Lux, Fabiola peppered us with questions. Scuffed Loafers and the bureaucrat we knew as Hansen captivated her, I assumed, because she and her late husband, a high-ranking Commission official, mingled with diplomats.

Belgian authorities, a mix of plain-clothes detectives, uniformed cops, and customs agents, corralled the bad guys. After Bog, Fabiola, and Hansen freed us, we darted out to freedom rubbing the legs of our human heroes. Bog described our escape from Châtelain, our race to Saint-Gilles, and the abandoned van. "We must go to the parvis, *now*," he said. After conferring with authorities, we were off. But where was Ivanovich and, for that matter, Claus?

We crowded into Hansen's fancy black Jaguar. Its pristine interior made me purr with delight. Fabiola directed Bog into the front seat, preferring to ride with her "furry friends." Bog fastened his seat belt and Auguste jumped into his lap. At my insistence, Penelope curled up in Fabiola's lap and purred with delight. I remained lapless.

On the drive into the city, Fabiola and Hansen briefed us. Fabiola had managed to lock Jacques in the basement before calling police. "But not before Rex, the rats, and my hatpin drove him utterly insane," she said with girlish giggle. "He'll welcome the safety of a jail cell.

"By the way," she added. "Amazing what a hatpin can get out of people. He muttered about being blackmailed into aiding the traffickers. Some cosmetics tycoon has photos of his nasty deeds. Who knows if it's true? Told him to save it for confession."

"It's probably true," Bog said, sharing what we knew about Claus.

He detailed Pierre's dinner party, the floodlit billboard, and the science behind the villains' relentless pursuit of animals and littermates. "Fluff thought she wanted their fur. Truth is, she wants their blood."

Horror swept across Fabiola's face. "Wicked woman! Scoundrels all. But the perfect segue to Hansen. After phoning the police, I contacted him. You see, my husband had mentored a young man named Hansen. Both were passionate about animal rights and welfare. When you described the man's idealism, I knew it was him. Down to his saggy socks."

From behind the wheel, Hansen groaned. "I'm sitting right here."

We chuckled before Fabiola continued, "He recalled his conversation with that hideous imposter you call Scuffed Loafers."

"She's been on our radar for some time," Hansen said. "Her diplomatic credentials didn't add up. Doesn't surprise me that she's working with traffickers." Hansen added that her car's diplomatic registration helped authorities track her movements.

I smirked. "Might say the dummy never saw you coming."

"We'll put the entire gang out of business," Fabiola said. "Won't surprise me if they had a hand in my husband's accident."

Hansen elaborated. He and Fabiola's husband, Laurent, were investigating a European-wide ring of animal traffickers when Laurent's car turned up in a watery ditch. Investigators found an empty liquor bottle in the front seat. Testing revealed high traces of alcohol and narcotics in his blood. "All highly suspicious, but they covered their tracks well."

"Sounds like their methods," Bog said.

"Our focus was a shadowy Russian. Man known as Ivan the Terrible," Hansen said. "Slipped through our fingers." My eyes widened. Were he and Ivanovich the same person? "This case might give us justification to reopen that investigation."

We neared the parvis. My tail puffed with excitement. *At last, my family.* Bog pointed out the windshield. "There's the van." Strobing lights of three police cars didn't surprise us. Because of the urgency, authorities at the warehouse had alerted Saint-Gilles police.

When Hansen pulled his Jaguar up to the van, a dour-faced policeman approached the window. "No sign of any life," he said. Penelope gasped; my stomach sank. We were too late. "The van was completely cleared out," the policeman added. "No cats or containers anywhere."

My heart raced with joy. They all might still be alive. The trail, I knew, would lead to Claus and Ivan the Terrible.

Chapter 27
Caught Off Guard

"Go ahead, call me a scaredy cat. But I'm beside myself with fear."

Sharing Penelope's concern, I comforted her with a gentle headbutt. I'm certain we all felt the same. But nobody wanted to admit, at least out loud, that our odds of finding our loved ones were dismal. A clipped-wing canary had a better chance of being rescued by a vegan cat.

We circled the abandoned van countless times and scanned and sniffed the vicinity but turned up nothing. We were too distraught and focused on our mission to notice that the night air had turned chilly or that the fine mist had intensified into a steady drizzle. Huddled under a shared umbrella, Hansen and Fabiola exchanged contact information with police. The lead investigator promised to update them after forensic specialists processed the van at the impound station. The same team, he said, was across the parvis at that very moment sweeping the church and rectory for evidence. Both were considered crime scenes. "Rest assured," the detective added in conclusion, "we take murder very seriously."

Turning to Penelope and me, Auguste scoffed. "When the victim's another human."

I understood his frustration. How long had Pierre and his villainous conspirators been sending innocent animals to their deaths under the very noses of these same authorities? The world had too few caring humans like Bog, Fabiola, and Hansen.

"Well, my furry friends, there's nothing more we can do here tonight," Fabiola said. "Any longer, we'll catch pneumonia. Especially you, poor Fluff. With your short yellow dander, you look like a little chick."

Penelope lifted my dropping chin. "You're still adorable to me."

Fabiola instructed Hansen to drive us to her apartment. Hungry, exhausted, and soaking wet, we accepted her invitation despite grave concerns for the whereabouts of our loved ones. "Best get some rest and nourishment. We'll have a busy day tomorrow," she added, ushering us toward the sedan.

Hansen paused at the car door. "What happened to Bog?"

Fabiola scanned our surroundings. "Hope he didn't runoff because of his precarious residency status. He told me that uniforms made him nervous."

"I'm sure it's nothing to worry about," Hansen added. "He'll catch up with us. Seems resourceful and resilient."

Penelope and I looked to Auguste. Feline protocol dictated that he had responsibility for monitoring Bog, his designated human. Although the rule is unspoken, cats usually divvied up people amongst themselves. Auguste puckered his face. "Oh, boy. Epic fail. He musta popped off when we all jumped into the van. Coulda easily slipped away during all the ruckus. Now what are *we* going to do?"

We?

Although he was wrong about the pronoun, Auguste was right about the commotion. Police combing the scene for evidence pitched a fit when three felines strolled under their yellow security tape and hopped into the van. I mean, really! They actually believed that a uniform gave them exclusive rights to satisfy their curiosities. In any case, they made it abundantly clear that the crime scene was their territory. If we didn't behave ourselves, they said with their fingers wagging in our faces, they'd have no choice but to lock us up. *Lock us up!* Not the most sensitive of phrases given our recent near-death experience.

If Hansen and Fabiola hadn't plucked us from the van, the blue uniforms worn by the bossy officers would have been slashed to threads. The surly police were lucky to have escaped the melee with only a chorus of hisses delivered in three-part harmony.

Hansen was closing the front passenger door when Auguste bolted from the car. "Bog!" he shouted back over his shoulder. "Over there!"

Darting over the rain-splattered cobblestones, he made straight for a large, burly figure dressed in black. When the man paused in front of the Maison du Peuple, the café's interior lights illuminated his face—Bog.

He proceeded toward us, his expression somber, his gait slow. Penelope's voice rose with excitement. "Max is with him."

"And Grumps," I whispered, spotting a bundle in Bog's arms. True to his word, our human friend had returned to the rectory to collect Grumps. Auguste reached the pair under a street lamp. "Hey," I said. "That's not Max. It's Rex!"

Indeed, the critter lumbering beside Bog was none other than our old camp colleague, fellow adventurer, hero, and animalitarian. The leather purse at his neck, bulged. More donations for animal rescue, I assumed. The trio joined us at Hansen's Jaguar for a muted reunion. Rex's tail wagged slightly as he lowered his snout to greet Penelope and me. Patting his head, Fabiola praised his bravery for guarding Jacques.

We bowed our heads as Bog came forward with the neatly wrapped bundle. Cook, he said, had groomed the body, swaddling Grumps in Pierre's favorite cashmere throw. When Bog mentioned his intent to give Grumps a proper burial near the squatters' camp, Hansen shook his head. "Not tonight, friend. Weather's much too nasty. Best leave the ceremony for tomorrow." He gestured to his car's trunk, which popped open.

Fabiola offered another suggestion. "From what you've all said, Grumps loved adventure. Inspired it in others too." She cast an affectionate glance down to me. "He wouldn't be happy confined to one location. Even a place he loved as dearly as your camp." My eyes widened and my ears perked. "No," she added. "If you're all in agreement, I suggest we scatter the dear fellow's ashes across his beloved Brussels. Not only at camp—"

"But also at Châtelain," I interjected, puffing my tail. "Other markets too. And the road to Paris. And, oh, oh, oh, the palace gardens…"

Bog smiled down at me. "Most definitely the palace gardens."

Fabiola patted my head. "I'll pull some strings. The royal gardener's late wife was a dear friend. Grumps can spend eternity among the King's most precious roses."

"And his wildflowers. Don't forget the King's wildflowers," I said, purring with joy.

"Then it's a yes?" With a chorus of loud meows, Penelope, Auguste and I bobbed our heads. "Good," Fabiola replied. "He'll be safe with me until we make the arrangements." Bog lifted the cashmere bundle into the trunk.

Rex agreed to ride with us to Fabiola's apartment but declined the dinner invitation. He had "business," to attend to, something involving his rescue work.

"Aren't you afraid to be seen with us?" I asked. "We might spoil your tough-dog image."

He shrugged. "After all we've been through? Non-mixing rules seem silly. Never been prouder to be seen with cats. Aiding animals is a stronger bond than pack membership."

I cocked my head. "Sweet."

"*Sweet*? It's no such thing. Nobody calls ole Rexy boy sweet and gets away with it."

"Well, you can still call me Fluffy if you want."

His paw smack nearly knocked me over. "Nah! I'll call you Fluff. But if I slip, consider it a term of endearment. Deal?"

"Deal!"

Before jumping into the car, the furry among us shook the rain from our coats. The short drive gave us a chance to catch up. Tapping into his intuition, Bog translated the feline and canine languages for the humans. Because of their empathy for animals, Fabiola and Hansen seemed to understand bits of our sounds as well.

Bog turned to the backseat. "First things first, Rex. Tell us about Saint Michel."

The shepherd howled with delight. "Cops are swarmin' around like crows over a smashed squirrel. Higher up church types too. Jacques's nose deep in the litter box with both. Kept muttering about swarms of rats, packs of wolves, legions of pike-wielding old ladies, and a furry lady. Until they put cuffs on him, he whacked his crotch so hard I thought he'd neuter himself."

Penelope giggled. "And Benny and Clyde?"

"First sounds of police, they scurried into the wall." His bursts of laughter made him hiccup his words. "B...but n...not until they m... made good ole J...Jacques as m...mad as a rabid b...bat."

Fabiola scoffed. "Lunacy is much too lenient a punishment for the scoundrel. Better he endures the eternal torment of lucidity. Next visit to Saint Michel, that's what I'll do. Yes, I'll light a bonfire of candles beseeching our Lady for that very outcome."

With that much candlepower working against him, Father Jacques, I figured, was toast.

Auguste spoke from Bog's lap. "And Max? Last saw him in front of the rectory. Pouted like a hurt puppy when he couldn't go with us for a car ride."

Bog and Rex shared what they knew. After witnessing our abduction, Max took off to search for his half-brother. He ran only two streets when he collided with Rex. "We trotted back together," Rex said. "Hoped to learn where the traffickers took you." When they reached the rectory, the ambulance carrying Pierre's body had just pulled away. Handcuffed, Jean swore in Polish at a defiant Cook who police questioned but didn't detain. Swearing she wasn't involved in Pierre's shady dealings, she shouted, 'I'm not even a practicing

Catholic.' She announced her intent to testify against her husband, which prompted more curses from Jean.

"Feral humans at their worst," Rex added. "Max and I were about to rummage through the rectory when Bog popped up."

"What happened to Max?" Penelope asked.

Rex sighed. "Stayed with Cook. Says she's good to him. Great chef too. Keeps his water bowl full. Feeds him like clockwork. Couldn't argue with that. Rain didn't help matters. Dry, warm mattress versus camp's cold, soggy ground. You do the math."

"Dogs!" I exclaimed. "Domestication turns them into softies."

"Now, now," Bog said. "You might find yourself enjoying domesticity someday."

My eyes widened. I'd forgotten his wish to adopt me. I shook the thought from my head. Until my family was found, I wasn't going anywhere.

<hr />

Unlike the rectory's formal opulence, the spacious, high-ceilinged rooms of Fabiola's home were warm and welcoming. The guestroom in which Bog placed Grumps' body was as posh as any palace. The main parlor was painted yellow. Landscapes, portraits, and tapestries to tempt any feline claw adorned the walls. In front of a bow window, a polished table displayed antique-framed photos. Penelope eagerly pointed out travel photos of Fabiola and her late husband. Responding to my gasps of terror, she assured me that I needn't fear being squashed under the huge, limb-shattering feet of the pictured elephants, giraffes, or camels. "As long as you stay in Brussels with me," she added with a wink.

Upon seeing a photo of her late owner, Penelope teared up. But she grinned when she glanced to the table beside Fabiola's reading chair. I jumped up for a closer look. In the picture, Fabiola wore a fancy, frilly dress, dangling pearls, and a feather hat to entertain the surliest of felines. She sat with Penelope and Odysseus at a table set for a fancy tea. Behind cream-filled saucers, the Siamese siblings wore white-froth frowns and glared at the camera.

Ushering us into her dining room, Fabiola served up a scrumptious dinner of salmon and roast chicken. After licking our plates clean, we retired to the parlor. Auguste and I leaped from table to table. Plush carpets cushioned any falls. With Penelope curled up in her lap, Fabiola giggled at our antics. Her laughter grew louder with each successive sip of blackberry brandy. The domestic scene of love, affection, and camaraderie gave us a temporary respite from tragedy. Soft, satin cushions beckoned us for naps.

Human voices roused me from sleep. I cracked open my eyes as Hansen finished a phone call.

"Good news," he said. "We may have located your wife and daughter."

Bog jumped to his feet, nearly spilling Auguste to the floor. "I must go to them."

"I understand your exuberance, but it's not possible. Not tonight anyway. We believe they're in eastern Belgium, just this side of the German border. Once we confirm their identities and precise location, I'll personally facilitate a reunion."

"B…but I can't just sit here and do nothing."

"You have our word," Fabiola said. "We'll help when the time is right. Be patient a bit longer. First thing tomorrow, we'll head to Place Louise for some new clothes. You wouldn't want your wife thinking you've become a priest."

Reminded of his clerical attire, Bog chuckled. "You're right. There's also the cats' families to consider." He turned to Hansen. "Can't thank you enough. How did you get involved?" Hansen explained that when

Fabiola first contacted him and described our plight, she asked him to reach out to refugee assistance organizations.

"I'm expecting another call," Hansen added. "A reliable lead or so I'm told. They'll call my mobile or Fabiola's landline. Try not to get your hopes up. Could turn out to be bad information or worse, a con—"

The ringing phone on the reading table interrupted him. All of us jumped. Fabiola motioned to Hansen to answer. Given the late hour, the call obviously was the one he expected. From his exuberance, we knew it was good news. Looking on, Bog beamed with joy.

Hansen spoke into the phone, "They're with you now? Both of them? …Well of course, I'm sure he's anxious to speak to—"

Grabbing the phone, Bog practically bellowed into the receiver. Fabiola led Hansen to another room to give Bog privacy. Ever curious, we three cats lingered. Bog's expression and demeanor changed. He looked confused, angry, frightened. "Yes, I'm alone. Why?…You scoundrel…Put my wife on the phone. I need to hear her voice." He pressed the receiver to his ear; his face filled with anguish. "My dearest. Are you…Honey?…You devil. If you touch a single hair on their heads, I'll hunt you down…Yes, I understand. Thirty minutes." He stood in the middle of the room staring glassy-eyed at the phone in his hand.

Glaring at him, we begged for an explanation. Heaving a sigh, his hand squeezed his reddening forehead. His mind seemed to travel to another place before his gaze returned to his audience of three eager-eyed cats. "Ivanovich has my family. Guessing he's got yours too although he didn't say so. Wants to meet tonight. Has a deal."

Penelope stammered. "Y…you shouldn't g…go. He's d… dangerous."

"No choice. Not a word to anyone." He nodded to the other room. "Our families' lives are at stake." He grabbed the black overcoat and hurried out. Scurrying behind him, Auguste left the door ajar.

Penelope turned to me. "I know, dearest Fluff."

"*Oui, ma chérie.* I've no choice either." After kissing her head, I bolted out the door.

Chapter 28

Rendezvous

A single butt of my head opened the building's unlatched front door. I yowled up and down Rue Américaine for my brother. Frenzied yelps of a high-strung poodle and seductive caterwauls from invisible felines, however, were my only replies. A chubby rat, not one I recognized, emerged from the shadows to gnaw on a refuse bag. When we made eye contact, he darted away. Because the rendezvous point with Ivanovich was unknown to me, I had to catch my companions. But urgency must have quickened their steps. I caught only a fleeting glimpse of a ringed tail at the top of the street before it disappeared. I ran to the corner. At that late hour, Chaussée de Charleroi was quiet. There were few automobiles and the trams that traversed the center of the roadway were nearly empty.

Trams!

Bog and Auguste would surely hop a tram. But would they travel toward Place Stéphanie and central Brussels, or in the opposite direction toward Uccle? My street-level knowledge was limited. However, Grumps' adventure yarns had given me a general understanding of the capital's layout. "Leave details and minutiae to mapmakers and engineers," he said. "Let imagination and instinct guide you. Wandering and wonderment are art, not science."

The territory was too vast to cover on paw. I had to catch a tram, the right tram, or I'd miss this adventure, the vital rescue of family.

Was I too late? Had my companions already boarded? The nearest stop was in the direction taken by the fleeing tail I observed. A tram passed. Standing on my hind legs, I tried to peer inside but I was too short. Lowering my head, I hurried toward the stop. Dodging the few pedestrians in my path, I bolted blindly across intersections. In the center of the roadway on a dimly lit platform, two people waited. From that distance, either figure could have been Bog. Whether Auguste sat at their feet, I couldn't yet tell. I charged forward. Another tram passed, this one heading into the city center. Stopping at the station, it obscured my view. Did the people board? Could I hop on before it pulled away? Adrenaline fueled my sprint. I darted off the curb. A car horn blared and its brakes screeched, propelling me backward onto the sidewalk. As I tumbled to the ground, Pierre's untidy end flashed in my head.

The near-collision must have distracted the tram operator; the train idled in the station. I scurried onto the platform. Empty! Had Bog boarded? I had only a split second to decide. Heaving an anguished sigh, I prepared to spring aboard when a loud meow stopped me.

"No, Fluff!"

As the tram doors closed in my face, I turned toward the voice. Auguste stood on the sidewalk. He waited for a passing automobile before joining me on the platform. "And where did you think you were going?"

"T…to j…join you. Least I thought that's what I was doing. B… Bog. Why did you let him get on without you?"

Disappointment blotted Auguste's face. "He wasn't on that tram. He's heading that way." My brother nodded up Avenue Brugmann.

My whiskers twitched. "I don't understand. You ran after him. Did you miss the tram? Did the driver throw you off?"

He looked embarrassed. "Bog didn't want me to go with him."

My head shot up. "That can't be. After all you've been through together."

He shrugged. "Don't know what to tell you."

I pulled a face. "You're a cat. Sly, slinky, stealthy. Why didn't you sneak on board?"

His shoulders drooped. He lowered his head hiding tears that welled in his eyes. "Bog lifted me into his arms. I thought he was trying to hide me from the driver. When the doors started to close, he kissed my head, dropped me onto the platform, and jumped aboard. I stared after him until the tram disappeared." He patted his damp eyes. "Decided to head back to Fabiola's when I heard the commotion. I turned and *voilà*, there you were."

I nuzzled him. "Sorry, brother. I'm sure he had his reasons."

"He mentioned that Ivanovich said, no cops or cats."

"I'm sure he was thinking about your safety, too." Although I chose my words to console Auguste, Bog's actions did arouse my suspicions. He should have understood our need to be involved. The lives of our loved ones were also at stake.

Auguste sighed. "You're right. I'm probably overreacting. Bog hasn't let us down."

Not yet! I thought but left unspoken. *Wouldn't be the first human to abandon a furry companion.* "Got any clue where he's gone? Where he's meeting Ivanovich?"

He nodded. "Sure. Asked me if this tram went to Uccle."

I pawed the pavement. "Pity you don't know where in Uccle."

He flinched. "I most certainly do. Helden-Héros stop. Ivanovich is waiting for him off Avenue De Fré…at a bistro. I gave him directions. Before he abandoned me."

A grin swept over my face. I'd nearly forgotten that Auguste's early search for our family made him a near expert on Brussels. I whacked the side of his head. "Dear, glorious brother and cat about town, you're brilliant. We're back in business." I gazed up the road. "Here comes the next tram. Time to act like the cunning and clever cats we are. *Allons, mon frère!* Let's prowl!"

After eluding the tram driver, a game of cat and mouse where we were the mice, Auguste and I alighted in Uccle. The area had a different feel from Saint-Gilles. Farther from the city center, the night was darker and the air considerably fresher. Streets and sidewalks were litter free. My twitching nose didn't detect the mildest hint of kebabs, frites, hamburgers, or stale urine. Apartment blocks and homes were fancier, larger, and spread out. And around us, an abundance of greenery—trees, shrubs, manicured grass. A comfortable place for humans and their pets. Less so for strays in need of food, shelter, and companionship. From the safety of tree tops, uppity birds could tease hungry felines. The few vermin we saw were snobbish and thin. Too lean, bony, and surly to be worthy of a chase and chomp.

"Let's try over there," Auguste said. "That is if you're finished soaking in the sights. I swear, every place we go your eyes bug out like a German tourist." He nudged me with a playful headbutt. I followed his gaze to a restaurant about a hundred feet away. Other than a late-night convenience store ablaze in fluorescent light, the smart one-story bistro was the only place open. As an elegant couple exited, the white-haired man held the door for two blondes in very high heels who entered.

I turned to Auguste. "Promising. Looked like a poodle in one of those purses."

He groaned. "Wipe that grin off your face. Pets are one thing. Petite puppies especially. But cats? Street cats? Different breed altogether. Guessing we're each *cattus non gratis*."

"Huh?"

"Unwelcome, little brother."

I swatted the air with my paw. "Pshaw! We'll find a way in. Felines always do. Betting the kitchen is our magic door. Follow me, big brother."

An apron-clad employee sneaking a cigarette was our entry ticket. Puffing away and engrossed by his phone, he didn't see us scoot beneath his shower of ash. Staff inside the chaotic kitchen paid us no heed. They bristled under the yoke of the head chef, Russian by her accent, broad physique, brusque demeanor, and combat boots. I gazed, wide-eyed, to the plating station.

Succulent aromas of roasted meats, grilled fish, and fresh seafood nearly made me swoon.

Auguste nudged my backside. "You can't possibly be hungry after Fabiola's feast." His logic escaped me. I rolled my eyes but kept my catty retort to myself. Sometimes, he made me wonder if he were feline at all.

A swinging door led from the kitchen into the dining room. After nearly getting smacked in our pusses, Auguste and I pushed our way into the dining area. For two cats on the prowl, the ambience was ideal. Thick carpeting and soft music muffled our pattering paws while candlelight cast the dining room in shadows. The bar area was even more dimly lit.

Tables set close together and long white tablecloths provided cover as we scouted for Bog. Dodging dropped napkins, silverware, and dinner rolls as well as lethal heels, we circled the room. Except for snarls from the pampered poodle dining on filet amèricain, we snooped undetected. Voices spoke French, Flemish, and English, but Russian was dominant.

"Completely forgot," Auguste whispered, "the Russian Embassy is near."

"No wonder Ivanovich picked this place. Hope it's not a trap."

What did he want with Bog? Surely, a Russian businessman operating on the fringes of the law considered refugees and strays expendable. Several of his minions were already arrested or dead.

Police were on his trail. Why didn't he slip under the radar and head back to Moscow?

Our front paws froze in mid-step. From inside the bar, Bog and Ivanovich spoke in heavily accented English. Creeping toward their voices, we ducked under an unoccupied table. Two loud robust women at the next table threatened our reconnaissance. Timely delivery of cake slathered in whipped cream, however, hushed them. We hoped to hear Ivanovich's plan before they inhaled the entire dessert.

"You want me to do what?" Bog's tone was a mix of confusion and anger.

"Everything I tell you to do, exactly how I tell you to do it."

"And if I refuse? Or go to the police?"

"Haven't you ever seen a spy thriller?" Ivanovich's laugh made my tail puff. "Can't believe you're making me say it. You'll never see your beautiful wife and adorable little girl again."

"If I do as you say, you'll let them go?"

"Simple, yes?" Ivanovich slid a piece of paper across the table. "The address where we'll send your wife and daughter. After, of course, you do what we ask."

Auguste and I looked at each other. We didn't have to speak to understand what the other was thinking. What nasty business did he want Bog to do? Could Ivanovich be trusted? More importantly, what about our loved ones?

As if reading our minds, Bog spoke. "And the cats?"

"Cats?"

"Snatched from the van in Saint-Gilles."

Ivanovich yawned. "You sure you won't join me in a bit of vodka? It's the perfect—"

"You grabbed them. No one else would have..."

"Suit yourself," Ivanovich replied, downing the contents of the glass. "Then again, we both know you can't hold your liquor. Why concern yourself with those annoying cats? Isn't *your* family the priority?"

"Yes, but..."

Ivanovich held up his hand. "Stop! At exactly midnight, a car will plunge into the Vergotedok. An anonymous tip will send authorities to the canal where they'll fish out the Audi. Inside they'll find a body. IDs will tag him as, yours truly, the most-wanted and reviled Ivan the Terrible. You simply swear he's the man you knew as Ivanovich."

"Who is the dead man?"

"Tourist from Minsk whose great misfortune was picking Brussels for a holiday. Dead ringer for me. All inconsequential details."

"Nothing inconsequential about it. He's a human being. Nothing inconsequential about the hundreds of innocent animals you've also sent to their deaths. I want those four cats."

"*Was*. He *was* a human being. As for the animals you speak of, innocent or not, it's simply nature's way. Sucks to be the jungle's lowly beast. Would you rather we kept your daughter? Of course not. Forget the cats. You and your little family will live happily ever."

Bog seethed. "And you escape justice."

Ivanovich scoffed. "Justice? Quaint fairy-tale dreamed up to dupe the masses. The horde believes bad acts have consequences. Keeps everyone in line, yes? Like religion. Why do the rich and powerful play by a different set of rules? Because we can. Who do you think sets the damn rules?"

Bog shook his head. "Then you'll resume trafficking animals?"

Ivanovich shrugged. "Until there's no more money in it." He raised a glass of vodka. "Do we have a deal?"

"You leave me no choice."

"Don't even think of double crossing me. Making people disappear is one of our guilty pleasures. Think Minsk."

"I beg you, release those cats. Don't send them to Moscow."

"But they're not going to Moscow. Not anymore. You see, to ensure that the idiots on the police force connect the dots, your feline friends will be found in the car with the dead body. The smoking gun so to speak."

"You'll kill them?"

"Depends on their lungs. Perhaps the police will fish them out on time. Maybe I can poach them again. Wouldn't that be rich?"

"You bastard." Bog reached across the table. Two guys sitting on barstools hustled to Ivanovich's side. One patted the bulge in his suit, implying he was armed.

Ivanovich smiled. "Pleasure seeing you again, Mr. Bog. Time for you to go. Get a good night's sleep. Big day tomorrow. I suggest you remember my Embassy friends. They'll be keeping an eye on you and your family."

The guy with the concealed gun escorted Bog from the restaurant. "He won't be a problem," Ivanovich said to the man who remained. "Saw it in his eyes. He'll put family first."

The man smirked. "They always do."

"Now, get to Hotel Sevastopol. Wait for my signal tomorrow... about the wife and daughter." After downing a shot of vodka, the man left. A ghastly sneer swept across Ivanovich's face. He lifted a glass. "Come midnight, Ivan the Terrible will forever rest in peace."

Chapter 29

Cats As Cats Can

"My stomach's doing summersaults and he eats like a vulture," I said with a huff.

Auguste scoffed. "Vodka must flow through his veins."

Hidden by the tablecloth, my brother and I observed Ivanovich. In a matter of minutes, the villain scarfed down a half-dozen blini topped with fish eggs, slurped a bowl of beet soup dolloped with sour cream, and devoured a pile of pork cutlets and a mound of mashed potatoes smothered with mushrooms. Shaking my head with disgust and just a smidgen of envy, I turned to Auguste. "We need to go."

He groaned. "We're on our own, li'l brother. No human savior this time."

I knew he meant Bog. Although we witnessed our friend demand our family's return, in the end, he succumbed to Ivanovich's pressure. Can't say I blamed him. Nor, if he were brutally honest, could Auguste. Strays and street people had no power and few choices. What was anyone capable of doing if a loved one's life were at stake? Bog didn't owe us anything. He had his family to save; we had ours. Simply nature's way.

I poked my nose and whiskers out from our hiding place when I froze. The head chef marched toward our table, halting abruptly before Ivanovich. Her combat boots nearly crushed my twice-notched tail. "I trust the meal was to your liking."

He grunted in reply. "Excellent, Irina. Exactly like my dear mother used to make. Warms my heart to think that our Minsk friend got a taste of your culinary genius. Couldn't wish for a better last meal. Pity he didn't know it at the time. Nobody masks poison as creatively as you." His laugh made my fur crawl. "By the way, is your cellar finished?"

"To your exact specifications, Uncle."

"Good. We'll resume operations soon. Once the dust settles, of course." He sighed. "I swear, your mother is more Russian bear than Flemish fox. Never stops badgering me. Won't be surprised if Claus sends me to an early grave as she did my brother."

The chef's laugh sounded stilted, automated. She bowed her head. "Excuse me, we're about to close." Trudging away, she marshaled what few customers remained toward the exit.

Auguste and I stared at each other. The news that Claus was Ivanovich's sister-in-law made our jaws drop. We started to slink away when a ringing mobile stopped us. More badgering from Claus? Speaking into the phone, Ivanovich peppered his words with laughter. "My signature bait and switch. Once he makes the positive ID, he'll be of no further use. Definitely something more interesting than a car accident. The wife and daughter? Human trafficking isn't all that different from trafficking animals. More lucrative, too. What's that, horizontal diversification? Ha. Very clever." His sinister laugh, again, caused my tail to puff.

Auguste cringed. "Poor Bog. We must warn him."

I rolled my eyes. Our feline family came first; my brother's misplaced loyalty, second. I nudged him. "We gotta get outta here."

Neither of us had any desire to be the cellar's first customers. We started moving toward the kitchen when the lights brightened. A cleaning crew appeared armed with a vacuum, which prompted us to bolt toward the swinging door. Although savory morsels littered the kitchen floor, fears of poison curbed my appetite.

Emerging into the street, we had hope, however slim, of finding Bog. If he knew the details of Ivanovich's evil scheme, he might join forces with us again. However, sidewalks in front of the darkened restaurant were deserted except for a few straggling diners saying their good-byes. Bog and the dark-suited henchmen were gone.

As we headed to the tram platform, we spotted Ivanovich strolling up Avenue De Fré. When he turned into the sprawling grounds of the Russian embassy, my inner tiger filled my head with wild, untamed images. I pictured Auguste and me. Two stealth cats, lurking in dense shrubbery, tracking our unsuspecting prey, choosing the moment to pounce. We rip into him with our claws and teeth. The Russian was lucky that Brussels transport didn't respect the laws of the jungle. We had to catch a tram into the city center before it stopped operating for the night.

⸺ ◦《◉》◦ ⸺

Huddling under a passenger seat in the tram's last row, Auguste and I quibbled over our next steps. As one plan came together a new detail unraveled it. Whether a consequence of sibling rivalry or merely because we were stubborn felines, we struggled to reach agreement.

"Too many tasks and too much ground to cover," I said, countering Auguste's preference for going straight to the canal. "We need help."

He sighed. "You're right. And Penelope should know about the threat to her brother. Prepares her for the worst." I understood the unspoken message in his downcast expression. We too, should prepare ourselves for tragedy. I tried to shake the dark thoughts from my head.

Urgency forced consensus. Reconciled to our scheme, we hopped off the tram where we first boarded earlier that night—the platform nearest Fabiola's flat. At that late hour her street was quiet; windows of its many townhouses mostly dark. Yappy dogs were asleep and amorous felines had found willing partners or turned their attentions to vermin. Nearing Fabiola's door, we hopped over a trail of trash spilling from the same refuse bag I observed earlier. Tiny teeth marks were visible on the torn plastic.

An image of the timid rat I'd scared away brought a smile to my face. The chubby fellow hadn't given up. His determination stirred my confidence. Although strays and street creatures didn't enjoy power, influence, or prestige, we did possess grit, tenacity, and perseverance. Surrender wasn't an option. With my chin held high, I turned to Auguste. "No surrender for us, dear brother. We'll save our family. I know it."

His sullen expression reflected doubt.

———◦((◦))◦———

"Wherever did you run off to? We thought we lost—" Darting into the middle of the living room, our high-pitched cries interrupted Fabiola. With her hand still on the doorknob, she stared into our faces. "You need our help…now. That's it, isn't it?"

Before we could reply, Penelope bowled us over with an exuberant greeting. "Did you find Odysseus? Your family? Where's Bog? You see Ivanovich? Anybody hurt? You're not hurt, are you?"

I nuzzled her head. "*S'il vous plait, ma chérie.* Calm yourself. We'll tell you everything but we don't have much time. Our loved ones are in grave danger." As I spoke the antique clock on Fabiola's mantle chimed eleven times.

"Midnight!" Auguste bellowed, "We must get to the canal by midnight."

The terror reflected in Penelope's face pained me. "We need the humans' help, *ma chérie.*"

"And Bog," Auguste added. "We need to find him. He's in great danger."

Hansen and Fabiola grabbed their coats. They moved with urgency filling Auguste and me with surprise and confusion. "Remarkable," Penelope said. "Keen intuition. Almost as good as Bog. Must have to do with their love of animals."

Whatever the explanation, I welcomed their assistance. As Hansen fiddled with his phone, Fabiola dropped a bag of salmon treats and several hatpins into her handbag. Her furtive wink made us her silent accomplices. "Let's roll," she said, ushering us into the hall. Exchanging phone for key fob, Hansen waved the device in the air.

"We should notify the police," Fabiola added as she locked her front door.

"I'll phone from the car," Hansen replied as he led our entourage down the stairs.

We piled into the sleek Jaguar when a familiar figure trotted up Rue Américaine. Penelope and I rushed to greet Rex, his head high and his tail wagging.

I rubbed against his lowered snout. "We're glad to see you."

Auguste shouted from the car window, "You seen Bog?"

Rex shook his head. "Not since earlier tonight, when I left you right here. What's happened?"

Penelope sashayed through his legs. "We need your help."

"We need your help, *again*," Rex replied, lifting his nose into the air. "Felines in need of canine assistance. Why doesn't that surprise me?"

Auguste yowled, "Don't dilly-dally. We got to get to the other side of the city."

I nudged Penelope. "He's right. Get in the car. I'll explain everything to Rex. Won't be but a second."

The shepherd's head tilted from side to side as he listened to my briefing and request. "Got it! You can count on ole Rex." He began to dart away but stopped. He looked back at me and offered an affectionate wink. "Dogs are loyal to a fault, Fluffy."

As he pulled his car from the curb, Hansen instructed Fabiola to pull a map from the glove box. No sooner had she unfolded it than Auguste planted his nose on the canal, the exact spot where our loved ones soon would meet their ends. My twelve staccato meows informed them of the midnight deadline. The humans may not have comprehended everything, but what they did was sufficient. They understood, for example, that we were disappointed in Bog.

"Don't judge your friend too harshly," Hansen said. "Ivanovich is ruthless. Once he gets what he wants, he'll simply make Bog and his family disappear. Bog's seen him. The fact that he can identify the elusive Russian's face sealed his fate."

"Bog's not alone," Fabiola said. "We can identify Ivanovich also. Connect him to these heinous crimes."

Hansen turned to her, a smirk on his face. "*We?*"

"Well, *they*," she replied, nodding to the back seat. "The cats... Oh! I see your point."

Hansen snickered. "They'll lock us both away."

As the car wove through traffic along the inner Ring Road, Hansen telephoned a contact in the police department. Speaking fast, he requested immediate assistance at the Vergotedok. That section of the canal wasn't vast, but circumstances allowed no room for error.

Penelope pawed Hansen's head. "We there yet?"

I brushed my paw through his hair. "How much longer?" I dropped my nose over the seat toward Fabiola's purse. "Treats! What are you saving them for?"

Penelope mewled. "I need to use the litter box."

Leaping into the front seat, Auguste nudged Hansen's forearm. "Is this a Jaguar or a mule? Drive faster. It's past 11:30."

Hansen elbowed him. "I don't want to get us all killed. I'm sure you can see the irony."

Fabiola turned toward Hansen, a look of concern on her face. "You do know where you're going, don't you, dear?"

"Of course."

Auguste placed his nose against the windshield. "What the... Why'd you exit the Ring Road? It's the fastest route." To make his point, he traced the Ring Road on the map in Fabiola's lap with his paw.

"Shortcut," Hansen snapped in reply.

Auguste hissed loudly. "Big mistake."

Agitated, Penelope and I crowded into the front seat. Our meows added to the growing chorus of complaints. Hansen seethed. His face turned red; the vein at his temple throbbed. "I wish everyone would sit down, be quiet, and let me drive. Shall I pullover, stop the car? I'll do it. I'm warning you." He glanced at Fabiola, a silent plea for help.

Picking up Penelope, Fabiola whispered into her ear. Nodding her understanding, Penelope jumped into the back seat. "Fluff, Auguste, come back here."

I complied without hesitation. Auguste, however, required firmer coaxing including a nudge to his backside. Penelope and I wedged him between us as Fabiola showered us with salmon treats. Even with his mouth full, Auguste managed to mumble his displeasure with Hansen's slow and meandering driving.

In addition to bribing us with treats, Fabiola engaged us in small talk—a diversionary tactic to keep us occupied and out of, quite literally, Hansen's hair. "I'm elated," she said. "We'll save your families and put that villain out of business and in prison."

"He's dangerous," Hansen replied. "Shudder to think how many poor animals he's killed. Who knows what other vile schemes he's involved with? Human trafficking isn't all that different from trafficking animals. More lucrative too. Bet he's mastered the benefits of horizontal diversification."

As he spoke, Auguste and I turned to each other. Our eyes grew to the size of saucers. The hair on our backs stood straight up. Those words! His words! *Horizontal diversification.* The exact words Ivanovich parroted during his phone call at Irina's. This was no coincidence. The co-conspirator with whom he bantered wasn't Claus or some other unknown villain. No, the person on the other end of the phone was Hansen. No angel or savior, the man at the wheel was a devil. What was he planning to do with us? How could we warn Fabiola without alerting him? How could we escape?

Distracted by this revelation, we hadn't noticed that the car had come to a complete stop. "Damn!" Hansen exclaimed, lifting his hands from the wheel. "We're lost."

Fabiola gasped. We three felines gaped out the car's windows. Hansen had navigated us down a dark, dead-end street. I turned to Auguste but even he didn't know where we were.

Hansen waved his phone in the air. "Can't get a signal and GPS doesn't recognize our location." His acting was flawless.

Fabiola fretted. "Don't worry, kitties, the police will watch the canal. Your loved ones will be fine." Turning to Hansen, she fluttered the map in his face. "We can use this. Back us out of here, dear."

"Afraid I can't do that."

She flinched. But before she could say anything, Hansen thumbed out the back window. "Another car's blocking us. We're stuck."

"We've no time for such nonsense. I'll tell the driver to move." She began opening her door but Hansen pulled her back.

"Can't let you do that."

The changing expression on her face informed us that she was processing the odd chain of events. Without our saying a word, she recognized his betrayal. "Fiend. And after all my husband did for you. Why?"

He shrugged. "Money and my life. I'm a mid-level bureaucrat with expensive tastes. Didn't want to end up like your husband. Idealists, as Ivanovich warned, die young and poor. *C'est la vie politique.*"

Auguste and I added our hisses to Fabiola's sharp rebuke. Penelope's shudder sent my gaze following hers out the back window. Two dark-suited figures brooded and smoked outside the other car, dead ringers for the guys at Irina's restaurant.

Auguste groaned. "Hansen must have called them instead of the police. Probably tracked us through his phone."

Hansen laughed in Fabiola's face. "Texted them from your flat. Don't worry. Wait won't be much longer." He pointed to the dashboard clock—11:45. "These Russians have good manners. After their smoke break, they'll take you all off my hands. Ivanovich's niece, I hear, is quite the chef."

I heaved a sigh. "Sorry, brother."

"For what?"

"You wanted to head straight to the canal. We'd have been there by now. If our family dies—"

He whacked me. "Feel better? Now get over it, li'l brother. Focus. We gotta get to the canal. No surrender, remember?"

Penelope whimpered. "But we're trapped."

"Not for long, *ma chérie*." With claws extended, I hurled myself at Hansen's head. Following my lead, the others attacked as well. He swatted at us in a mad frenzy. One blow batted Auguste to the floor. Another made Penelope wince, enraging me. We continued to pummel him. Reeking of sweat and fear, he reached for his phone. Auguste swatted it to Fabiola's feet. Penelope bit his earlobe. My scratch to his cheek drew blood. *Open the door*, I thought. *Open the damn door*. Still, with arms flailing he held his ground.

"Ow, ow! Ouch!" he screamed. "Stop, stop." His attention and hands shifted to his legs. Fabiola stabbed his thigh and calf with hatpins. Her relentless attack prompted Hansen to blare the car horn. Another hatpin volley prodded him to open the car door. He tumbled backwards onto the pavement. Blood streamed from gashes on his face and stained his tattered trousers.

"Run, my kittens, run," Fabiola shouted. She picked up the mobile phone from the floor and dialed the police. "I'll be fine."

The burst of cool night air jolted us. Jumping from the car one-by-one, we pounced on Hansen's battered head. His winces sounded like a cat's squeaky toy. Finally getting a chance to relieve herself, Penelope aimed at Hansen's face. Reacting to the chaos, the dark-suited men dashed toward us. Darting past them, we avoided their outstretched arms. "Grab them," one shouted. Leaving Hansen behind, both sprinted after us, their leather-soled shoes clicking over the pavement.

Panting heavily, I turned to Auguste. "Where are we?"

"No clue. Keep running. Wait, wait. Up there." Before us bathed in light, a gilt angel stood atop a tall spire. "The Town Hall in the Grand Place," he shouted in jubilation. "The gold statue is Michael the Archangel slaying a demon."

"And so shall we slay a demon, dear brother, so shall we."

"I can get us to the canal from here," he added.

Auguste led us over damp cobble-stones. We ran so fast that my chest hurt. My two companions looked winded. Still, we darted ahead. The determination of three small cats on a life and death mission proved too much for our human pursuers. The race was, now, only with the clock. My heart thumped so loudly that I barely heard the tolling bells.

Auguste gasped. "Midnight!"

Penelope whimpered. "We're too late. We're too late."

"Keep running," I shouted, reminded of the chubby, intrepid rat. "Don't give up."

After several more twists and turns and agonizing minutes, we reached the canal. The air carried the chill and odor of stale water. Our efforts were in vain. We were too late. Flooded with despair, we plodded toward the embankment. The canal was blacker than the night sky and stiller than death itself. Sitting side-by-side, the three of us gazed into the dark void. The watery tomb held our loved ones. Words and meows escaped us.

Penelope broke the silence. "Over there! Pretty blue lights."

On a street leading to the canal, a paneled truck pulled forward revealing a large police presence. Several uniformed officers stood around a dark sedan. Something else caught my attention. A figure in dark clothing. Tall and burly, the man faced away from us.

My heart raced again. "Could it be?"

Auguste was on his feet. "Follow me."

Renewed hope fueled our sprint toward the officers and mystery man pelted by strobes of blue light. We neared the outer edge of the scene. The man turned, his face battered, bloody, unrecognizable. We inched forward. My heart sank. It wasn't Bog. Instead, I recognized one of the henchmen from the restaurant. Although small consolation, our loved ones' murderer had been apprehended. But how?

"Auguste, Fluff, Penelope."

Startled by the familiar voice, we turned. Bog! He was also bruised and bloodied but not nearly as battered as the man in custody. We dashed forward. When we neared, he opened the back door of a police vehicle.

"What the... Is it your cruel intent to freeze us to death? Such incivility. Will my ordeal never end?"

Penelope gasped. "Odysseus!"

My neck stiffened; my eyes widened. On the bench seat beside Odysseus were three sleeping cats—a clump of white and black fur. At long last, Auguste and I had been reunited with Mama Vanille, Licorice, and Lily.

Chapter 30
End of a Cat Tale

"Whoa, boys. Not so fast."
Bristling at Bog's command, Auguste and I looked past his raised palm for an explanation. Afterall, he allowed a squealing Penelope to nuzzle, paw, and lick her brother to the point of torment. So much so that Odysseus had to pry himself free. Jumping from the police car, he plopped onto the ground to fluff his fur.

"Your family's been through a lot," Bog said. "No telling how long they were in that crate. They're dehydrated, weak."

Craning my neck around his crouched figure, I peered into the backseat. "B...but, are they okay? Are they going to die?"

"You're a vet. Can't you do anything?" Auguste's expression and tone had attitude.

Bog's dark eyes sparked with kindness. He attempted to pat the top of our heads but we backed away. "They're alive. That's the good news. Cleaned them the best I could. They'll need medicated baths. Nourishment and fresh air too. We'll know more once they've been to the clinic. For now, take it slow."

I yowled. "Can we see them? Get closer?"

Bog snatched me up in his arms. "Course you can. That I can do. But one at a time. You're next," he added with a smile for Auguste. Hoisting me into the car, Bog lowered me near my mother. "Gentle," he whispered, "gentle."

Although droopy and glazed, Mama's eyes seemed to flicker with recognition despite my dandelion-yellow color. I dropped my nose into her fur. A soft whimper escaped my mouth. Mama Vanille's familiar purr and scent transported me back in time. I recalled the cardboard box, our humble but cozy home where she made us feel safe, secure, and loved. And although our father absconded when she needed him most, the stories she shared about him spoke only of his bravery and goodness. I licked her cheek. "Rest well, dear mother. Your little Fluff loves you."

Her eyes closed; her breathing slowed. I choked back tears. Licorice and Lily lifted their heads. They appeared weak like Mama but not nearly as fragile. I pawed their heads uncertain if they remembered me. "Rest dear brother. Sleep sweet sister. You're safe."

Before Bog could lift Auguste into the car, a police detective waded into our midst, speaking into a mobile phone. His rolled eyes, clenched teeth, and pulled face signaled frustration with the person on the other end. "*Oui, Madame...oui,* several cats. No, can't say with certainty they're the ones you ask about... *Non, Madame Severns, non.* Can't very well ask them, can I?"

Penelope mewled. "Fabiola. That's Fabiola on the phone."

Taking her outburst as our cue, the rest of us raised a chorus of meows. The detective lowered the phone nearer our mouths. Returning the device to his face, he tried to ask questions but Fabiola kept interrupting. He huffed. "*Oui, Madame,* two tabby cats...yes, yes, one beautiful Siamese and... *oui, oui,* a chubby one with much, as you say, catitude." Gazing down to a bristling Odysseus, the man chuckled. "*Oui,* they're all here. And as you heard for yourself, they're *bien, madame, très bien* if not a bit offkey."

Bog waved his hand in the man's face. "I know Madame Severns. May I speak to her?"

Four pairs of feline ears rotated toward the conversation but Bog turned his back. Returning the phone to the detective, he crouched down. Mustering a closed-mouth smile, he looked into our eyes.

"Fabiola's fine. A little ruffled but nothing, she said, that a hair stylist, manicurist, and snifter of blackberry brandy can't remedy."

Odysseus purred. "*Mon dieu*, how I idolize that woman. Precisely how I feel after being trapped in that car's squalid trunk. We shall book the spa *ensemble*, together."

Bog snickered. "She sends her love."

"And Hansen?" I asked.

"She told me all about the devil. He was arrested. Taken to the hospital. She mentioned your courage, too." I spotted awe and admiration in his face. "Anxious to hear details. Told her we'll come to her flat. No need to venture out at this hour."

After allowing Auguste to see our family, Bog set him on the ground next to the rest of us felines. My brother's feelings wavered between anger and admiration. Would he forgive, forget, and seek his designated human's lap again? Or would he pee in his shoe?

Curious to know everything that happened, we stared up wide-eyed and anxious at Bog. I remained suspicious. To test his loyalties, I planned to ask a series of loaded questions. I glared at him. "Did Ivanovich push the car toward the canal?"

Odysseus's ears perked. "As a matter of fact—"

I swatted him so hard that he fell over. "Gee whiskers! Sorry, Odie. Let Bog answer, okay?"

As Penelope helped her brother to his feet, Auguste groaned. "No games, li'l brother. You know Ivanovich wasn't anywhere near the canal tonight. Truth be told," he said, turning to Bog. "We followed you to the restaurant. Saw and heard everything."

"And then some," I added. "And then some. Don't forget the rest of the story."

Snorts peppered Bog's chuckles. "Rascals. Why doesn't that surprise me? Were you all there?" Adopting a sheepish expression, Penelope gestured to Auguste and me. Following her extended paw, Bog met my icy glare. His grin vanished. "Oh! You heard *everything*."

"Yes, everything," I replied. "*Everything*."

He drew in a deep breath. "Explains your boys' tone. And why Fluff keeps giving me the stink eye. I can explain."

Odysseus heaved a sigh. "I wish someone would explain. Unless you'd rather me regale you with my epic tale of intrigue and woe. Guaranteed to captivate you. Only say the word."

"*No!*" we all replied in unison.

He bobbled his head from side to side. "Your loss. You'll have to wait. Read about it in my memoir. And don't expect courtesy copies either."

Bog assumed an earnest expression. "After leaving the restaurant, my conscience nagged at me. I couldn't let Ivanovich escape justice. He'd go on killing. Not only Odysseus and your family, but others. I fled my home to escape cruelty. I couldn't ask for sanctuary while turning a blind eye to brutality. I had to stop him. Otherwise, my hands would be as bloody as his."

"Sound and sensible thinking for which I'm eternally grateful," said Odysseus.

"Your family?" Penelope asked with a whimper. "What about them?"

His gaze wandered over our heads. "Had to do what was right…no matter the consequences." He sighed. "Fast forward to the restaurant. Ivanovich was so full of himself. Bragged about his scheme. Gave the exact time and location. I intended to stop them from sinking the car into the canal." He pointed to his bloody face. "Got this trying to get away from his henchman. Tailed me all the way here."

I gasped. "So, you saved Odysseus and our family."

He shook his head. "That was my plan. When I got here, the goon on my tail and his buddy teamed up. Knocked me out cold. But not before I bloodied them both. Sent one to the hospital, or so they tell me." He nodded to the group of plain-clothes detectives.

Odysseus gasped. "Just like an American gangster film."

Auguste pawed Bog. "If not you, then who stopped the car?"

Shifting his gaze, Bog stared at his feet. "Afraid I've got some bad news."

The four of us froze. My heart raced. "It's Rex. Something's happened to him."

Bog's neck stiffened. "How did you know?"

Pangs of guilt stirred within me. "Before we left Fabiola's, I asked him to help. Told him about the car and the canal. Is he..."

Bog heaved a sigh. "I'm very sorry."

Auguste meowed. "But how? What happened?"

Penelope swatted my brother. "Bog was knocked out, remember?"

Bog nodded. "But when I came round, Rex's human friends filled me in. You remember? The couple with the grooming salon." How could any of us forget the sphinxlike tuxedo cat and Rex's mysterious money pouches?

I cocked my head. "The groomers were here?"

"After you spoke to Rex," Bog said, "he ran to the salon. Shared what you told him. Asked them to call authorities before he ran off. The groomers and police came here together. In time to arrest Ivanovich's thugs. But too late to help the boys."

"Boys?" Penelope asked.

"Wouldn't you know it," he replied with an affectionate snicker. "In addition to the groomers, ole Rex recruited his brother Max."

"Both were here?" I asked. "Does that mean Max is also..."

"He'll pull through," Bog replied. "Broken leg, maybe two. Otherwise, fine. Police took away Rex's remains and Max just before you got here. Groomers went too. Same emergency clinic police are taking your family." He nodded to the car with my mama and siblings.

Responding to our persistent swats, he shared additional details. "Groomers said that when they pulled up, they saw a car rolling downhill toward the water. It gained speed. From out of nowhere, a barrel hurled into the car's path. The car hit it and veered. That's when they spotted Rex and Max. Watched in horror as the car struck both dogs. Plowed into more barrels before stopping at the edge of the canal.

"Rex and Max pushed that initial barrel," Bog added. "And that's the whole tragic story. When I came to, I told police about Ivanovich and his scheme. Including the murdered tourist from Minsk and the feline cargo they'd find in the trunk."

Auguste sighed. "Poor Rex. A true hero."

Odysseus sniffled. "Like a brother to me."

Penelope choked back tears. "A selfless animalitarian to the very end."

I recalled our last meeting. Rex running down the sidewalk, his proud snout and tail held high. His affectionate wink and parting words: 'Dogs are loyal to a fault.' Tears streaked my cheeks. "We'll never forget him. Best of the best."

"We'll make Rex an honorary cat. Yes, that's precisely what we'll do," Odysseus added.

News of our friend's death gutted us. Huddled in a mass of grieving fur, we accepted Bog's soft pets to our heads. "You boys said there was more to the story. What else did you hear after I left the restaurant?"

I turned to Auguste. His eyes were as wide as I imagined mine to be. Our family reunion and news of Rex's death had distracted us. "*Merde*! We forgot."

"After you identified the body," Auguste added, "Ivanovich planned to kill you."

I nodded. "Never intended to release your family. Said they'd be trafficked like cats."

"But not for cosmetics," Auguste added.

Bog seethed. "I'll kill him."

"We know where they're holding them. Your wife and daughter," I said.

Bog's expression shifted from surprise to joy to concern. "Where are they? Ivanovich will use them as leverage. If he doesn't know already, he'll soon learn that his plot has failed."

"And that the police caught two of his guys," Auguste added.

Bog's darting eyes suggested a mind racing with scenarios. "He knows they won't talk. They fear him more than they do the police. I'm the one he'll want to stop." Bog shuddered; fear flashed in his eyes.

"He'll send me a message. I must save my family. Where are they?"

"Hotel Sevastopol," I replied.

"Near Gare du Midi," Auguste added. "I know the very place."

With a shout, Bog summoned two detectives. He planned to plead for their help to save his wife and daughter. As we waited for the man and woman, Auguste and I shared what we also learned about Claus, Irina's toxic cooking, and the restaurant's refurbished basement. "To top it off," I said, "Ivanovich walked into the Russian embassy as if he owned the place."

The detectives' appearance halted our conversation. Bog made his case. Both seemed to listen, the woman taking notes. But neither grew agitated by the account. The man shrugged. "Afraid we can't run all over Brussels on a search and rescue mission for undocumented migrants. Especially when you won't tell us how you came by this information."

Bog pressed his temples; his complexion reddened. He couldn't risk telling them that felines had fed him the facts. They'd discount everything he said or worse, lock him up. "What about Ivanovich?" he said. "I told you he was involved. Arrest him. If you don't, he'll hurt my family."

"We'll check out your story," the woman said. "If he's inside the embassy as you say, he'll claim diplomatic immunity. We'll request an interview at his earliest convenience. We can hope he chooses to cooperate."

"B...but my family's life is in danger." He started to tell them about Irina and Claus when they cut him off. The female detective put her hand on his shoulder. "With all due respect, sir. You might want to reconsider going to the hospital. You did take several blows to the head."

The man put his hand on Bog's other shoulder. "Every reasonable allegation will be investigated. But tonight, our hands are tied."

"Mine aren't. If you won't do anything, I will. Correction, *we* will." He nodded at the four of us. "Come on, friends."

The man gripped Bog's arm. "Afraid we can't let you go, sir. There's the matter of an official statement. This is a murder investigation."

Bog bellowed, "Let me go or there'll be more murders." I worried he meant the detectives. In retrospect, maybe he did.

"Sir, please calm down," the woman said. "We haven't yet established your role in this incident. And I hoped not to mention the fact that you're in this country illegally."

Wriggling free of their clutches, Bog seethed with anger. He looked as if he might strike them.

"Wait!" I exclaimed. "Over there."

My high-pitched cry drew everyone's attention. Whether or not they understood my hearty meows, all eyes followed my extended paw. After a loud gasp, Bog ran. The detectives hustled after him. So did we felines.

Penelope called to me, "Is that…"

"Yes," I replied. "Bog's wife and daughter. Least I assume so."

Odysseus panted as he tried to keep up. "A miracle. That's what it is, a miracle. Those candles and marble statues back at Saint Michel do make wishes come true."

"But how?" asked Auguste, running at my side.

"That's how." I nodded ahead. Accompanying the woman and girl was a parade of familiar faces: Peter and Sarah, my first human friends at camp; Lucinda and Lucky from the market circuit; and Rex's brother Brutus and the rest of the DeVilles. Scurrying to keep up were the indomitable rat brothers, Benny and Clyde. There were unfamiliar faces too, people I figured were part of Rex's animal rescue network. Together, they must have stormed the hotel to free Bog's family.

Auguste turned to me. "Don't tell me, li'l brother…"

I grinned. "Yup, ole Rex."

In addition to telling him about the canal plot, I informed Rex where the traffickers were holding Bog's wife and daughter. True to his noble breed, the resourceful canine managed to shepherd a broad alliance to pull off one final, spectacular rescue.

Chapter 31

The Cat Jumped Over the Moon

"**I**'m utterly and unequivocally exhausted."

Odysseus's unsolicited lament prompted Fabiola and me to look up from our respective books: hers a thick legal volume concerning extradition and diplomatic immunity; mine, *The Adventures of Huckleberry Finn* tucked inside a dictionary. We glanced to the living room's sunniest corner where Odie had nestled onto the plush cushion of a wingback chair. Reclining on his back, the drowsy Siamese stretched his front paws over his head. He emitted a loud yawn.

"How exactly have you exerted yourself?" I asked. "Are you counting the second helping of salmon pâté, the third trip to the litter box, the fourth teacake, or your languid stroll from sofa to chair? Didn't you just awaken from your second nap of the morning."

"My third, actually. Kind of you to watch me like a hawk." His tone suggested that the hawk he had in mind was a doomed bird writhing in his clenched jaws. "You, dear Fluff, may derive euphoric satisfaction from burying your nose in dusty books all day. But such sedentary activity is better suited to the canine lifestyle. It would bore me. I must keep active. The reason why I'm such a fervent daydreamer." His declaration ended with another yawn. "See? Simply talking about my armchair adventures makes me sleepy."

"Nap well," Fabiola added. "We've a big afternoon ahead of us. The limousine arrives promptly at two." Offering a soft giggle, she winked at me before returning to her book. A true diplomat, she avoided inserting herself into our feline squabbles. The serene look on her face, her sparkling blue eyes, and a propensity to hum throughout the day made it clear to Penelope, Odysseus, and me that she was delighted to have cats under her roof again.

Mention of our big afternoon caused my heart to race. Ever since Fabiola proposed the gathering, a celebration of sorts, anticipation gripped me. Originally, she proposed a very proper and fashionable tea at the Horta Museum. Odysseus pounced on the idea. He proposed a string quartet to entertain and a menu of salmon paste sandwiches, French patisserie, scones with strawberry jam, and saucers brimming with cream. Penelope and I burst his bubble. The venue, we said, was too staid and stodgy for the eclectic mix of guests. Once we reminded her that rat brothers Benny and Clyde were among our guests, Fabiola came around to our way of thinking.

We settled on a private tent at Châtelain. The market's vendors would provide flowers, wine, and a feast of meats, fishes, cheeses, and other savories. Roast fowl from the royal family of chicken was at the top of my list. For entertainment, Fabiola engaged a small—in number and stature—band of circus musicians. "Can't stand the clowns," she said. "But the band is darling."

The prospect of a reunion with old friends excited me. It had been ages since I brushed up against their legs, jumped into their laps, or inhaled their scents. The chaotic scene at the Brussels canal was three months in the past, enough time for Penelope's and my fur to return to their natural colors. The days following that climactic night were a frenzied blur. Fabiola had little time for tummy rubs, chin scratches, or lap naps. The first several weeks were filled with trips to the clinic to visit my family and Max. Memorials for Rex and Grumps also occupied our time. We spread their ashes throughout Brussels including the palace gardens.

In addition, we fielded numerous requests for interviews with law enforcement agencies. The criminal investigation of the traffickers spanned local, federal, and international jurisdictions. Due to credibility concerns, we feline witnesses operated in the background, channeling relevant information through Bog and Fabiola. Investigators, they reported, were astonished with their amazing memories and attention to detail. Authorities were able to build strong cases against Hansen, Big Suit, and Scuffed Loafers. Prosecutors had been very close to getting Vaclav and Grabowski to flip against Ivanovich, but toxic mushrooms allowed the pair to escape justice altogether. The source of the fatal food poisoning dumbfounded police. Claus and her Saint Albert cosmetics line emerged from the scandal unscathed. Her wealth, Fabiola explained, bought influential friends. Claus' pledge of a new factory and hundreds of Belgian jobs didn't hurt. She leaned into the crisis. She spearheaded a European campaign promoting the ethical treatment of animals and launched a line of faux-fur apparel. Ivanovich vanished. Rumors circulated that he led his criminal network from Moscow and had moved from trafficking to hacking and ransomware.

Immigration officials conducted extensive interviews with Bog and his family. To assist, Fabiola hired an experienced attorney. Because of his role in breaking up the international trafficking ring, an angle that Fabiola had her friends in the media play up, Bog was hailed as a hero. The government granted the entire family asylum.

Domestic arrangements also needed to be ironed out. Fabiola made it clear that her human and furry friends were not returning to the squatters' camp. One by one, pieces fell into place. Fabiola opened her home to Penelope and Odysseus. Peter and Sarah started a fleet of food trucks and rented an apartment off the Parvis de Saint-Gilles. The grateful couple adopted Mama Vanille, Licorice, and Lily once the three were strong enough to leave the clinic. Bog and his family rented a simple flat near Gare du Midi. It came as no surprise when they adopted Auguste. Even more than I, he resembled the cat left behind when they fled their homeland. My brother boasted of being pampered beyond his humblest expectations.

The owners of the grooming salon hired Bog as a veterinarian for their rescue network. A flood of contributions in Rex's memory endowed the position. The couple said that once the trafficking business hit news outlets, donations poured in from around the world. Additional funding meant time off and an occasional smile for the inscrutable tuxedo cat. An Abyssinian and a Persian shared sentry duties, taking shifts outside the salon.

As for me, I had no shortage of adoption opportunities. Bog, Peter and Sarah, Lucinda, and even the Queen of Chicken offered me a home. Given my affection for Penelope, I accepted Fabiola's offer. In addition to heaping plates of salmon pâté, I devoured her library of books, which included an entire shelf of adventure yarns. The library also allowed me to expand my vocabulary. If I hoped to ever understand Odysseus, I needed to master three, four, and even five syllable words. Besides, something he said at the canal planted a seed. He spoke about writing his memoir. If he could do it, so could I. The human-centric literary world could benefit from a fresh feline perspective especially one rich in adventure as mine promised to be. Humans have made a royal mess of the world. They don't listen to each other. Maybe, just maybe, they will listen to cats.

⸻ «◊» ⸻

No sooner had the limo driver opened the car door than Penelope, Odysseus, and I purred with anticipation. We scampered toward the large pink and blue tent set up on the edge of Châtelain Market. Flowers, streamers, and balloons gave it a festive air. Inside, I gazed around with wide-eyed wonder. Familiar faces sat at tables topped with white linen, fine china, and crystal. Centerpieces featured wildflowers, dandelions, catnip and squeaky cat toys.

Bog and his wife looked like established Brussels residents. In the arms of their giggling daughter, Auguste purred with excitement. He grew chubbier each time I saw him. Peter and Sarah were there, doting over Mama Vanille, Licorice, and Lily. At a table to themselves, Lucky and Lucinda served Benny and Clyde. With manners of gentlemen, the rat brothers nibbled off china saucers. The groomers, tuxedo cat, and other two- and four-footed members of the animal rescue network were also in attendance. Out of respect to Rex, Fabiola extended an invitation to his brother, Brutus. The rest of the DeVilles weren't invited but showed up nonetheless. Running around the tent, they refused to sit, heel, and obey. Brutus sat with Max who looked spiffy in his police vest. After his heroics at the canal, Brussels Police recruited him for their elite K-9 patrol. He jumped at the opportunity since he no longer had a home. Fearing Ivanovich and his toxic niece, Cook absconded to an undisclosed location.

Guests hushed when Fabiola entered the tent pushing a pram. The musicians, which included a fiddle plunking tabby, a beagle on the trumpet, and a mouse playing the piccolo, sent up a grand musical flourish. After the cheers and music subsided, a blushing Fabiola spoke. "*Merci beaucoup, mes amies, merci.* And now the moment you've all been waiting for. I present, for the first time in public, four Siamese tigers. Penelope and Fluff's newborns." From the pram she lifted two of our five-week-old kittens. The sight of the bundles of fur prompted a chorus of oohs and ahhs. "Here's the smallest."

"But his fur's no less soft or fluffy because there's less of it," I said, blowing a kiss to my mother who always comforted me with those words.

"On the contrary," Mama replied, "because there's less of it, his downy coat's the most precious of all."

Fabiola held him to my face. "Looks just like Papa. We're thinking of calling him Fluff Two."

"How about Puhi?" shouted a spritely woman with twinkling blue eyes who sat at the groomers' table. "Means fluffy in my native Slovenian."

A name for our youngest kitten wasn't the only thing garnered from the rescue people. Their Eastern European operatives found the Russian lab where my papa and dozens of other strays had been taken. During their raid and rescue mission, the operatives learned that a unique blood mutation made our papa invaluable to cosmetics research. That fact drove Ivanovich and Claus' desire to get their hands on Mama Vanille, my littermates, and me. In the chaos, Papa escaped. But not before they snapped a photo. Not only was Papa the spitting image of Auguste and me, Lucky identified him as the same tabby caught in the snare with him. The rescue network had scouts looking for him, but I knew Papa was heading for Brussels.

———◦((◦))◦———

On the drive home from the party, despite Fabiola's loud snoring, Odysseus fell asleep in her lap. Because of the excitement from their first outing, our four kittens snoozed soundly. When they reached twelve weeks of age, Bog and his family would adopt one and Peter and Sarah another. Both families decided to name their male kittens, Rex. To Penelope's and my delight, Fabiola couldn't part with them all. She decided to keep the oldest and youngest, a gray female and the runt male who resembled me.

I nuzzled Penelope's cheek. "You know, *ma chérie…*"

"I believe I do, my dearest." She looked at me, kindness in her eyes. "You can't stay."

I flinched. "Gee whiskers! How did you know?"

She laughed softly. "Who knows you better than I? Between your vocabulary lessons, you sneak in one adventure tale after another. I saw how your gaze wandered outside the tent during the party. The market still excites you. You're bursting with wanderlust. And, of course, there's now the matter of finding your father."

I twitched my whiskers. "*Bien sûr*, certainly. Grumps' dream burns inside me. First, I find Papa. Then, I take the road to Waterloo. Maybe even Paris." I studied her face. There was no anger or anguish. "Aren't you sad?"

"Of course. Maybe not as much as you anticipated or even wanted. I'm more happy than sad. Pleased to see you follow your destiny."

I brushed a tear from her eye. "I worried you wouldn't understand."

"Domesticity isn't for every cat, especially a wildflower like you. Letting go is a form of love. If you tire of wandering or want that warm hearth you dreamed of, Fabiola will open her door."

"And you?"

She caressed my cheek. "You know better than to ask, *mon chéri*. My heart will always have a cherished place for you." Embracing each other, we cried tears of joy and sadness.

"One more thing," she added. "I know a little fellow who shares his papa's wanderlust." I cocked my head, uncertain what she was implying. "My dearest," she said, "when our kittens are old enough, you will take Puhi with you. Only a matter of time before he sets his big green eyes on adventure. A mother knows. I'd much rather my two loves seek adventure *ensemble*, together."

"Sweet Penelope, in my search for heaven, I've learned it's not a place. *Ma chérie*, you are my heaven."

Acknowledgments

I offer sincere thanks to:

My husband Jim. Our marvelous journey never grows stale. His love, patience, and support know no bounds. As he often says, "It's for life, baby." Together, we not only survived the pandemic, we also thrived.

My editor, Julie Kendrick. A keen eye for detail, love of good grammar and compelling story telling, and affection for cats of all kinds made her the perfect editor for this book.

My cover designer, Susan Jackson O'Leary. Once again, her talent helped create the perfect cover.

The Barrington Writers Workshop. For over ten years, this dedicated group of skilled writers has offered this author friendship, professional advice and enrichment, and respectful criticism. Before the pandemic hit, their reading and critique of several early chapters guided me.

Friends and family who continue to support my writing with unconditional enthusiasm, encouragement, and genuine interest. My creative journey has revealed to me the truest meaning of friendship.

My most loyal fans. Although their number may be small, their impact is mighty. They buoy my spirit, confidence, and resolve to keep writing. I'm eternally grateful.

The wonderful pets whose love, loyalty, and companionship have blessed and enhanced my life. Fluffy, Gentry, Kiltie, Kona, Simba, Jack, and Sadie, cuddly canines all. Then came Puhi. Our first and purely accidental cat. Not only did the precocious Bruxellois feline enter our Brussels garden and life, he burrowed his way into Jim's and my hearts. His unconditional love and antics brighten our days. His unknown lineage and adventures inspired this story.

CPSIA information can be obtained
at www.ICGtesting.com
Printed in the USA
LVHW081541251121
704451LV00011B/558